"Princess."

Lightning fast, she spun. A shiny object shot toward him. He misted, reappearing on the opposite side of the alley. Raine anticipated his move and pivoted to face him so fast her ponytail flicked in a wide arc before settling behind her head.

He had the strongest urge to wrap it around his fist and yank.

"I told you I'd kick your ass if you called me that again." She sneered.

A smirk curled on his lips. "And I told you I didn't care."

In fact, he cared more for her reaction and how much he pissed her off.

Her chest lifted with a deep inhale. The black tank top she wore did nothing to hide her taut, defined figure, luring his gaze to her—

"Eyes up here, Hell boy." She pointed two fingers at her deep violet eyes. "I've killed Fallen for much less. Like this one." She slid her shoe through the ex-Fallen residue on the dirty concrete beside her. "He called me pretty and paid for it with his soul."

She was batshit crazy. And so fucking hot.

Any Fallen who approached her must have a death wish. *Check.*

Untamed

by

Cassie Laelyn

The Fallen Guardians

Untamed

Cover Art by *Diana Carlile*

The Wild Rose Press, Inc.
PO Box 708
Adams Basin, NY 14410-0708
Visit us at www.thewildrosepress.com

Publishing History
First Edition, 2022
Trade Paperback ISBN 978-1-5092-4066-1
Digital ISBN 978-1-5092-4067-8

Published in the United States of America

Dedication

For you, because an existence without you would be
utterly soulless.

Acknowledgments

To be honest, as I write these acknowledgments, I'm kind of speechless. I mean, I'm writing acknowledgments for another Fallen Guardians book! This series has received more love than I ever could've imagined and it's all thanks to you, my readers. So, this acknowledgment is for you. Thank you for your continued support and for falling in love with these exiled angels and giving them wings to soar off the pages into your heart. And for, well, even liking Blaine!

Thank you also for patiently waiting for Raine's book. I hope you love her story, her badass attitude, and her obsession with shiny objects. Between you and me, I have a serious case of shoe envy!

As always, a huge thank you to every person who read, reviewed, or promoted the Fallen Guardians. Your support means the world to me.

The end is beginning, my friends. Strap in and enjoy the ride.

Cassie x

P.S. Reader support is the lifeblood for any series. If you loved reading *Untamed*, please consider leaving a review, recommending it to your friends or requesting your local library to purchase a copy. Thank you x

Glossary of Terms

Ariel – Angels of Nature who regenerate flora using angelic magic, often in the aftermath of a natural catastrophe such as a wildfire. Ariel have bronze wings.

Azrael – Angels of Death who transport souls from the mortal realm to their final resting place in either the Heavens or Hell. Azrael have silvery-gray wings.

Chosen – A mortal created by Fate; whose destiny restores the balance in Fate's favor.

Dumahel – Half angel, half mortal, Dumahel possess the power to enter and manipulate dreams. They are rare and always born as twins.

Fallen – Once angels of the Heavens, Fallen now reside in the many realms in Hell and give their allegiance to the current ruler of Hell. Fallen have crimson wings.

Guardians – Fate's warriors, tasked with protecting Chosen mortals, so they can fulfill their fated destiny. Fate exiled the Guardians to the mortal world over three hundred years ago. They have black wings.

Purah – Crystalline water from the Eternal Fountain, found in the Heavens. Purah is toxic to Fallen.

Raziel – Angels who cast magic, commonly used to disguise the immortal world from mortal eyes.

Tartirim – A realm in the Heavens where Fate imprisons angelic souls that require intense rehabilitation.

PROLOGUE

Blaine
Fifty mortal years ago

Fire licked the gates of Hell. The flames stretched high above the thick black iron, lapping the humid air as though desperate for salvation. How pathetic. Clearly, Fate flaunted her power when creating these gates. Any ordinary immortal would've simply built a wall. After all, this was a kingdom.

Just not hers.

The mortal male trembled beside him. Former mortal. Well, technically once he entered the gates, he'd become a former mortal. Semantics.

"Please."

Now the poor lad begged. Why did mortals do that? It never changed the outcome.

He glanced at the male's pale face, wide, terrified eyes, and quivering bottom lip. "Perhaps next time you should rethink your extracurricular activities. Oh, wait." He paused, mainly to drag out the suspense. "There won't be a next time."

The male all but fainted.

He was quite over babysitting such annoying creatures. "It's more fun once you're inside the gates. Think of it as an endless tropical vacation without the…vacation."

Before the mortal whined any further, Blaine shoved him forward. "Now, chop-chop. I'd like to return to the mortal realm this century."

As the male trudged forward, Blaine flipped up the collar of his leather jacket and strode toward the gates with a spring in his step. At will, they swung inward, welcoming them to Hell.

"Honey." He chuckled at his own singsong tone. "I'm home."

Just kidding.

Hell wasn't his home any longer. Since his deal with Zath, he'd acquired himself a lovely, if a tad musty, residence in the mortal realm. The best part about the new location? That brotherhood of good Samaritans moped around looking for him and it thrilled him to know he was right under their noses, and they had no idea. He enjoyed their little game of Guardian and Fallen, even if the odds were in his favor.

Besides, he couldn't engage phase two of his I-Fell-from-the-Heavens plan without them, so location was everything.

Before phase two though, he needed to move a few pieces on his proverbial chessboard and pay a visit to Zath.

Current ruler of Hell.

After strolling through the gates, Blaine continued down the main street. It resembled any ordinary street in the mortal realm in the aftermath of say, an explosion. Fire, crumbled cobblestone, decrepit buildings that barely remained standing.

Fate took it a little too far with that oversized, scorching sun blazing on the back of his neck. He was more of a winter immortal himself.

Trailing behind him, the mortal sobbed but kept pace. Blaine ignored the antics. In hindsight, perhaps the male shouldn't have beat that child, putting himself on Blaine's radar.

No point in dwelling on the past. Nothing good ever came from it.

Oh, wait. Yes, it did.

Various shopfronts flanked the main street, adding to the mortal realm illusion. Grabbing the male by the collar of his dirty white shirt, he dragged him through the entrance on the left, misting himself and Mr. Not-so-upstanding Citizen to Zath's lair.

Lair.

He liked that word.

He paused while the mortal leaned to one side and emptied the contents of his last meal on the burned, blackened ground. Misting dissolved his body into individual cells, down to a molecular level, becoming nothing but fragments of light traveling through the universe, or in this case, the many realms of Hell, before it reformed on the other side.

When the mortal wiped the cuff of his shirt over his mouth and straightened, albeit paler than before, Blaine continued along the rocky path toward their destination.

Ash fluttered in the air like dirty, burned snowflakes. Here, the sun barely rose above the horizon, as though forever rising, or setting, casting the volcanic landscape in gloomy shades of red and purple.

Cresting the small hill, he spotted Zath's lair. Zath could use a touch of Fate's powers to fix up the place. A lair should ooze power and nobility, but instead, this castle resembled nothing but a decrepit pile of firestone and rubble. Zath had spent centuries in this realm with the sole focus on regenerating his powers.

No king should be so single-minded.

Two Fallen guarded the entrance, standing before oversized iron gates, a smaller version of the fiery gates, without the fire. One Fallen eyed the mortal stumbling along behind Blaine. The other Fallen gave Blaine a curt nod.

After all, he was Zath's most regular visitor.

His only visitor.

The gates swung inward, and he strolled through with the mortal in tow.

The castle was one expansive open space, no doors or windows, minimal furniture, and an oversized rectangular dais positioned in the center. Dark stains surrounded it on the stone floor.

A pretentious throne made of mortal bones loomed on the other side of the dais, positioned on a raised platform.

He figured Zath used the throne as a coping mechanism after Fate stripped his powers and imprisoned him here. As though positioning it on a raised platform made him feel more superior than his visitors. More powerful.

Even if Zath somehow reacquired his full powers, he was no match for Fate.

He was no match for Blaine.

The poor mortal squeaked when he spotted Zath sitting on the throne. Blaine rolled his eyes.

"You brought me another mortal." Zath's voice boomed off the stone walls. "I want an Ariel."

Blaine presented the male with a wave of his arm. "Let's not be ungrateful now. A Fallen in your…predicament cannot be choosy."

Zath rose from his throne. His fiery eyes flamed hotter as he descended to the dais. Behind Zath's back, his limp, torn wings resembled gossamer sinew with fractured bones and open infected wounds. Over the centuries, they'd slowly regrown but never possessed enough power to completely heal. Harvesting mortal souls aided the healing process but was nothing compared to the power of an Ariel's.

Blaine wasn't stupid.

When he acquired an Ariel, the power would be for himself, not Zath.

The king of Hell thought Blaine was an ally. Fool on him. Zath was yet another puppet in Blaine's revenge plot against Fate and wouldn't ever step foot in the mortal realm again.

Fate imprisoned Zath here for a reason and Blaine intended to finish that job.

Zath braced his palms on the dais. "Approach."

Blaine held up a finger, halting the mortal from taking another step. "About our deal."

Zath's narrow gaze snapped to Blaine. All that crimson inside his pupils was rather sickly. He hoped his eyes didn't turn out like that.

"I granted your freedom in the mortal realm in exchange for souls."

"That is true." Blaine remained where he stood. When negotiating with the king of Hell, he was wise to stay out of reach in case Zath retaliated.

Zath slammed his fist on the dais. "Give me the mortal," he roared.

Desperation looked good on no one, especially a so-called king.

"Grant my request," Blaine countered.

Blaine negotiated with Zath only when it suited him. A little deal here and there made Zath think he had a worthy ally. If Zath discovered Blaine's true intentions, his entire plan would unravel at the seams.

Zath straightened, eyeing the mortal with that sickening crimson gaze. "What?"

"I'm in need of a reliable sidekick. It seems the mortal realm is rather boring with no one to wreak havoc with. And you're stuck here—" He circled his finger in the air around what remained of Zath's wings. "Regenerating."

"Take another Devoid." Zath's lips curled in a snarl. "Now give me the mortal."

"Devoid are so…weak." He drew out the last word, making a point Zath would understand. "Actually, I'd rather grab a Fallen from the Infernal Pits."

This deal was risky, he knew that. But Zath's thirst for power was his greatest weakness, and ultimately his downfall. No victorious king should allow his desire for power to overshadow his quest for revenge.

Zath would be wise to remember that.

"A Fallen." Zath sneered.

Not just any Fallen.

Zath waved his hand to the right of the dais, producing a glowing red portal, pulsing in the air. A gateway to the Infernal Pits. Blaine could've done that himself, but that would've revealed his powers. And now wasn't the time for showing off.

"One Fallen. Now, give me the mortal."

Blaine shoved the mortal toward the dais, breaking the compulsion that kept him frozen in place. "Your fate awaits. Enjoy."

As the mortal screamed and Zath's sinister chuckle boomed in the stale air, Blaine stepped through the portal to collect the one Fallen crucial to his plan. The only one who could unleash Hell.

Chapter ONE

Raine
Present day

Raine smoothed the file along the length of the boot dagger. Not her preferred weapon, still, the simple blade had many uses. Stabbing, maiming, slitting and her favorite, gutting. Just like all the others she forged, this dagger would end up in the blackened heart of a Fallen and knowing Aric, he'd require a replacement next week.

It didn't matter. She'd forged weapons for centuries and would continue until Fate ended her immortality.

Which, given her progress of late, would be sooner rather than later.

Tonight, she'd hid down here in the armory for hours. Mortals would call her antisocial, but what did they know? Socializing was an excuse for needing company and she functioned just fine without it.

Twisting the dagger, she angled the file along the blade, sharpening both edges. Flames from the nearby furnace flickered along the polished surface, making the metal reflect a kaleidoscope of colors over the ceiling. But this dagger wasn't any ordinary blade. Made of Purah, from the Eternal Fountain in the Heavens, the dagger was more powerful than any mortal blade,

8

capable of killing a Fallen, sending its scummy soul back to Hell.

Where it belonged.

Someone punched the pin code on the armory door. A second later, a clunk disengaged the lock and the door swung inward. All she asked for was a few hours of solitude, but he never left her alone.

Without bothering to turn around, she acknowledged her brother with a chin tip.

"How goes it, sis?" River asked, strolling around the opposite side of the workbench to stand before her.

Today, he'd outdone himself in the wardrobe department. The mortal realm had benefits, like the male who designed the red patent pumps currently hugging her feet. Or the local gin distillery which crafted tarty concoctions that made socializing somewhat bearable.

But her brother's obsession with bright colors had become nauseating.

Aric would no doubt give River shit about this outfit all day long.

"Another palm tree shirt?" she grumbled, lifting her gaze to River's.

His moss-green eyes brightened as though she'd given him a compliment.

"The store had a sale." He tugged the hem, admiring the floral print explosion splattered across his torso. "Tayla said this one brings out my eyes."

She deadpanned her brother. "As in, makes others want to gouge them out?"

River screwed up his face. He couldn't care less what others thought of him and she envied that. How nice it would be to never disappoint anyone.

She continued perfecting the dagger, sweeping the file along the curved edge right to the tip and back up again. Tension trickled through her shoulders, down her arm, releasing through her fingertips with each smooth stroke. She flipped the blade and repeated the process on the other side, ensuring both edges were identical.

Her brother knew her well enough not to interrupt or she'd likely stab him.

She never had but today might be the day.

When she sensed River's body hum with pent-up energy because he hadn't spoken for two and a half minutes, she placed the file on the workbench and crossed to the furnace.

"You're off patrol tonight." The words burst from River's mouth as though he'd held his breath the entire time she filed the blade.

With her back to him, she nodded while connecting the dagger to a large metal rod, before inserting it into the freezing chamber. The final step. She'd already transformed the liquid Purah into a solid before shaping the blade. A few seconds was all it needed for the Purah to crystalize, turning it into the most lethal weapon in this realm.

Well, second most lethal.

She'd made so many of them now, she could do it in her sleep.

River dragged out a stool, setting himself up for the long haul. If she had any hope of leaving this realm, she first needed to shake her brother. If she tried to run, he'd track her down, she knew that, but if she had a head start...

River cleared his throat.

Removing the rod from the chamber, she unclasped

the dagger with her gloved hand and placed it on the workbench while it warmed back to room temperature. She made the mistake of lifting her gaze to her brother's. He narrowed his eyes. He was the one person in the entire universe that knew her better than she knew herself.

"Spit it out, River."

He twisted his mouth. Something he often did when not wanting to deliver bad news.

"The girls are looking for you."

She groaned. The women in the house treated her as though she were part of their sisterhood. Some elite group of warrior women taking over the world. They forced her to partake in what they called "girl nights," subjecting her to endless movies and salty, buttery popcorn while her badass reputation slithered down the drain one romantic comedy at a time.

"I'm busy."

In the beginning, she'd engaged in those activities with Tayla. Not because she was the only other female in the household, but she felt an overwhelming need to make amends for the car accident which took Tayla's life.

*If I'd driven instead...*But she hadn't.

Even though Fate granted Tayla immortality in the mortal realm, Raine still had a twisted obligation to make things right. As the household grew and other soulmates joined their forsaken crew, she somehow lost the ability to say no.

They clearly knew that. Why else would they continue to ask her?

From under the bench, most likely from his pocket, River plonked a packet of candied snakes on the workbench and ripped it open. He riffled through the contents until he found his favorite color and tossed it in his mouth.

"Hailee chose that new movie with some hot Australian dude in it. Luckily EJ is on patrol tonight." He chuckled with a mouthful of candy.

"I said I'm busy."

River huffed a breath. "They're trying to include you. They just want to be your friend."

He offered her a snake, and she cocked a brow. Was she the only person in this realm who knew the toxic effects of sugar? She never ate it and had no idea why River kept offering. "I don't need friends. It's not like I'm hanging around here forever."

"Maybe not, but while you're here, you could…" He threw another candy in his mouth and took his time chewing it. "At least make an effort."

That just pissed her off.

Make an effort? All she'd done since she arrived here was make effort after effort. Every week she forged Aric a new set of daggers. Raven said he'd never fought with a better short sword than the one she made him. A few months ago, she even endured a hellish road trip across the country with EJ to escort Hailee to the Guardian mansion.

What more did they want from her?

Her fingers curled around the handle of the finished dagger. In one swift motion, she flicked her arm out to the side. The blade shot across the armory before the tip slammed against the stone wall and flopped to the floor with a clunk.

Never deterred, River continued, "You were going out tonight, weren't you?"

Yup.

She couldn't hide anything from him. Never could.

Without answering, she shoved away from the workbench and crossed to retrieve the dagger off the floor. She turned it this way and that, inspecting the blade for fractures in the Purah. Nothing.

The dagger remained one perfect piece.

She was the best forger in history. Why would Fate risk losing that?

Back across from River, she jammed the dagger into the workbench before she threw it again and then needed to forge another for Aric's patrol tonight.

She glared at River. How could two siblings, created from the same power be complete opposites in so many ways? He was so heavenly. She…wasn't.

He nodded in understanding even though she hadn't said a word. "It takes forever to travel around this realm without misting. I didn't realize how difficult it would be for you." He paused. "We need to think outside the box. What about a plane?" Excitement lit his eyes. "The Guardians need their own private jet."

There he went again, trying to solve her problem. This mess was hers, not his.

She rolled her eyes. " 'Cause asking for a jet isn't obvious."

His expression fell.

And there she went, deflating his happy bubble. Again.

"I still think you should risk telling Raven. He'd help. He seems like a cool boss. I think all the Guardians would help. They like you."

Here we go.

"I can't."

They'd had this same conversation countless times.

She strode to the long rectangular basin on one side of the armory, her heels tapping on the floor in time with her pounding pulse. Roughly the size of a small dining table, waist height and made of black and gray stone, the basin contained the last remaining Purah in this realm.

The Guardians threw around their weapons as though they had an endless supply because the black stone gave the illusion of a bottomless pit. Newsflash, they didn't.

When the heavenly water ran out, they were all screwed.

Including the entire mortal realm.

Leaning over the edge, she trailed her finger along the top of the liquid, setting off a mesmerizing display of color. Pink, yellow, blue, and silver glittered across every surface in the armory, including her skin-tight black pants. Apparel suitable for running, flying and kicking a Fallen's ass.

She spun to face River. "Have you checked this lately? At the rate Aric goes through daggers, we'll be lucky to have enough Purah for three more months."

His shoulders dropped. "It's cool, sis. We'll figure it out."

Nothing ever fazed him.

The only thing she hated more than small talk was her brother's carefree attitude.

She snatched a weapon from her belt. Mortals referred to them as throwing stars, or ninja stars, but the correct title in the Heavens was Kiel. Star of heavenly fire and ice. The hole in the center perfectly crafted to twirl the star around her index finger. Cool Purah instantly warmed to her body temperature. Her shoulders lightened with each spin, and her breath steadied.

Back at the workbench, she faced her brother. "We've been in the mortal realm for over two years and haven't found a single clue. What makes you so sure we even will? What if Fate set this whole thing up just so I'd fail? She did it to EJ for centuries. Who says she hasn't done the same thing to us?"

River lifted one shoulder. "I just know."

Correction, she hated her brother's faith in Fate more than she hated his carefree attitude. She'd had a similar level of faith once. All that disappeared the second Fate banished them here on an impossible mission.

She stopped spinning the Kiel and scraped the point along the workbench, the vibration shuddering through her hand and up her arm. Tiny chunks and indentations marred the wood where she'd dug a Kiel or ten into it over the years.

Instead of kumbayaing around a metaphorical campfire with a sisterhood, what she needed tonight was to get out of the armory and stab something or someone. Aric was usually up for a spar, and they raged on the same level. That all stopped when he got his soulmate back. Now he played happy family.

Everyone in this whole fucked-up realm played happy family.

Everyone except her.

She clipped the Kiel back onto her belt, gathered her forging tools into a leather pouch before rolling them up and securing them with a tie. "May as well accept that Fate tricked us. We have roughly three months left before she retaliates."

Before River replied, she stormed out of the armory, leaving her brother to his sickly-sweet candy and equally revolting positive attitude.

Chapter TWO

Slater

Slater scooped the broken chair off the floor and tossed it. It sailed through the air until it collided with a lantern, knocking it off the wall. Glass shattered in every direction.

Even without a broken lantern, the living room resembled the aftermath of that mortal rave party he attended some time ago, minus red plastic cups littering the floor. Instead of pulsing, colored lights, black Fallen blood dotted almost every surface. Given the destruction, anyone would think the Guardians had outnumbered them when they attacked. But he'd interrogated a surviving Fallen and that wasn't the case. Only two Guardians had stormed Blaine's castle in Hell.

Two measly Guardians.

How in the fiery Hell did they enter the gates without Falling?

He sensed Blaine a moment before the Fallen strolled into the living room.

He didn't bother with pleasantries. "This is what you get for trusting that backstabbing traitor while you made me stay in the mortal realm. I should've been here, and you know it."

In the center of the room, ground zero of the

destruction, Blaine surveyed the damage to his precious underworld hideaway. "I sense a hint of resentment behind that snarky tone of yours."

Slater scoffed. Resentment didn't begin to cover it. Why bother having a second-in-command if Blaine left him out of the battle zone? He was the best, most skilled fighter Blaine had on his side, yet time and time again, Blaine tasked him with matters in the mortal realm.

He belonged in Hell not mingling with mortals.

Foam spilled from slashes in the leather as Blaine sank into an armchair. The Guardians sure did a number on the joint.

"Remind me to send my brother and his Boy Scouts the bill." Blaine held out his palm and a short glass materialized in his hand with a few shots of liquor in it. He downed it in one go. "I think it's time for a story…"

Slater crossed his arms over his chest. "I'm not in the mood for a story."

Ignoring him, Blaine motioned to the remaining armchair.

He grimaced at the dark stains of Fallen blood and faint sticky residue that remained when Purah entered a Fallen's heart and their body exploded into mist. "I'd rather stand."

"Suit yourself." Blaine crossed one leg, resting his ankle on his knee. "Once upon a time there lived an angel."

"Shocking."

Blaine side-eyed him before continuing. "This angel wasn't just any angel. He was an Azrael with a thirst for life. He wanted more from his immortality than the task assigned to him by Fate."

"Get on with it."

"One bright and sunny day…no, actually, I think it was a bit cloudy…anyhoo, a dark angel approached the Azrael and offered him all he'd ever hoped for. Power, recognition, the chance for freedom."

A shudder ran down his spine.

"Of course, the Azrael accepted the deal, without knowing the dark angel who offered it possessed neither the means nor the power to grant such a deal. In fact, that dark angel had gone behind the queen's back with that same offer to many others. Unfortunately for the Azrael, the queen eventually tracked down all that sought to betray her and cast them from the Heavens before they chose to Fall. Upon entering the fiery kingdom, the Azrael discovered the dark angel's true plan, so vastly different to the one he'd promised. In an act of rebellion, the Azrael refused to give his allegiance to the new king, resulting in his imprisonment to the deepest depths of Hell."

Although impossible, the black bands marring Slater's forearms heated. Bile rose in his throat.

Blaine summoned a refill in his tumbler and swirled the golden liquid before sipping. "Shortly after the Azrael's imprisonment—"

"Centuries after."

Blaine waved his hand in the air. "My story, my timeline."

No, my story.

"Sometime after, a Fallen angel approached the Azrael with a different deal, one which ensured his freedom from the Infernal Pits. Do you recall the terms of that deal?"

"You wanted me to recruit Dumahel twins."

"Not just any Dumahel twins." Blaine swung his gaze to Slater, narrowing his eyes. "You're free of the Infernal Pits, and yet, I am now missing the Dumahel you acquired."

That wasn't the only thing missing.

Blaine's tone hardened, just as it had when he approached him in the Infernal Pits. "Instead of focusing on the state of affairs in the living room, how about you redirect your attention to finding Ebony."

"I've already looked."

Crimson flames simmered in Blaine's pupils. "Look again."

"Asher took her when he misted away after the Guardians attacked."

That twin did nothing but cause trouble ever since Blaine recruited her. As for her father, Blaine should've never trusted the Fallen with such an important immortal.

The whole reason Blaine recruited the Dumahel was to use her dreamwalking powers to connect with Fate. He'd done that. Why bother keeping her any longer? Unless he planned another visit.

Or a dreamwalk with another immortal.

As for his true mission…that would take time. Centuries even.

"I hope your field trip to the Heavens was worth it." He grew more impatient by the second. "This isn't on me, Blaine. You left me in the mortal realm. This is all on you."

"Perhaps."

Perhaps. Slater lowered his arms and rounded the couch to stand before Blaine. Sitting down still wasn't an option. What would it take for Blaine to admit defeat? Time and time again, his plans came apart at the hands of the Guardians. Surely, he saw that.

"You've been in Hell for almost four mortal centuries, Blaine. Do you truly believe you can still win this war?"

"The end is beginning, my friend."

Before he questioned Blaine further, Peyton strolled into the living room. Since she Fell from the Heavens, he'd trained her in both battle and wits. He needed someone he could trust in Hell when Blaine tasked him with meaningless missions in the mortal realm. If it were up to him, he'd avoid that realm at all costs. Especially of late.

He'd made a lot of enemies since leaving the Heavens, and more than one of them was currently after his wings.

"You requested to see me, my lord?"

Slater snorted. *My lord?* The only thing bigger than Blaine's ego was…nothing.

"Which two Guardians entered the gates?"

Peyton hesitated a moment before answering. "Only one Guardian entered the gates. The other was an Azrael. EJ and Cole."

Slater's eyebrows flew up. EJ storming through the fiery gates to rescue his soulmate didn't surprise him. After all, Blaine had held EJ's soulmate captive until she agreed to connect him with Fate.

But Cole? Cunning bastard.

"Cole must've protected EJ with Azrael shadows," Slater said.

Blaine leaned forward to place his glass down but paused, staring at broken wood over the floor that once resembled a table. Redirecting, he placed the glass on the floor before standing. "Did you see Asher leave with the Dumahel?" Blaine asked Peyton.

She shook her head. "I came to warn you that EJ was in Hell but…" She frowned. "By the time I got here, Asher and Ebony were gone, as were Cole and EJ."

Slater noted the slight twitch of her fingers. What was she hiding?

Blaine stepped forward, but Peyton held her ground. He might have trained her, but she was still no match for Blaine.

"Strange how you didn't get here before them, considering you're familiar with the gateways."

Exactly.

Blaine held her stare for a moment before addressing Slater. "It seems the Guardians have upped their game. See, Slater, I told you the end is beginning. Perhaps you need to match their efforts." He tapped a finger on his chin. "Or perhaps what you need is motivation in the form of a sidekick? That worked for me once."

No. The last thing he needed was a sidekick. "I'm perfectly capable of finding them myself. I work better alone."

"I recruited you as my second-in-command because I was led to believe you were the most skilled tracker Fate ever created. However, I thought you would be more…capable."

Before Slater, Blaine's second in commands were Devoid—soulless former mortals who sold their soul to the devil so to speak. Zath, devil, same thing. Mortals referred to them as zombies, although they resided in

Hell. No wonder Blaine's plans never worked.

Since freeing him from the Infernal Pits, Slater had been Blaine's longest-serving second. But even he wasn't naïve enough to think Blaine wouldn't replace him in a heartbeat if it served his revenge against Fate.

Which made Blaine a cunning and lethal leader.

An even more dangerous and deranged king who'd do whatever it took to fulfil his plan. Including sacrificing his own army.

He hardened his tone to make his point. "I found the Dumahel once and I'll do it again."

He had to find the twin before Blaine realized what else Asher had in his possession. Something a hell of a lot more priceless than a Dumahel with dreamwalking powers.

Peyton lifted her chin. "Let me find them instead."

The corner of Blaine's mouth curled in a smirk that Slater had witnessed many times. A smirk reminding him of Blaine's powers, and his position in Hell.

He needed to walk a fine line. If Blaine imprisoned him back in the Infernal Pits, no one would come for him. Devoid, under Zath's command, would torture him again for the rest of eternity. He'd never gain his freedom.

He couldn't let that happen. He needed to complete his mission.

That, and only that, kept him toeing the line.

"I said I'd find them," he snarled, about to lose his cool.

Blaine stared at him long and hard. "Perhaps you should find the Dumahel before Peyton earns a promotion."

Chapter THREE

Raine dashed down a side street, hunting a Fallen. A dimly lit alley in the dead of night was no hindrance to her sight. She'd spot those crimson eyes a mile away. Frigid wind stung her cheeks, burning a path into her lungs with each sharp inhale.

Ever since she'd found the Fallen corrupting a mortal outside SubZero, the local club, she'd chased it across town.

She veered around the corner—

The Fallen slashed a dagger at her, but she was quicker. She leaped sideways, spinning in a tight circle, the blade missing her by less than an inch. The Fallen stalked forward, all cocky and obviously brain-dead.

The idiot clearly didn't know who she was.

She ate cocky Fallen for breakfast.

She didn't bother mentally calling for assistance from the other Guardians, nor did she assess a fight strategy. She could take down this guy with her eyes closed.

In fact, maybe she'd try that.

One day. Not tonight. Tonight, she needed information first.

"I've heard about you. The Guardian's bitch."

This loser was dumber than she thought. If he'd truly heard of her, he wouldn't stick around to fight her. That just proved his stupidity.

She rolled her eyes. "Bitch? How original."

She'd heard all the names Fallen and angels taunted her with. *Whatever*. They should fear her. Especially considering she could gut any immortal like a fish in less time than it took for them to unfurl their wings.

Every so often, she came across a Fallen she considered a skilled warrior, a worthy opponent for a minute or so. Others were like this dropkick, full of themselves and overestimating their capabilities.

The Fallen stalked forward. "Such a shame the Guardians left one of their own unprotected."

She scoffed. This Fallen's overconfidence would result in his death quicker than she'd like. The Guardians didn't need to fight Fallen in cliquey groups. Fate created warriors, not beauty queens.

Killing this loser would do the universe a favor. Otherwise, his ego might squash the whole fucking planet.

But she wasn't ready to return to the Guardian residence yet. This Fallen gave her an excuse to stay out, which was why she'd chased him and let him think he had the upper hand. Fool. He also hadn't given her any information, so for now, his soul remained inside that filthy body.

"You're the one without a weapon, asshole."

He threw his head back and laughed. "I don't need a weapon to fight one Guardian."

The Fallen unfurled his wings. Moonlight reflected the dark crimson feathers, like blood splattered over a perfectly good set of wings. Sharp, black, poisonous talons curled from the tip of each wing. If only she had those, they'd make fighting a hell of a lot more entertaining. Especially for her.

Instead, she settled for throwing a Kiel.

She slipped one from her belt and twirled it around her index finger, just itching to use it. Made from Purah, the Kiel would mist that disgusting idiot's soul back to the depths of Hell for a few centuries. By the time he regenerated and made it back to the mortal realm, she'd be long gone. In fact, the entire realm might no longer exist.

She stepped back and the Fallen matched a step toward her. Crimson flames fired in his pupils as that cocky grin widened on his face.

How easily Fallen allowed their emotions to rule them.

"You're too pretty for a Guardian. Come and join me in Hell."

Vomit. "Does that line work on all angels?"

The idiot lifted one shoulder. "Only the crazy ones."

Before he finished the sentence, the Fallen flipped his wing outward and aimed the talon at her. Now, he got with the program instead of trying to seduce her.

She shot her arm in an arc across her body, blocking the talon, slicing the Kiel along the inside of his wing. The Fallen grunted. Purah sizzled a path like lava across his flesh, the smell sweet satisfaction.

Adrenaline coiled in her limbs. She leaned forward slightly, distributing her weight to the balls of her feet, readying herself. The stupid Fallen didn't learn his lesson. He struck again, but she anticipated every move.

As his other wing shot toward her head, she dipped, unsheathed the dagger from her ankle and spun in one swift movement. The Fallen's wing curled around her. Before he knew what hit him, she drove the dagger into his flesh until it hit bone. Then she shoved harder. The Fallen roared as the dagger shattered the bone, rendering his wing useless.

Talons were nothing without wings to direct them.

She moved to slip under the Fallen's wing, but he snagged her ponytail, ripping it backward. She stumbled. With a kick, she shoved the tip of her shiny black pump into the loser's balls.

With a yelp, he released her hair and bent over at the waist, clutching his groin.

Fallen were still males with a weakness between their legs.

Before the Fallen recovered, she grabbed his thick, curly hair, using it to twist him and shove him face-first against the brick wall. She pressed the dagger to the soft flesh under his chin. A tiny droplet of black blood pooled at the tip. One wrong move and she'd slice right through his jugular.

"Tell me what you know about the Empryen?"

His eyes went wide.

"You're crazy," he spluttered.

"Again, not very original."

She redirected the dagger, trailing it down his back between his wings, effortlessly slicing flesh all the way to his belt. The guy should've worn a shirt.

Or Purah proof vest.

His uninjured wing jerked toward her. Just before the talon struck, she flipped the dagger in her hand and shoved it through the flesh, impaling his wing to the brick wall.

The Fallen screamed in agony.

Not so tough now.

"Last chance," she growled.

"I don't know what you're talking about."

They never did. But someone must and until she found out who had information, she'd never stop.

Done here, she tore her dagger free. The Fallen collapsed to his knees, shuddering in pain. In one swift movement, she spun, extended her leg and side-kicked the asshole in the head. Something crunched, probably his neck. The Fallen's head fell to one side, his body followed, smacking the ground.

Standing there, she stared at the Fallen's unblinking gaze. Wide eyes rimmed with crimson glowed in the darkness of the alley. She should've let him win a bit more to prolong the fight. This loser was the only Fallen she'd found tonight and now she had no excuse but to return to the Guardian residence.

This early at night, there was still potential for someone to corner her into socializing. If she had to watch another sappy romance, she wouldn't need a Fallen to stab her, she'd do it herself. With her pumps.

She crouched beside the Fallen. Even with a broken neck, the idiot's soul wouldn't return to Hell until she finished him with Purah. If she left him here, his immortality would eventually heal the broken bones and he'd wake to cause more havoc. Sitting here twiddling her thumbs while she waited for him to heal, just so she could kill him again, wasn't her thing. Patience never was.

She straightened. Instead of using her dagger, this time she opted for her secret weapon of choice. A weapon that equaled her frustration level tonight.

By the Fallen's side, she lifted her foot and jabbed the heel of her pump in the Fallen's chest, stabbing him in the heart. Less than a second later, the Fallen exploded into mist, coating the ground in a fine glossy substance.

A gust of wind would carry it away by morning.

And then she'd start all over again until she got the answers she sought. The answers this realm depended on.

Bracing one hand on the brick wall, she lifted her foot to slip off her shoe and wipe the black Fallen blood on her pants before putting it back on.

What the hell did she do now?

Hanging out in a dingy alley for the next four hours was up there with movie nights. No thanks.

A prickle sparked along her nape, bringing a grin to her face.

Just when she thought her night was over, another Fallen landed on her radar.

Chapter FOUR

Leaving Hell, Slater misted to the mortal realm. Summit Creek to be precise. The small town where Blaine decided he needed a permanent residence because his brother and the other Guardians lived here.

Instead of misting to Blaine's place, he materialized in town to walk off the frustration coiling inside him. He welcomed the cool change in temperature accompanying the breeze drifting down the street. Stuck in the hothouse for centuries was enough to convert any immortal to loving winter.

This late at night, not many mortals ventured to the outskirts of town. He'd been in the realm long enough to figure out their habits and the times when he could fly or fight. Not that he fought much these days.

Or tracked.

Both skills he'd mastered, yet as of late, rarely used.

As he strode down the pavement, Blaine's threat back in Hell lingered in his mind. He wasn't naïve enough to think just because he'd fought alongside the Fallen that Blaine wouldn't replace him. Absolutely Blaine would. And then he'd find himself stuck in the Infernal Pits for eternity.

His hands curled into tight fists.

He needed to end this before it was too late. But what he needed most was to keep a level head.

Mid-step, he paused, sensing a flare in his blood. A sure sign a Guardian was nearby.

The Guardians made a point of keeping their battles off the street and away from mortals. So far, they hadn't targeted him. Probably because they thought Blaine would retaliate and their holy quest to return their beloved brother to the Heavens would fail.

A quest they needed to lose, no matter the consequences.

He needed Blaine in Hell. He'd made a vow to keep him there.

Cocking his head, he scanned the street, searching for the Guardian. They must be hunting a random Fallen stupid enough to prey on mortals. Blaine gave clear instructions to his Fallen army to remain in Hell. Regeneration in Hell took centuries. If the Guardians kept sending their souls to the Pits, they'd wipe out Blaine's entire army in the next twelve mortal months. Blaine would have to start all over again. He didn't have that time to waste.

Neither of them did.

Besides, he had no loyalty to the Guardians, regardless of their relationship to Blaine. He'd also avoid returning to the Pits at all costs.

Not locating the threat, he continued down the street—

A flash of platinum hair darted around a corner on the opposite side of the street. He spun just in time to spot the Guardian.

Not just any Guardian. He recognized that hair, that lethal body, that deadly power.

Raine.

He had two choices. Pursue her or…pursue her.

Turned out he only wanted one thing.

His blood heated at the thought of their reunion. He'd ached for this day for far too long to let the opportunity slip away.

Crossing the deserted road, he strode in Raine's direction just as she disappeared around a corner leading to a dead end. Given she couldn't mist, he'd catch her as she tried to exit.

The closer he ventured to the alley, the more he overheard the conversation. A Fallen had her cornered. Or so he thought. Raine's cut-throat reputation was legendary in Hell. He'd experienced her wrath firsthand to know not just any Fallen could overpower her.

Leaning his shoulder against the brick wall, he settled in, listening to the action unfold. With one hand, he summoned a thin veil of shadows to conceal his presence, in case Raine darted around the corner. He didn't want to ruin their moment. He wanted to fully appreciate her reaction when she saw him.

The Fallen tormented Raine with words that coiled a nasty flash of heat through his center. His shadows darkened, curling around him, aching to join the fight. But he held them back. Raine could take on one Fallen without his help.

Still, the motherfucker kept at it, baiting Raine instead of engaging with something other than words. Clearly, not trained by him or Blaine.

Just as he considered stepping free of his shadows and ending the Fallen himself, Raine lashed out, and the Fallen got what he deserved.

The scent of burned flesh carried in the air, drifting his way. As much as he ached to watch her end that Fallen, he hung back in his shadows. If she knew he was there, she'd aim for him instead.

Which he also ached for, just not yet.

Their fight had been brewing ever since he attacked the Guardian mansion a few months ago and she got all up in his face for calling her "princess." The memory brought a grin to his face. He hadn't had that much fun in…forever.

And that encounter had consumed his thoughts ever since.

What he'd give to have her all fired up again and take that snarky aggression out on him.

When the Fallen made no further grunts or whines, he lowered the veil of shadows and stepped free, rounding the corner into the alley.

Raine had her back to him as she slipped her shoe back on.

"Princess."

Lightning fast, she spun. A shiny object shot toward him. He misted, reappearing on the opposite side of the alley. Raine anticipated his move and pivoted to face him so fast her ponytail flew in a wide arc before settling behind her head.

He had the strongest urge to wrap it around his fist and yank.

"I told you I'd kick your ass if you called me that again." She sneered.

A smirk curled on his lips. "And I told you I didn't care."

In fact, he cared more for her reaction and how much he pissed her off.

Her chest lifted with a deep inhale. The black tank top she wore did nothing to hide her taut, defined figure, luring his gaze to her—

"Eyes up here, Hell boy." She pointed two fingers at her deep violet eyes. "I've killed Fallen for much less. Like this one." She slid her shoe through the ex-Fallen residue on the dirty concrete beside her. "He called me pretty and paid for it with his soul."

She was batshit crazy and so fucking hot.

Any Fallen who approached her must have a death wish. *Check.*

He inched closer, not at all intimidated by this fiery princess. Excited, awakened maybe, but not intimidated. Raine held her ground, feet slightly apart, twirling a Kiel around her index finger as though the whole situation bored her. He sensed she was far from bored. While anticipating his next move, he bet she considered the thousand different ways to stab him. Again.

"You are pretty." He tilted his head slightly to one side, studying those wild, violet eyes. "In a psychotic murderous way."

"And here I thought you were incapable of compliments."

He held back a smirk.

"I heard you've been playing happy family with your Hell buddies."

She'd heard nothing. He'd made sure of that.

He shrugged one shoulder. "Something like that. Blaine's pissed about his castle by the way. You might want to deliver that message to your boy-band."

She paused the spinning Kiel with her thumb, and he couldn't stop himself. His gaze zeroed in, expecting a drop of blood, thirsted for it even, but it never came. She played with those Kiel so often she probably had tiny cuts on every finger.

Cuts to match his scars.

"I'm not your messenger. Do it yourself," she snapped.

His lip curled as a wild rush of heat flooded his blood. "I heard you've been looking for the Empryen."

Reports from the Fallen she'd maimed and sent back to Hell with their balls shoved down their throats said a crazy Guardian was after it. Only one was crazy enough to actually hunt for it.

Hunting was his role, not hers.

"What do you know about it?"

Her breath hitched when he misted, reappearing right in front of her, so close only her dagger could slither between them.

"Why do you want it?"

She narrowed her eyes, staring him down as though she were a good foot taller than him, not the other way around. The Kiel in her hand remained motionless under her thumb.

His pulse quickened more than he liked in situations like this. Tormenting this pretty princess was his latest obsession, but he needed to keep his head in the game. Otherwise, she'd chop it off, gift wrap it in a bloody box and express mail it to Blaine for shits and giggles.

"This twisted game you're playing is over."

"Oh, sweetheart." He leaned in, whispering against her rosy lips, while the sharp edge of her Kiel dug into his thigh. "Our game's over when I say it is."

She held his stare, her breath tingled his lips, sending a delicious burn through his body. He could continue this game between them for another few centuries; in fact, the thought alone made him quiver in anticipation.

If only he had the time.

Her violet eyes deepened a split second before she spun, almost slapping him in the face with her ponytail. He remained still, watching her walk away. Just like all their previous encounters.

Raine 0. Slater 1.

At the end of the alley, she crouched and scooped her dagger off the ground. Quicker than he anticipated, she whirled around and threw it at him again. The dagger slammed into his chest before he misted. He grunted, stumbling backward. Fire burned through his torso, flooding his blood in a rush of toxic Purah.

It wouldn't kill him unless it reached his heart, but it hurt like hell.

Looking down, he gaped at the blade lodged between his ribs, less than an inch below his heart. A fraction higher and his corporeal form would explode into mist, landing his ass back in the Pits.

Even now, the muscles surrounding his heart spasmed, reacting to the poison entering his bloodstream.

"You missed." He grunted, gripping the hilt, and ripping the dagger free. Blood oozed from the wound, sliding down the inside of his shirt.

She glared at him. "I never miss."

As Raine turned away and exited the alley, a smile crept on his lips. Why would he want their game to end? Just when things were heating up.

He wiped the dagger on his thigh and flipped it in his hand as his body tingled, beginning to heal, and neutralizing the Purah in his system. Guess he'd live another day.

Raine 1. Slater 1.

Chapter FIVE

Raine threw several Kiel at a helpless tree one after the other, so fast her arm barely stilled. Each one lodged deep in the bark snug against the one before. She'd been at it for hours, throwing, collecting, throwing again until late in the afternoon.

Her back-alley encounter with Slater last week still rattled her more than she'd admit. Seeing him again made her blood boil. Like all Fallen, he deserved to rot in Hell for the rest of eternity, but she sensed he knew something about the Empryen. Until she found out what, she couldn't end him. She needed every bit of information she could get her hands on. Once he gave her what she needed, she'd send his soul to the Infernal Pits in miniature pieces for calling her a princess.

She was far from a princess.

Just because she'd spent her time in the Heavens holed up in a tower away from others, didn't mean she needed a prince to swoop in and rescue her. She managed just fine by herself.

Stupid mortal sentiments.

Grabbing the top Kiel from the pile in her palm, she pinched it between her finger and thumb and threw it at the tree, not even waiting for the crisp breeze to still. It shot true, straight through the air with the precision of a bullet, perfectly balanced, each point filed to the exact right angle to create the most lethal spin known to immortals and mortals. The Kiel slammed into the bark beside the previous one with less than a breadth of air between them, as though all the stars connected as one.

She sensed Raven approach from behind her.

"Your aim is unparalleled."

Tell me something I don't know.

She turned to face him as he strode toward her with twin short swords hanging from his hands. He twisted his wrist this way and that, obviously testing their weight. The swords were perfect. She already knew that, too.

"I dunno how you do it, Raine, but these are exactly the right balance."

She lifted a shoulder.

"Fancy a spar so I can test them out?"

She tipped her chin. Raven tossed a sword and she caught it. The second it landed in her palm, the Purah regulated to her body temperature. Forged with Raven in mind, it wasn't the right weight or size for her, but she'd make do.

She couldn't exactly spar with a Kiel.

Raven raised his sword and gave her a curt nod. She advanced. Without wasting time, she swung the sword at him. It whizzed through the air, clanging at the last second with his as he blocked her strike. He flipped his wrist, swinging back at her. She blocked it. Back and forth they parried, establishing a rhythm of strike then counterstrike. Raven got the upper hand, forcing her backward, only for her to change direction and return the favor.

She admired not just Raven's swordsmanship, but his equally fierce leadership. He didn't take any bullshit, but also wasn't one of those assholes that felt the need to assert his authority at every opportunity. Maybe River was right. Perhaps Raven would understand.

Would he help if he knew?

She and River had gotten nowhere since Fate banished them here. Maybe they did need help before the Guardians lost this war. But could she trust them? Fate had aided the Guardians more in the time she'd been here than ever before. Had Fate done that just to rub it in her face? To remind her of Fate's power, while Raine remained imprisoned in the mortal realm, unable to complete the one mission Fate created her for?

But she'd just gotten her first lead. Slater knew something. She needed to find him and figure out—

Raven lunged. She raised the sword to block his strike, but he twisted and kicked out a leg. The world flipped. Air punched from her lungs as her back slammed to the dirt. Raven towered over her, his sword at the hollow of her neck.

Fuck.

Her breaths punched in and out, pulse racing. Slater had a lot to answer for. Firstly, the knowledge he kept from her about the Empryen, and now, ambushing her thoughts which resulted in her back in the dirt with a sword at her throat.

"What's up with you?" Raven lowered his sword and offered his hand to pull her up. "It usually takes more than that to knock you over."

She grunted. Stupid Slater. "Even I have bad days."

He paused, didn't leave like she hoped he would.

She tossed the sword back to him and diverted to the tree trunk to remove the Kiel.

Raven waited. He still didn't get the hint.

"Ever since the Fallen attacked here a few months ago, you haven't been yourself. Is there anything you need to tell me?"

If she were her brother, she'd blurt it all out. Why they were in the mortal realm, what happened for Fate to banish them here. She'd ask for help to figure out who betrayed Fate.

Raven was loyal and, to her, more loyal and a stronger leader than their almighty queen. But even he couldn't help in this situation. This battle was hers to fight and it had nothing to do with why Fate sent him and the other Guardians here.

Though, at the rate she progressed with her mission, her battle would soon collide with his and they'd both fail.

In the end, she wasn't River. Therefore, she'd do this herself.

"I'm fine."

She yanked the Kiel from the tree trunk, made her way back to the starting point and threw them again as though Raven hadn't even interrupted her session.

"Raine." His voice deepened, laced with power and assertion.

She halted, arm cocked, ready to throw.

"If there's something going on, tell me. You and River are part of this fucked-up family, and we protect our own."

She knew he meant it, not just because like all angels, Raven couldn't lie, but also because she'd witnessed firsthand the bond between the Guardians. Strange sensations tugged in her chest, almost convincing her to tell him.

She'd never had a problem with loyalty before, never considered breaking a vow. But the moment some asshole fucked up her existence, everything changed. She felt more connected to the immortals inside the Guardian household, including the ones without wings, than her fellow angels back in the Heavens and she'd protect every one of them with her soul.

But even she couldn't protect them from the inevitable.

"It's nothing for you to worry over."

Not a lie if she believed it.

Raven remained silent for so long she glanced over her shoulder to see if he'd left. He hadn't. Silence was one of his many weapons. All the others caved under the pressure, but not her. She enjoyed silence as much as she enjoyed sharp, shiny objects.

Raven held her stare. As her throat thickened, she turned away and resumed throwing the Kiel. She couldn't allow anything else to distract her. Not Raven, not the females in the household, and definitely not the one Fallen who was always one step ahead of her.

In three months, it all wouldn't exist.

Raven finally sighed. "Meeting in ten. Fate sent EJ a new vision and I think it's linked to the shitstorm that happened in Hell."

She nodded without turning around. " 'kay."

She waited until Raven exited the forest and was halfway back to the mansion before she exhaled, allowing her shoulders to sag under the weight of Fate's overwhelming expectations.

Chapter SIX

Slater materialized in Pahadim, a hidden realm in Hell that he thought only he knew about. The two Fallen he'd acquired on a fake order from Blaine materialized beside him a second later.

The realm resembled a vast desert. Dirty soot fluttered in the air, while volcanoes spewed fiery lava into endless rivers. A blazing sun loomed in the sky, so big it could melt him in a heartbeat if he were a mortal.

Not that mortals came here.

He'd arrived in this realm shortly after his Fall. Originally, he came here with the naïve intention of hiding from Zath until the time came to act. But that motherfucker had found him. Since Blaine freed him from the Infernal Pits, he'd only come back a handful of times.

Clearly, he'd become complacent.

If only he had Blaine's patience.

"Where do we start searching?" the Fallen beside him asked.

He didn't even know their names, had just plucked them from outside Blaine's Hell mansion. Like loyal Fallen, they wouldn't dare defy him. His position as Blaine's second came with perks even with the threat of demotion hanging over him.

"Search the caverns," he replied. "Start with that one." He pointed to the nearest volcano.

Fallen One nodded before misting. Fallen Two stepped forward.

"Take the far one on the right."

Fallen Two misted as instructed.

Slater held back. It felt like forever since he'd used his tracking abilities. Outstretching his palm, he summoned the shadows swirling inside his body. Dark gray clouds of fog pooled at his palm, intensifying, swirling into the air above his hand. He rarely used his shadows in Hell. As an angel, he'd used them to escort souls to the gates or, on occasion, to hide his existence in the mortal realm. But only a few Azrael had the ability to track souls with them. Though, as a Fallen Azrael, he could only track Fallen souls.

Pity. Tracking the one he truly needed would take half the time if he could use shadows.

As the shadows curled around him, consuming his body in darkness, he lowered one knee on the red dirt and spoke the soul he wanted. "Asher, Fallen Azrael, father of Fallen Dumahel Ebony."

Names were powerful in Hell, and he used them as a beacon to the soul.

He waited seconds, minutes, he couldn't tell. In Hell, time moved differently than in the mortal realm.

These days he traveled between the two so often he wouldn't even know the day or month.

"Asher," he spoke again.

The shadows continued swirling around his body, intensifying as he poured more energy and power into them. They loomed in front of him, dark and ominous.

No light. No beacon.

No trace.

All Azrael had the ability to cloak their soul using

shadows. He bet Asher did exactly that.

Closing his palm, the shadows vanished in an instant as he lowered his head into his hands.

Asher wasn't in this realm.

He'd searched almost every realm in Hell looking for the traitor and came up empty. His position as Blaine's second was in serious jeopardy. At this rate, Blaine would likely hand him over to Zath just to prove a point.

He couldn't let that happen. He'd never return to the Pits. Ever.

But he needed to find Asher before Blaine realized the true cost of the Fallen's betrayal. Losing a Dumahel was one thing, but Asher threatened to destroy plans set in motion centuries ago.

The other two Fallen materialized beside him. He straightened, hoping like hell he'd been wrong and that they'd found Asher hiding in an abandoned cavern in one of the volcanoes.

"I found nothing. No evidence any Fallen have been here," Number One said.

He turned to Number Two on the slim chance he'd had more success.

"Same," said the other.

Slater inhaled a lungful of stale, hot air as the dim spark inside him snuffed out.

The only place he hadn't thoroughly searched was the mortal realm because he didn't think Asher would be stupid enough to hide his daughter right under the nose of the Guardians. Including her twin sister, who was a Guardian's soulmate. He was out of time. If he didn't locate Asher soon, word would get out and then she'd discover his screw-up.

If he thought all Hell would break loose if Blaine found out, he had nothing on her.

He needed to find Asher before Blaine realized just what he'd stolen, and he needed help to do it. Blaine wouldn't agree, but he was out of options.

Not just his position was at stake.

So was his soul.

Chapter SEVEN

Raine arrived in the war room ahead of everyone else. A room on the second floor where Raven discussed useless strategy. Planning wouldn't help them defeat the Fallen, nor would it aid in returning Blaine to the Heavens. Planning also wouldn't give her information on the Empryen.

She preferred action. Ambushing Fallen in back alleys and torturing information out of them. Unless they pissed her off, and in that case, she sent their soul back in pieces and hunted the next one.

Standing off to one side, she leaned against a side table in her usual spot and tried to compose herself. Since sparring with Raven earlier, she'd showered and changed. The last thing she wanted was one of the Guardians suspecting she was more on edge than usual.

Raven called the meeting because EJ had received a new vision from Fate. Most likely another Chosen.

When Fate banished her to this realm, she decided Raine wouldn't receive a Chosen assignment—a mortal created by Fate to fulfil an extraordinary destiny and contribute to Fate's plan for the universe. Which was just fine. As of late, Chosen assignments led the Guardians to their soulmates. Not exactly something she wanted or needed right now. Or ever. Having someone else monitor her every move would seriously put a kink in her destiny.

Besides, she wouldn't be here long anyway. No point in forming attachments.

Her mission in this realm was to recover the item stolen from Fate. How in the Heavens Fate let that happen, she'd never know. But until then, she didn't need any distractions or mortals getting in her way.

Though, she hadn't anticipated being in this realm for long. But the longer she stayed with the other Guardians, the more they'd become suspicious that she was the only one that had not received a Chosen assignment. Since the beginning of time, the Guardians had protected Chosen.

She needed to finish her real mission before they caught on.

Besides, if she couldn't recover the Empryen, protecting those fragile mortals was pointless. If that happened, no extraordinary mortal path was powerful enough to save this realm.

It would all end, her and the Guardians included.

As the rumble of Raven and Aric's voices traveled up the hallway, she straightened, lifting her chin as they strode into the room.

Aric acknowledged her with a nod. "Raven said he finally got one up on you."

First time for everything.

"Felt sorry for him."

Aric barked a laugh and slapped Raven on the shoulder before taking his seat.

Raven scoffed. "I'd expect you to take it easy on Tayla because she's still learning, but not me."

Tayla excelled at every self-defense lesson she put her through. After the Fallen attacked the property a few months back, she'd upped her lessons with Tayla and the others. Guardians or not, no one should think they were safe.

She cocked a brow at Raven. "Tayla's kicking ass lately. I'd watch out if I were you."

Raven relaxed in the chair with a satisfied smirk.

Aric laughed again. He shouldn't. She trained Willow just as hard.

Before Raven said anything further, the others filed into the room. She chose that moment to admire her new shiny pumps. The special order had arrived in the post yesterday. After buying so many from the mortal designer, he now sent her his special editions before they hit the stores. The mortal realm came with some perks.

This pair was inky black, as though dipped in oil and covered in a thick coat of gloss. With a tapered point and a thin strap around her ankles, they were heavenly on her feet.

Until she dipped the heel in Purah, she wouldn't wear them outside and certainly not when she hunted Fallen.

"Oh, my, Raine. Are they new? They're gorgeous."

She lifted her gaze at Hailee's voice. The Dumahel cooed at Raine's shoes as though they were a mortal baby. Hailee was the only other member of the household who appreciated stylish footwear.

A pang behind her ribs made her recall River's words the other day. If she had more time, she'd make an effort with the other females, for her brother's sake. But time wasn't on her side. They only had a few months left, so no point forging bonds when she'd only break them.

She forced a smile that hurt her cheeks, so River

didn't give her shit about it later.

"I need a pair that color," Hailee said, continuing their one-sided conversation.

"I wish I could walk in them." Tayla laughed.

For the love of Fate, now Tayla had joined the awkwardness. See? Exactly why she avoided gatherings. Now they were both in her space and gushing over her shoes.

Raine shifted her feet slightly, a subtle hint that her shoes were no longer up for conversation or display. When they continued to the table to take their seats beside one another, muscles tightened in her chest, probably in relief. She exhaled a deep breath and glanced across the table at her brother.

His bright green eyes lit when he smiled back. As though he'd caught her playing nice. Which, he hadn't. She didn't play nice with anyone. But she excelled at pretending, and if that made his time here a little less awful, then...whatever.

Being kind came with a price. Everyone expected it and sooner or later they'd realize kindness wouldn't save them when this realm ceased to exist.

Or when someone betrayed them.

"Right, let's get this show on the road." Raven turned to EJ. "Tell everyone about the vision."

EJ leaned back in his chair, his hand in Hailee's. "I dunno, Rave. I don't think it was a vision. I mean, Fate has never sent me a vision of a Fallen before. Except for that time with Red." He glanced at Willow. "Though technically she wasn't a Fallen, so it doesn't count. This was totally different. He was in this...wasteland. Like, I dunno, a desert or something only a million times worse."

"Do you think it's in the mortal realm? Or could it be a realm in Hell?" Willow asked.

Willow spent time in Hell after she Fell. If only Fate sent the vision to her, they'd have more answers.

EJ shrugged. "The place is like nothing I've seen. But if the vision is of a different realm in Hell, I'd like to have a quiet word with our fearless queen. What does Fate expect me to do if that dumbass Fallen is stuck in Hell? All puns intended."

"Leave him there?" Aric grumbled.

Raven leaned forward, his forearms on the table. "Given he's a Fallen and not a mortal, this isn't a Chosen vision. It's strange why Fate would suddenly send you a vision of him. Could he be using shadows to hide a Chosen? Or plan to? Do you sense anyone else in the vision? Any indication he cloaked a soul?"

EJ shook his head. "Nope. Just Slater."

Something caught in Raine's throat, making her cough.

"Did you say Fate sent a vision of Slater?" River asked, because clearly she couldn't speak.

What the actual fuck? Why would Fate send EJ a vision of Slater just after he'd asked her about the Empryen? She eyed her brother. She'd only told him of her...run-in with Slater and how he had information on the Empryen. On the outside, River perfected his goofy self, but she sensed he was just as shocked as her.

Holy shit.

Her pulse spiked and she inhaled through her nose to steady her breaths. Had someone turned up the heat? Off came her fingerless gloves, and she held them in her sweaty palm.

"Yep. The vision was Slater in this wasteland

place, crouching on the ground, his head lowered, those gross crimson wings unfurled behind him. I had the biggest urge to kick him and laugh as he face-planted in the dirt."

You and me both.

"You're definitely sure, bro? Slater?" River asked.

"I didn't get a look at his face, but I'd recognize that baldie anywhere. Why? You know something I don't?"

She ripped a Kiel from her belt and twirled it around her finger. It didn't help. She spun it faster, watching the Purah whirl around and around until the motions blurred together in a shiny circle.

"Raine?" Raven's voice echoed in her head from a faraway land.

She couldn't stop the spinning. Something pounded in her ears. She needed to get out of here before she told them. Before she said something she couldn't take back.

Then River would pay for her mistake.

Without answering, she fled from the war room.

Chapter EIGHT

Slater hid in a dimly lit corner of the SubZero nightclub, cloaked by his own shadows. Having searched many of the realms in Hell, besides the one he refused to return to, he failed to locate Asher and his daughter. To complete his mission, and maintain his position with Blaine, he needed to find those two Fallen, as well as the other item Asher stole when he decided to betray Blaine.

When had Asher revoked his allegiance to Blaine? And which side, or more importantly, who, did he now align himself with? Zath? Or had Asher discovered the true value of the item he stole and decided to try his luck taking on the prince of Hell on his own?

Just because Asher was a Fallen Azrael didn't mean he had the power or skill to overturn Zath. He probably didn't even know the location of Zath's realm. Asher was probably scared shitless, hiding behind his shadows, praying no one realized what he stole. He likely didn't even know its potential.

As if Slater wouldn't find out.

And now, he wouldn't let that traitor get away with what belonged to him.

Slater was the best tracker Fate ever created. Everyone knew that. The only thing on Asher's side was even Slater couldn't track a soul cloaked in shadows. But he'd find a way and get it back by any means necessary. To do that, he wasn't above a little bargain of his own. Which was how he found himself in this nightclub waiting for a Guardian to show. Preferably EJ, but he wasn't picky, any Guardian besides Aric would do. He and Aric didn't get along so well these days.

Had they ever? Not really.

As the mortal saying went, in times of war, he needed to keep his allies close and his enemies closer.

Thumping music blared in his ears, while sticky, humid air coated his exposed arms in a thin layer of sweat. Mortals threw their limbs back and forth to a rhythm of their own, not necessarily in time with the beat. Finally, he understood the attraction to a place like this. How one could lose themselves in the sounds, the sensations, the gritty need. It added a sweet layer to the wrath simmering beneath the surface of his skin. He'd been to this club before but never bothered lingering long enough to experience the thrill. If the Guardians didn't show, maybe he'd stay here until dawn.

Narrowing his eyes, he zeroed in on the sea of bodies crammed together beneath the flickering, colorful lights. His gaze snagged a blonde he had no interest in approaching. Lately, he had a liking for blondes. Only, he preferred ones that wouldn't break when he touched them, unlike these fragile mortals.

A tingle through his blood alerted him to the presence of the enemy.

Still cloaked, he leaned around the corner and scanned for the Guardians. From his position, he could see the entire club, everything from the entrance all the way to the rear sectioned-off area where they usually congregated. A door at the rear swung open and…bingo. EJ strolled into the club with his soulmate hanging on his arm. She looked just like her Fallen twin, only more…heavenly.

Slater waited until they sat at a table in the roped-off area before he dropped his shadows and stepped free of the cloak. As expected, EJ sprung up, no doubt sensing the presence of a Fallen. Without drawing a weapon or quickening his pace, he shoved through the mortals on his way to the Guardian. The moment EJ spotted him, he ushered his soulmate slightly behind him as though Slater was a threat. Usually, he was, but not tonight.

With the flick of his hand, he brushed off the mortal who tried to stop him from entering the roped-off area. The guy backed away, hands in the air, surrendering. Smart.

At the table, he inclined his head at the Guardian. "EJ."

"Get bored in Hell, Slater?"

"Something like that. I want to speak to Raven."

EJ screwed up his face. "Why the hell would I let you do that?"

"I have information he'll be interested in." He tipped his chin to EJ's soulmate, standing behind him with a murderous scowl on her face. He couldn't remember her name. "It involves her twin."

The Dumahel pushed EJ aside. "What's happened to Ebony?"

She not only had the same features as her sister but also the same feistiness. "Sorry, darling, this is between us."

"Watch your mouth, baldie," EJ snapped, stepping closer. "She's my soulmate, which means she's one of us. Which also means I'll slice your soul into tiny pieces if you speak to her like that again."

The corner of his lip twitched. "It's strange seeing you all...domesticated."

"That's a big word for you. Sure you know the meaning of it?"

Before he replied, EJ's soulmate threw her hands in the air. "Enough! What happened to Ebony?"

"Get your Guardian to call his leader."

The Dumahel glared at her soulmate. Less than a second later, EJ snatched a cell from his back pocket.

Ruled by a soulmate. What a joke.

"Frickin' Fate," EJ mumbled, holding the cell against his ear. "Rave? Slater's here at the club. He's got information on Hailee's sister."

Hailee. That was her name.

EJ slid the cell back into his pocket. "Rave's on his way. Go wait outside where you belong."

"Nah, I'm good. I'll wait right here." He pulled out a chair and settled at the table. "What's decent to drink?"

Even though Hailee sat back down, EJ remained standing with his arms crossed.

"You won't be here long enough to find out."

"I'm not here to cause a scene so you can drop the hostility," he replied.

"That'd be a first."

Liar. Scenes were the last thing Slater caused. He much preferred sticking to the shadows rather than out in the open like Blaine or EJ.

He was only here for one thing. To recover what was his. Once he had it, he'd leave everyone alone. The Guardians were no threat to him. While he was Blaine's second, they wouldn't dare send his soul to the Pits in case it ruined their chances of saving their former brother.

A waiter approached the table but a curt shake of the head from EJ diverted the guy in the opposite direction. Fine. He didn't want a drink anyhow.

Raven must've flown, because in hardly any time he stormed through the same rear door EJ and Hailee entered through earlier. Raven and Blaine were so alike. The way they exuded power, authority, and strength as though this world should bow at their feet.

Fate clearly had her favorites.

He hoped this trade of information worked to his benefit. If not, he could kiss his freedom goodbye and say hello to an eternity of torture and misery.

A slight buzz zipped through his blood when he realized Raven brought the cavalry with him. And not just anyone.

Raine.

Her gaze locked on his as she strode to the table, projecting a different kind of lethal power compared to Raven. Raine's was more like…deadly grace. He had no doubt she could hack his soul to pieces, whereas EJ was all smoke and mirrors.

Tonight, she had her hair pulled into a high knot with what resembled metal chopsticks crisscrossed through the center. He knew better than to assume she made them with anything but Purah.

Another weapon to stab him with.

At the table, Raven didn't waste a second. "Slater, I didn't expect you above ground for a while."

Reluctantly, he forced his gaze off Raine and stood facing Raven. "I thought you'd appreciate the heads-up."

"On what?"

Every cell in his body sizzled under the weight of Raine's stare. The way she looked at him like she wanted to cut him into bite-sized pieces and feast on his flesh created a delicious burn through his blood.

But now wasn't the time for distractions. For this plan to work, he needed to tread carefully.

"After EJ's little stunt in Hell—" He side-eyed the Guardian. "—Asher took the Dumahel twin and vanished."

"And? He's her father. What's that got to do with us?" Raven asked, gripping the backrest of a chair.

Shit. Good point. He hadn't thought of that.

He needed their help to find the Fallen Azrael but couldn't tell them why. Getting that weapon back before Asher used it wasn't something he wanted to share with the Guardians just yet. Nor did he want to reveal why he needed it. He only had a limited window before she found out he'd screwed up. When that happened, Raine cutting him into pieces would be the least of his worries.

Instead of revealing any of that, and risking Raven blabbing to Blaine, he addressed the Dumahel. "Your father betrayed Blaine and now Blaine's out for his soul. If Ebony isn't careful, she'll find herself in the crossfire. I'd hate for you to lose another of your family."

Besides her father, but nothing would save that Fallen now.

"That's rich coming from you, considering you didn't stop him from killing my mother." Hailee shot back.

EJ reached for her hand as her voice cracked.

Even though Hailee was just as snarky as her sister, matters of the heart always trumped the head. He would know.

"This time you can stop him."

"Like you care about what happens to Asher," Raven grumbled. "What's in it for you?"

Bingo.

He straightened. "An extra set of eyes in the mortal realm. I can't be everywhere at once and I suspect there's a leak in Blaine's…supporters. That's the only way Asher could've misted from Hell undetected." With the most powerful weapon in the universe, but he left that part out, as well as the fact Blaine had built an army in Hell. No need to give away all their secrets.

Raven thought for a moment, his gaze darted to EJ and back to Slater. "We'll keep an eye out for Asher and the twin but don't think we're doing this as a favor for you."

Deal done. He didn't care how they justified it, so long as it happened.

He turned to leave but stopped to look back at Raven. "If you find him, save us all the hassle and take him out."

Raven gave a curt nod.

Plan set in motion, he left the club through the rear door the Guardians seemed to prefer. Before he entered the dimly lit corridor, his gaze slid back to the table and locked on Raine's. The corner of his lip twitched as her eyes narrowed. No doubt he'd see her again sooner or later.

He hoped for the former.

Chapter NINE

Counting in her head, Raine waited a whole twenty-three seconds before releasing a breath and sinking into a chair. EJ, Raven, and Hailee barely noticed her as they debated the merits of joining forces with Slater to help catch a rogue Fallen. A Fallen hunting another Fallen. If that weren't the most absurd mission she'd ever heard of, she didn't know what was.

Why were they even bothering to discuss it?

From what she overheard of the conversation, Hailee was for it, Raven was hesitant even though he had already agreed, and EJ couldn't decide between his Guardian duty to kill the dickhead and saving his soulmate's sister from eternal death.

Who cared? One less Fallen in this realm, the better.

She couldn't wait to get out of here. Besides the filthy mortals gawking at her or undressing her with their eyes, the shitty music blasting from every corner, and the sweaty odor lingering in the air, sitting here wasted time she didn't have. She'd been back and forth to Blaine's decrepit mansion all week searching for Slater with no success. He knew something about the Empryen, and she needed that information.

More than that, she hated the fact he knew something she didn't.

Since she arrived in the mortal realm just over two

years ago, she'd searched for the Empryen with no luck. Then one day Slater ambushed the Guardian mansion, and since then, had relished in tormenting her at every moment. Figuring out his motives, and where he spent his downtime was her next logical step. He probably misted to Hell like most Fallen, but a strange pulse in her blood told her that wasn't the case. He frustrated her to no end, especially since he always seemed one move ahead of her.

Enough.

She needed to increase her efforts. Time was no longer on her side, if it ever was. When the Purah ran out, and the Guardians had no weapons capable of killing a Fallen, the Fallen would win.

She would fail.

This realm would burn to ash. Just as Fate predicted.

"Raine?"

She jolted as Raven said her name. They all stared at her as though waiting for her answer.

For the love of Fate, Slater muddled her thoughts even when he wasn't here.

"Yup?" she replied, shaking off the annoyance.

"I asked what you thought of Slater?"

Her fist clenched under the table. What did she think of Slater? How long did they have? "He's an untrustworthy piece of shit."

That summed it up. Nice work.

EJ leaned back in his chair and laughed. "Tell us something we don't know."

Raven narrowed his eyes, the blue darkening around the rim. "Do you two have a history I should know about?"

How the Fate did she answer that? The others didn't know why Fate banished her and River to the mortal realm, nor did they know her mission, and she wasn't about to tell them. Not even Raven. Her own brother didn't even know the full story. If they did, the whole plan would blow up in her face. Fate made sure of that.

She snatched a Kiel from her belt and pinched it between her fingers. The Purah warmed beneath her touch, tingling her skin. "Slater's a Fallen. You can't trust any of them."

She lifted her chin, projecting confidence she didn't feel in her bones. That damn Fallen.

Raven didn't seem convinced, especially considering she kept avoiding his question. "You think it's a trap?"

She made the mistake of glancing at Hailee. Her eyes were glassy as though on the verge of tears, and the way she clutched EJ's hand, made her reconsider her answer to Raven. Did she think what Slater proposed was a trap? *Likely.* Did she trust him? *Not one bit.* But should they at least try to save Hailee's twin from imminent death before the entire mortal realm burned to the ground?

Whatever.

"If it means killing another Fallen, then I'm in."

****

After they left the club, Raven ordered an emergency meeting back at the Guardian residence. Turned out, the count was unanimous. They'd help Slater hunt down Asher. Like her, they all suspected Slater's request was a trap, but they agreed for the sake of saving Hailee's twin.

That mission seemed all too familiar.

Hadn't Hailee just gone to Hell to save her sister only to find out her sister set her up? If that were River, she would've dragged him out by the collar of his palm tree shirt. On second thought, she would've made him leave the shirt in Hell.

After the meeting ended and the others left the room, Raine held back. The four walls caved in on her and squeezed the air from her lungs. Hatred coiled in her muscles, threatening to consume her emotions. How dare that Fallen turn up at the club and expect the Guardians to help him fix whatever shit he'd gotten himself into. She bet his ploy had nothing to do with Ebony's wellbeing.

Clearly, he faked his concern well.

She couldn't care less about finding Asher or saving Hailee's twin. They'd both made their choices. All she wanted was information on the Empryen, and Slater stood in her way. The sooner she tortured the knowledge out of him, the sooner she could end his soul and send it back to Hell where it belonged.

The sooner she could complete her mission and get out of this realm.

If only she knew where to find him. He'd struck a deal with the Guardians, so surely, he'd stay in this realm for the time being. Knowing his twisted sense of humor, he probably wanted her to chase him. Since he'd baited her last week, she had searched for him, but now that stopped.

Now, she'd hunt him.

Storming out of the war room, she swung by her room, stocked up on weapons, then headed downstairs. When no one questioned her, she slipped out the front door into the darkness and nearly tripped over River sitting on the top step. He had his long legs stretched out in front of him, back resting against a post. Even if he weren't blocking her path, all that florescent clothing made him hard to miss.

He glanced up at her. "Where are you headin', sis?"

She loved her brother, but by Fate, he annoyed her sometimes. "I don't need a babysitter, River."

He peered out at the darkness. "Fate sent EJ a vision of Slater. No instructions or hints, just a Fallen hangin' out in Hell or wherever."

He popped a candy in his mouth and chewed. She tapped her foot, impatient for this conversation to end.

"That was after Slater confessed to you that he has information on the you-know-what. And Fate also sent the vision before Slater requested help from the Guardians to find Asher."

Using her foot, she shoved her brother's legs off the step and descended to the gravel path, knowing River would follow her. When they were out of earshot of the Guardian mansion, she turned to her brother. "I presume either Fate has become impatient, or she's realized how little time we have left."

He nodded. "I figured the same. But what's with the vision? In the vision, Slater was in Hell, but he's clearly not, considering you just saw him at the club. And why would Fate send a vision to EJ when she wanted you to keep your mission a secret?" He thought for a moment, staring at the cloudless night. "Do you think she heard me suggest that you tell Raven?"

"Paranoid much?"

"She's a little scary when she's mad." He frowned

at her. "Unless…Slater doesn't just know about the Empryen…what if he has it?"

Something she'd also considered. But how the Fate did he steal it? "Your guess is as good as mine. But Raven's not stupid. Slater won't fool him with his request for help. Fate probably sent the vision to tell me to hurry up."

River popped another candy in his mouth and slowly nodded. Thank Fate he was immortal, otherwise he'd need a lifetime of dental work.

"I still think you should risk telling Raven."

"That's not an option, especially now. We have no idea if Fate will follow through with her threat. It's not worth it."

They stood together in silence for the longest time. Probably a record for her brother. He hadn't been that silent in his entire existence.

She unfurled her wings, sighing as a rush of euphoria swept through her blood. "I'll check in when I come back."

River stuffed the bag of candies in his pocket. "I'll come with you."

She fanned out her wings in a wide arc, stretching the muscles, preparing for flight. Wrapping things up inside with the Guardians took longer than she anticipated, which left her only a couple of hours of darkness. She needed to take advantage of it to find Slater.

He wouldn't return to Hell so soon after his proposition to Raven. No, that loser enjoyed the chase, and she hated the fact she gave him exactly what he craved.

Once she got the information, she'd have no further

use for him.

Bye-bye, Slater.

"I'm fine, River. I'll be back by sunrise."

His mouth set in a firm, grim line but he didn't argue.

Once he nodded, she launched into the sky. The fresh air did her lungs good and cleared her head. How one Fallen could irritate her so much, she'd never know.

First stop tonight on the hunt for Slater was Blaine's decrepit mansion on the outskirts of Summit Creek. She'd been back and forth there all week but found nothing. In fact, she hadn't encountered any Fallen there at all. Had Blaine and his buddies abandoned the place for somewhere else? Or were they all hiding out in Hell like Hailee said?

Flying took a few minutes. She used that time to get herself in the right frame of mind. To hunt Slater, she needed to think like him. He could be anywhere, and given she no longer possessed the ability to mist, it made finding him a slow and arduous process.

Landing in the nearby forest, she paused only a moment to fold her wings behind her and slip a Kiel from her belt. Stalking through the trees, she spotted the three-story mansion wrapped in leafless vines. Gothic wasn't exactly her style despite what others thought.

No smoke billowed from either chimney, and the drapes were drawn on all the windows. Willow had spent some time here while she was on Team Blaine. She'd given a detailed layout of the floor plan and told them Blaine cloaked the inside under a Raziel spell. A shudder ran through her when she thought of how Blaine got his hands on one of those.

At the tree line, she stretched out her senses. The still night air remained quiet as though it anticipated her ambush and was too scared to move. Dark shadows swirled around the mansion, the only light coming from the crescent moon low in the sky.

She sensed no Fallen nearby or inside. But if the Raziel cloak still worked, it would prevent her from sensing past the barrier.

Tonight, she'd go inside.

The time for chasing from the sidelines had come to an end.

With her weight on the balls of her feet so her heels didn't get stuck in the grass, she dashed across the lawn. She slipped around the corner of the building, intending to sneak in the front door but didn't get the chance.

Slater wasn't stupid. He also wasn't in Hell.

He'd waited for her.

Her steps faltered as Slater moved free from a shadow beside a pillar.

Tonight, he wore more current century attire, likely not to stand out at the nightclub. Or perhaps because she made fun of his leather pants a few months ago. Even though she figured he favored Azrael shadows over any other weapon, she still scanned his leather jacket searching for bulges in the fabric that suggested he concealed something that might harm her. It had nothing to do with how his form-fitting shirt accentuated his muscular physique. She appreciated a male immortal as much as anyone, just not one she wanted to kill.

Slater portrayed the part of a tall, dark, and handsome immortal with the deepest brown eyes she'd ever seen. But hidden under all that perfection was the soul of a traitor.

When this war was over, she'd remember only that.

She marched right up to him, pressing the point of the Kiel against his surprisingly firm chest. "What's your angle, Slater?"

Even with her four-inch fighting heels, she tilted her head up to meet his gaze. Why was he so tall and broad, putting her at a height disadvantage?

He glared down at her, though his eyes sparked with amusement. "I knew you'd come."

She cursed herself for playing right into his hands even though he'd left her no other choice.

By now, she'd perfected what EJ called her resting bitch face. She wouldn't reveal how much her encounters with this Fallen affected her, nor would she let him know how much she wanted to stab him.

She'd surprise him with that knowledge later.

"Why not use a Fallen to do your dirty work rather than the Guardians?"

She narrowed her eyes, waiting for his answer or a spark of Fallen emotion. His irises remained their usual brown and didn't change crimson like when a Fallen lost control. Slater never lost control of anything.

She hated that.

"I don't need the Guardians' help, princess. I met with them to set up this little encounter with you. Although, I didn't expect you to come to the club. Had I known, I could've saved you the trip here."

He inched closer, forcing the Kiel through his shirt, piercing his skin until she had no choice but to lower her arm before it injected his blood with Purah. Only because his motive intrigued her. It had nothing to do with not wanting to hurt him.

Because she did want to hurt him. A lot.

His front brushed against hers in the lightest touch and she scoffed to mask the stir in her belly. "That's stupid of you, considering I want to grant you a thousand deaths with my bare hands."

His body consumed her personal space, just as he had in the alley. Like then, the air around them thickened, squeezing her lungs. Her hand curled into a tight fist, wanting to strangle the breath from him.

She didn't retreat, even though every part of her body screamed to turn and run. A natural response for an angel.

She wasn't just any angel.

"I have a deal for you."

Her lip curled in a snarl that she couldn't hold back. "Unless it ends in your soul returning to Hell where it belongs, I'm not interested."

When his hand reached out to brush her cheek, she whacked away his arm then shoved his shoulders. He didn't move an inch. She reached for the dagger at her hip, but he snagged her wrists. In the next second, he slammed her against the pillar, pinning her arms above her head.

Her pulse raced as she struggled against his hold, trying to free herself. All that perfectly crafted muscle coiled into a stone force even she couldn't move.

He leaned in, dangerously close. "Not even if it means getting your sword back?"

She froze.

Surely, she misheard.

"Now I have your attention," he murmured, his tone a low, deep rumble. "Work with me and you'll get it back."

"Why would I trust you?"

With him distracted by her question, she shifted slightly, ready to knee him in the balls.

"Because I know who you are, princess." He smirked. "The *real* you."

Except for her brother, no one outside the Heavens knew her true identity.

Slater knew nothing. How could he?

"I need your...expertise to track Asher."

She shoved against his hands again and this time he released her, taking half a step back. Not far enough.

"I don't know what you're talking about," she said through clenched teeth.

"I thought you couldn't lie?"

She stared at him. He couldn't. No way he knew the real her. If he did, that meant someone told him...Fate...

Her hand tightened around the Kiel, slicing her palm until it drew blood.

Fate. Fate sent EJ a vision. How convenient she did that right before Slater requested help from the Guardians.

Did Fate tell Slater? *No.* She couldn't have. Fate hadn't left her sanctuary since Blaine Fell and from what she knew, Slater Fell long before Blaine.

Fate wouldn't risk misting to this realm to meet with a Fallen. Would she?

She glared at the Fallen before her. If he truly knew who she was, then she needed to end him now. She couldn't risk it. No one could know she was in the mortal realm. Especially not a Fallen.

Right before she flipped the Kiel and aimed it at

his heart, Slater reached behind his back and produced a dagger, offering her the hilt. Not just any dagger, but the one she lodged in his chest the other night in the alley.

"I've kept your secret."

Her heart slammed inside her chest.

He knew. He fucking knew. How the Fate did he know?

This situation was all kinds of screwed up. Just because he knew her secret and hadn't exposed her, didn't mean he wouldn't. Nor did it mean he wouldn't hold it against her as leverage, just as he did now.

The bastard was better off dead.

She eyed the dagger in his hand. How quickly could she snatch it and slam it into his heart?

"You probably stole it."

He smirked. "Why would I want your help if I stole it?"

Because the sword was useless without her.

She searched those big, brown, Fallen eyes for something resembling the truth. Whether she cared to admit it or not, he had a point. Why would he seek out the Guardians if he already had the sword? Either he told the truth, or he played a risky game to trick her, which would end in his death.

But...if he spoke the truth, this was a solid lead. Her first since arriving in this realm.

After she got the sword back, she could finally complete her destiny. Taking the sword to its rightful place would grant the Guardians more time to complete their mission. It would save this world.

It would save River.

Was all that worth working with a traitorous

Fallen? A traitorous Azrael? She wasn't so easily convinced.

Even so, caution was the key. Just because Slater had information and agreed to share it with her, didn't mean he'd magically changed back into an angel. He was still a Fallen.

Wait a minute. He had information on the Empryen.

She lifted her chin. "What's in it for you?"

"I made a vow I intend to keep."

She scoffed. "That's rich coming from a Fallen."

He shrugged. "It makes no difference to me whether you believe what I say."

His brutal honesty threw her.

Was she actually considering a deal with a Fallen?

Her breath punched in and out. She hated Fallen more than she hated girly chick-flicks, and she sure as the Heavens couldn't trust him. Fallen were immortals conditioned for betrayal and broken trust.

But to date, she'd gotten nowhere. Slater forced her to play right into his hands by dangling the only thing she'd fight for. This might be her only chance.

Gritting her teeth, she snatched the dagger out of Slater's hand. "I'll gut you before we even find Asher."

"Maybe." He smirked, lowering his mouth to her ear. For some reason, she refrained from disfiguring it. "But it'll be one helluva way to go out."

Chapter TEN

Slater materialized on the roof of Blaine's mortal castle. He'd spent the day acquiring weapons. Fighting another Azrael solely with shadows wouldn't work in his favor. He could ask Raine, he knew she forged weapons for the Guardians, but given their rivalry, she'd likely make him a blade from a rare form of Purah that leaked into his skin causing his soul a slow and painful banishment back to Hell.

That would put a serious dent on his freedom.

First, he needed to warm up his frosty princess before she trusted him enough to make him a weapon. Before he trusted her enough to make him a weapon. Until then, he'd rely on a special sect of mortals that knew of the immortal world. Some worked with the Guardians trying to eliminate Fallen, others preferred to play for both sides, hedging their bets on whoever had control at the time.

At the edge of the roof, he stilled, casting his senses in a wide arc in case someone was dumb enough to ambush him or snoop around the mansion. Coming up empty, he unfurled his wings, stepped off the edge, and landed on the dirt. Misting directly inside was impossible given the Raziel cloak Blaine had on the place. It stopped random Fallen from entering, and if Fate ever granted the Guardians back their misting powers, it kept them out, too. Every visitor entered through the door like a mortal.

He swung open the front door but stopped when he sensed others inside.

For fuck's sake, why was she here?

Slamming the door shut behind him, he stormed into the living room on a new mission to inflict as much pain as possible. When Blaine spotted him, he relaxed back in a leather armchair. The Fallen out for his position sat across from Blaine as though already victorious.

Like hell she was.

Halting beside the couch, wicked pain throbbed in his temples. He hadn't slept since returning to the mortal world and although he didn't need much, he could really use a fucking night off.

All this misting back and forth between realms played havoc with his brain.

"What do you want?" he snapped at Peyton, though he directed the question to them both.

Peyton scowled.

To think he trained her so he had an ally in Hell he could trust. Now it seemed she was just another immortal in his existence that threatened to betray him. These days the list was a mile fucking long.

He'd send his soul back to the Infernal Pits himself before he let Peyton or any other Fallen steal his position with Blaine. Everything depended on him being beside Blaine.

Blaine chuckled, though the look in his eyes was far from humorous. "Have you found the Dumahel?"

He turned to face Blaine, maybe then Peyton would get the hint and run back to Hell. "You've been in Hell too long. Things move slower in the mortal realm."

"I don't care for excuses, Slater."

Before he said something he'd regret, he grabbed a glass from the side table, taking his sweet time pouring himself a drink. Anything so Blaine didn't notice how his words affected him. He owed that Fallen a great deal of debt and for that reason alone, he supported Blaine's quest for revenge.

After all, it fit nicely with his own mission.

But he hoped it wouldn't come to that.

He took a long sip of bourbon. "What's the real reason Peyton is here?"

Blaine flipped his boots up on the coffee table. "I won't let this quest fail. Two Fallen are better than one."

A Fallen and an angel were even better, but he kept that bit to himself. Before Raine had agreed, she'd made it clear if he told anyone, their deal was off. He needed her. To track down Asher before the two most powerful immortals found out what Asher stole, he needed Raine's…unique skills. So, for now, their deal remained between them.

"Besides," Blaine continued, "Peyton could use some familiarity with the mortal realm."

Like hell she could. "My personal tours are closed for the holidays. I suggest you try again next century."

Blaine tilted his head, studying him and the weight of his stare unsettled him more than he liked.

"What are you hiding?"

He took a long draw of bourbon, steadying his emotions. If Blaine found out, all Hell would break loose. Literally.

It looked like he needed to babysit Peyton.

After refilling his glass, he took a seat across from

Peyton on the other couch. "The mortal news this morning reported a mysterious death on a subway. A mortal with black marks beneath his skin. The authorities think it's some new kind of drug, but—"

"Azrael shadows." Blaine finished his sentence.

He nodded.

Peyton shifted on the couch. "An Azrael took a soul, so what?"

He studied the glass in his hand. "Syphoning a mortal soul doesn't leave a mark. But when an Azrael uses shadows to manipulate a mortal's mind, that infects the blood."

"Leaving lines beneath the skin." Peyton nodded in understanding.

Manipulating any soul wasn't something he did often. Despite what others thought. Removing memories or manipulating free will fell into the same bucket as torture. Just because he was a Fallen didn't mean others deserved the same trauma he experienced. Those memories alone would haunt him for the rest of eternity.

Although impossible, the thick black scars marring his wrists heated, stealing his breath. *Heat flashed along his skin, sulfur burned the insides of his nostrils with each inhale, sharp hisses surrounded him as Devoid dipped metal rods in hellfire preparing to—*

Pain burst in his hand, vanishing the memory. The tumbler shattered. Glass shards scattered in every direction, over him, the floor, and the couch.

Peyton leaped to her feet. "What the hell?"

Not the first episode he'd had since Blaine freed him, but they usually came when he was alone with his thoughts, not in a room with others. The more he ached for freedom, the worse the memories got.

"No need to panic. It's nothing." He stood and shook the glass off his pants.

Blood dripped from slices in his palm. He pinched a jagged piece of glass and slid it from his skin, dropping it on the floor by the small pool of blood.

Drip, drip, drip...

Curling his toes inside his boots, he inhaled a deep breath through his nose to steady the nausea.

Every Azrael had the ability to syphon a soul from a mortal body and escort it to its final resting place in either the Heavens or Hell. But when Fate created some angels, she did so with a little extra zing, like him. He was the best immortal tracker because he also had the ability to syphon emotion. He not only felt and experienced what a mortal felt right before they died, but he also used that emotion to track any connection to others.

In a single strike, he could annihilate an entire family.

But his ability to feel was also his greatest weakness. Sometimes those emotions took hold and dug their sharp talons inside his soul, slowly torturing him.

Blaine waved a dish towel in front of his face. He took it and wrapped it around his hand until the skin began to tingle, healing the cuts and stopping the bleeding. Stepping over the glass, he made his way back to the side table and grabbed a new tumbler, pouring himself a fresh drink.

He turned to Blaine. "What's the situation in Aralim?"

Blaine created the realm as a base for his

operations. Hiding from Zath in plain sight was a risk, but he couldn't exactly build an army of Fallen in the mortal realm. Though, by now he should've had a Guardian and an Ariel on his team too, which would've made their presence in the mortal realm easier. That plan failed though when Willow returned to the Heavens.

Blaine waved his hand in the air, dismissing the concern. "There's no need to worry. The Guardians won't return, EJ has his soulmate safely tucked away in the mortal realm."

"Do you still need her?"

As a Dumahel, EJ's soulmate also possessed the ability to dreamwalk, but with angels, unlike her twin. A few months ago, Blaine used both twins to connect him and Fate in a dream. Blaine hadn't given him all the details of what occurred in the dream, but he presumed Blaine hadn't harmed Fate given the Guardians hadn't targeted them since and the universe hadn't vanished.

"The next time I meet with Fate will be the moment I knock her off that pretty throne. I won't need a light Dumahel to do that."

He leaned his ass against the side table and sipped the bourbon. "How will you get into the Heavens?"

Blaine waved his hand in the air again, which pissed him off. Why did he feel so left in the dark lately?

"Let me worry about that."

So many unanswered questions about Blaine's plans made him nervous. Even though Blaine released him from the Infernal Pits, could he really trust the Fallen?

Peyton crunched through broken glass as she wandered the living room. With only a couple of couches, a side table and a few scattered items left over from the previous owner, there wasn't much to look at.

No point in familiarizing herself with the place. She wasn't moving in.

He peered out the window at the fading light. He needed to get rid of them both before Raine came knocking. They'd agreed to meet here tonight, but if she found out Blaine and Peyton were also here, Raine would split. And his plan would go up in smoke.

Raine was more valuable than Blaine or Peyton right now.

"Isn't Peyton better utilized in Hell? She could search the realms looking for Asher in case he slips back in," he said to Blaine.

A slow smirk lifted on Blaine's face. "I have the gateways covered. If Asher returns to Hell, I'll know about it. Perhaps your concern should be tracking him in a realm so foreign to you."

He clenched and unclenched his fist. Blaine wouldn't let this go. He needed to think of another way to lose Peyton and be smart about it. "You're right. I could use the help." Just not hers.

Peyton smiled, her eyes clearly back on his position. Little did she know, he was onto her and wouldn't give up so easily.

"Excellent. I have some business to attend to back in Hell. Keep me updated."

Blaine strolled out the door, leaving him in the living room with an annoying sidekick.

What was the use of being second-in-command without any fucking autonomy?

Chapter ELEVEN

Raine slipped a dagger into the holster strapped on her thigh. The Purah blade was a warning to Slater and any other Fallen who wanted to test her patience tonight. She wasn't in the mood for games. The dagger wasn't her only weapon, just the only one visible.

If she intended to work with Slater, she needed to do so with her eyes wide open. He would, and could, betray her at the first possible opportunity.

She left her cell on the workbench in the armory, so the others didn't call. They could still track her through the Guardian bond linking them together, but usually they only relied on that in times of emergency.

Given she would be with Slater, nothing catastrophic would happen. Despite being a Fallen, he was a skilled fighter.

Before leaving the armory, she slipped off her shoes and dangled them from her fingers as she crept upstairs and snuck out the back door of the mansion. Outside, she put her shoes back on, unfurled her wings and took to the sky.

She'd agreed to meet Slater back at Blaine's mansion tonight so they could start the hunt for Asher. The sooner they found him, the better. Clearly, Slater had been hiding at the mansion all along, she just hadn't been able to see him through the cloak.

The brisk night air kept her thoughts clear and on

the task at hand. She'd never been this close to finding the Empryen. Nothing stood in her way now.

In no time, she descended through the patchy cloudbank. Stretching her wings, she slowed her speed and gently slipped between the trees to land on the outskirts of Blaine's estate—

A palm slapped over her mouth. Fire and brimstone slammed into her senses as hard and fast as the arm around her middle, holding her against a firm body.

Slater.

She jabbed her elbow into his ribs. He cursed but tightened his hold.

"Relax, princess," he whispered.

Relax? She didn't know the meaning of the word. Also, not calling her "princess" still hadn't got through his thick skull.

Lifting her leg, she moved to thrust her heel into Slater's shin. Before she got the chance, he knocked her foot out from beneath her and she toppled forward. At the last second, he twisted, taking the brunt of the fall, grunting as his back slammed on the ground with her on top of him. His damn hold around her middle never loosened.

"There's another Fallen here," he whispered.

She stilled. Exhaling a long breath, she steadied her heart rate to concentrate on the prickle at her nape, rather than the places where her body heated, pressed firmly against Slater's. She'd assumed the prickle was a result of Slater being nearby, but any Fallen would set off her angelic warning system. It couldn't determine how many threats, just that they were imminent.

Closing her eyes, she listened, stretching out her senses for sounds of another Fallen.

Of course, Slater could've lied to her. But why would he?

When she detected no threat besides the lump of muscle she lay on, she reached for a Kiel clipped to her belt, knowing Slater would anticipate her move. He shifted his arm to snag her hand before she grabbed the Kiel, and she took advantage of his distraction. She clutched his wrist, twisted out of his hold, and leaped to her feet in one swift move. Before he stood, she placed the pointy, Purah-dipped heel of her shoe at the hollow of his neck.

"Don't lie to me."

He smirked, seeming unfazed that she could end his corporal form with the slightest push of her foot.

"As much as I like you rattled, and let's be clear, I fucking like you rattled, I'm not lying." He lifted an arm and pointed behind him toward the mansion. "There is a Fallen inside."

Fallen could, and did lie, but again she sensed Slater told the truth. Fate only knew why. But what would he gain by tricking her? If he wanted to harm her, he wouldn't have warned her about the other Fallen. Nor stopped her from walking into a trap when she exited the forest.

Why was he so infuriating?

With a groan, she stepped back, allowing him to stand. "I made it clear that we do this alone."

Slater brushed dirt from the back of his pants. "Blaine sent her."

Her? A strange sour taste floated up the back of her throat. "Get rid of her."

"I tried, but it won't be that simple." He peered toward the mansion. "Let's just say she has an invested interest in proving to Blaine that she can find Asher before me."

She rolled her eyes. Babysitting wasn't her responsibility, and she sure as Fate didn't need someone knowing about her deal with Slater. Too much was at stake. The more immortals involved, the greater the risk of failure.

She gritted her teeth, glaring at Slater. "Fix this or you're on your own."

He closed the distance between them so fast she had no time to retreat. Why did she let her guard down with him around? No other Fallen, or immortal, ever gained the upper hand on her. Why him?

"You'll help me because you want the Empryen back."

Again, he dangled the one thing she wanted above everything else. Again, she sensed herself falling into his trap.

She shoved his chest, pushing him backward. "How do I even know Asher has it? How do I know you're not lying?"

"You'll have to trust me."

"I'll never trust you. You're a Fallen. You probably stole it yourself and stashed it away in Hell while I help you find Asher."

Something flashed in his eyes too quick to decipher.

Slater angled his head, staring down at her in a challenge. One she was more than ready for.

"Treat me like the villain all you want, princess. I am, and I make no apology for it. But I don't have the Empryen."

She scoffed and lifted her gaze to the Heavens as

though Fate would help her. *Doubt it.*

He inched closer, forcing her gaze back to his. "For this to work, at some point, you'll have to trust me."

"Yeah, when the Heavens Fall."

Which might be sooner than everyone thought.

Movement between the trees to her left caught her attention. She slipped the Kiel from her belt, preparing for attack. Slater followed her line of sight and swore under his breath but didn't call his shadows.

"We have to meet somewhere else."

Through the trees, she glimpsed another Fallen stride around the corner of Blaine's mansion. From this distance, all she spotted was a female with raven hair braided back from her face, and a slender frame clothed in black military wear.

Slater had told the truth.

Facing her, Slater moved slightly, blocking her view of the Fallen. Or blocking the Fallen's view of her?

"I'm not scared of a Fallen."

She stepped aside, but he matched it.

"This particular Fallen has a hidden agenda, one I intend to figure out before you go all stabby on her."

"I don't go stabby."

Slater cocked a brow.

She stared up at him, waiting for the explanation that never came.

"Until I know what she's up to, she can't be trusted."

"Neither can you."

He remained silent while that same emotion as before once again flashed over his features. Guilt? Satisfaction? Before she identified it, it vanished.

"We can't meet tonight, or here again. I need to tie up some loose ends. Meet me behind the mortal nightclub tomorrow night. I have somewhere safe we can go."

"What if I don't want to?"

He grinned as though he found her comment adorable. He didn't believe a word she said and perhaps, neither did she.

Slater turned to leave but she snagged his jacket, holding him back. "Once I get the Empryen, we're done. Does your puny Fallen brain understand?"

"Keep telling yourself that, princess."

Before she punched him in the face, Slater misted and reappeared behind the other Fallen. As the female spun to face Slater, Raine turned and ran in the opposite direction for the first time in her existence.

Chapter TWELVE

Raine waited by the pool table while the other Guardians filed into the room. EJ beelined to the bar and snatched various bottles to make cocktails. That immortal should've been a bartender.

River diverted to her. "Any news?"

She shook her head as both a warning and answer. Discussing her mission within earshot of the others was too risky, even if everyone was involved in other conversations, someone might overhear. Speaking telepathically to her brother was an option, but again, if another Guardian wanted to, they could intercept.

River got the hint and continued to the couch to sit beside Tayla.

Standing on her own, the air was cooler, not as suffocating.

The Guardians converged on and around the couches as EJ handed out a variety of drinks as though this were an ordinary Friday night. But it was far from it.

Fate sent EJ another vision.

Raven called the meeting to discuss their way forward, but little did they know, she already had a plan. She just couldn't share it with them.

What she needed was to figure out a way to combine the two.

The second Gabe strode into the room, she

stiffened. Had Fate told the Archangel the real reason why she and River were in the mortal realm? Could she confide in him?

Probably not.

Gabe gave her a slight bow. "Raine."

She tipped her chin. "Gabe."

He proceeded to the center of the room to join the others. "EJ, tell me about the vision."

"That baldie Fallen was still in the wasteland, but this time the vision came from the front."

EJ handed her a martini glass before moving back to Gabe.

She placed the glass on the edge of the pool table before her shaky fingers dropped it. Leaning forward, she focused on EJ's words, to decipher every clue. The others thought this vision was for them or for EJ. Perhaps a Chosen vision. But she and River knew better.

Fate sent EJ this vision as a message to her.

A message to hurry the fuck up.

EJ continued, "This time when I saw Slater, he had his hands wrapped around the hilt of one helluva spectacular sword, the point shoved in the dirt."

Icy chills slithered down her spine. An imaginary steel vise squeezed her chest. She didn't dare let her gaze slip off EJ, not even when she sensed River watching her, gauging her reaction. If she looked at her brother now, she'd fall apart.

"Describe the sword," Gabe said to EJ.

"Bright. Glowing like River's shirts, only brighter. I didn't think that was possible." He chuckled, though no one joined in. "Umm, long with a black hilt. And it had weird black markings down the blade."

Shit.

Holy fuck.

She slipped a Kiel from her belt, curling her fingers between the points.

Raven turned to Gabe. "Could it be?"

Gabe's mouth formed a thin, grim line. "I believe so, though I'm unsure why Fate would send the vision. I'm also unsure why a Fallen would be in possession of such a powerful weapon."

Her heart raced, sucking air from her lungs. She reached for the side of the pool table to steady herself as sudden dizziness swept through her body.

Raven paced back and forth, hands on his hips. "What the hell does it mean? How could a Fallen have it?" He paused and spun back to EJ. "It can't be a vision. A Fallen couldn't get their hands on the Empryen."

EJ gasped. "Hang on, did you say the Empryen? I thought that was something Fate made up. I've never even seen it."

Raven clapped EJ's shoulder. "It's as real as you and me, my man."

EJ swore under his breath before reaching for a bottle of vodka.

She twirled the Kiel around her index finger, assessing the information. Slater had the Empryen. He'd lied to her. Why the Fate did he need to hunt Asher if he already had the sword?

Fate had just increased the stakes. She'd also broken her one and only rule: tell no one. If Fate sent EJ a vision of Slater with the Empryen, she effectively told the Guardians. Should she tell them the rest?

Would Fate still punish River if she did?

The Kiel spun faster. Around and around her finger it flew until the motions blurred into one.

Was this another twisted message from Fate? If Fate sent the vision as a warning, it confirmed Slater had the Empryen, likely in Hell, the only place Raine couldn't reach it.

If that were true, how would she complete her mission? She'd have to somehow convince Slater to bring it to the mortal realm.

Raven placed his drink on the bar top. "If Slater has the Empryen in Hell, why did he approach us about Asher?"

"Unless Asher found out and Slater needs to eliminate the liability?" Aric said from his spot on the barstool.

Raven slowly shook his head. "It doesn't make sense." He braced his hands on the back of the couch, behind Tayla. "Until we figure out what's going on, we need to get to Asher before Slater does."

"Agreed."

She stilled the Kiel with her thumb. Now was her chance. She could volunteer to track down Asher. It gave her the perfect opportunity to skip Fallen patrols, an excuse to leave the Guardians for periods of time, and a solid explanation why someone would spot her with Slater.

Way better than telling them and risking River's immortality.

She'd screwed up. She'd gotten herself and River into this mess and she sure as Fate wouldn't rely on another Guardian to save them.

While Raven and the others brainstormed a plan, she side-eyed her brother. He gave her a slight nod, and that was all the reassurance she needed.

"I'll do it."

The conversation halted and all gazes swung to her.

She straightened, slipping the Kiel back in her belt. "I'll track down Asher."

Raven tilted his head as though about to question her. She never gave him the chance. "There's nothing else to do around here. I forge the weapons to feel useful 'cause there's never enough Fallen to kill. I'd love nothing more than to take that asshole down."

EJ choked on his drink. The others stared at her as though she'd cartwheeled from one side of the room to the other wearing a pink tutu. She ignored them to address Raven. He was the only one she needed to convince. He had the final say.

She cleared her throat. Why was it so dry? "Honesty, I could use a change of scenery."

Raven was quiet for a moment. "All right, but I want two Guardians. There might not be any Fallen around town these days, but you can bet your ass Asher isn't the only Fallen involved in this. And if he betrayed Slater, or whatever the hell happened, there's more at stake than we first thought." He turned to Aric. "You up for it?"

What the actual fuck? She didn't need another Guardian to get the job done. She was as capable, if not more, than any other Guardian. Battle tactics were Aric's greatest skill, he'd figure out her ulterior motive before she had the chance to change her shoes. For this mission, she needed someone she could lose.

River stood. "What about me? I know I'm not the first choice 'cause I don't look all tough and scary like Aric, but Raine and I work great together." He flashed a big smile. "It's a sibling thing."

Raven studied River and she sent a silent thank you to her brother for once again saving her ass.

"Okay." Raven straightened, glancing between her and River. "Report back every step of the way and if you need backup, make sure you ask."

She nodded.

River, on the other hand, didn't know when to quit. "We'll need access to funds."

"I'll hook you up," EJ answered.

"Given we can't mist, we might also need a plane."

In one swift movement, she unclipped the Kiel and threw it at her brother. He anticipated her shot and plucked it from the air without taking his gaze off EJ.

Shithead.

"How about you fly like the rest of us, sunshine?"

River slipped the Kiel on his pinkie and shrugged. "It was worth a try."

She shook her head but couldn't help the smile curving on her lips. In his own way, so none of the Guardians suspected a damn thing, River had given her the perfect alibi. No longer would she need to hide another secret or pretend to patrol for Fallen while she searched for clues. She could hunt Asher...then end Slater for lying to her.

Most importantly, she could discuss the Empryen without fear of Fate retaliating.

River tossed her the Kiel and she caught it, slipping it back in her belt.

As she turned to leave, EJ's voice whispered in her mind. *Fate needs Ebony alive.*

Chapter THIRTEEN

Slater stood in an abandoned corner of a parking lot, shadows swirling around his body to conceal his presence. The last thing he needed was a Guardian showing up asking questions, or wrongly assuming he wanted to fight.

Night fell more than an hour ago and Raine still hadn't shown. She didn't seem like the type to turn up late. Was she testing him? Or had she backed out of their arrangement? After Peyton's stunt, he wouldn't blame her. But he also suspected she wasn't one to quit. After all, she'd managed to get herself to the mortal realm so she could get the sword back after it…fell into the wrong hands.

Fell being the operative word.

If only he'd ended Asher when he had the chance. Then none of this would have happened.

He dug the toe of his boot into the gravel. How long would he wait? His options were limited, and without Raine and her…talents, his chance of recovering the sword was slim.

Raine probably wanted to make him stand here to prove that he needed her more than she needed him. True, but that didn't mean he couldn't find Asher on his own. Working together was just more efficient. Which was why he'd stand in this shitty parking lot all night and wait for her to show.

In fact, he'd endured centuries of torture in the Infernal Pits for that sword. A few more hours were nothing.

Three mortals mingled around a car. He lifted his hand, sweeping a wispy shadow of compulsion toward the closest one, sending them all on their way into the club. Best that nothing spooked his feisty princess.

Withdrawing the shadow, he returned to kicking the dirt.

Fire flashed through his blood, drawing a closed-lip smile. A second later, crunching gravel signified Raine's approach. He straightened but kept his shadows in play while she strode around the corner toward him as though she saw right through his cloak. With all that leather, she looked straight-up deadly. Skin-tight black pants, jacket, and a pair of heels that reminded him of his Fallen wings. Crimson.

To a mortal, she hid most of her Purah weapons well, but for him, he spotted them all. The foreign sight of a shopping bag dangling from her fingertips made him chuckle. No matter how hard she tried, she'd never fit in in this ordinary realm.

She was far from ordinary.

When Raine was within a few feet of him, he snapped his palms shut and vanished the shadows.

Without a flinch, she pinned him with a hard stare. "You lied to me."

Her sass was off the charts tonight. "You'll have to be more specific, princess."

"You told me you didn't have the Empryen."

He pushed off the wall and moved into her space. The smell of dark stormy nights slammed his senses, and nearly knocked him on his ass. He inhaled a deep breath, sifting through the layers. Beneath the earthy harshness, buried deep at the bottom, were undercurrents of something sweet. Soft. Peony? Night jasmine? Whatever it was, the smell lit his blood, swirling fire beneath his skin until it consumed every cell in his body like nothing he'd ever experienced.

It took his brain a moment to respond, as though he'd resurfaced from the depths of the ocean and taken his first gulp of air.

He shook his head, clearing the forbidden thoughts. What the hell just happened?

Raine cocked her brow, waiting for an answer. He couldn't tell her, not yet.

"I don't have it. Did the Guardians tell you I do?"

She narrowed her glare, searching his eyes for the longest moment. "Just know that if you lied to me, I will follow through with my threat to gut you."

He smirked. "I never doubted it."

Clearly, she knew more than she told him but wasn't ready to share. That made two of them.

She glanced at the sky and exhaled an annoyed huff. "Did you lose your sidekick?"

"Sure did." He tipped his chin at the bag. "Did the Guardians pack you a goodie bag?"

The thought of the Guardians knowing Raine was with him thrilled him more than he cared to admit. A sweet sense of satisfaction that she told them about their arrangement. That they knew he'd convinced one of their own to pair up with him.

Instead of answering, she dusted the point of her shoe on the back of her calf. "Stop stalling, Slater. Tell me how you know about the Empryen."

Convincing her to do more than work with him

would take time, he knew that. But maybe longer than he first anticipated.

He held out his hand. "I'll show you."

She screwed up her face as though he'd offered her a rusty nail instead of a shiny dagger. No doubt she'd still manage to stab him with it regardless of the weapon.

"I'd rather fly."

"Princess, we don't have the time to fly. Besides, why have a power if you never use it?" He bent down, hovering mere inches from her face, and lowered his voice. "Like you."

She glared at him as he straightened.

Raine 1. Slater 2.

"Sooner or later, you'll trust me."

"I'll never trust you."

Not when I'll break that trust. But he couldn't focus on that until the time came.

He offered his hand again.

"How do I know you won't mist me to Hell?"

He sighed a deep breath. "Because that wouldn't be half as fun as having you in the mortal realm."

Her upper lip curled in a sneer. "You don't have me."

"Yet."

"Ever."

He laughed. "We'll see."

Raine 1. Slater 3. He excelled at this game of theirs.

Wicked thoughts of claiming his icy princess shot a burst of heat right to his groin. Pity that wouldn't happen this century.

Instead, he feigned impatience. "Sometime tonight

would be good. I can only send Peyton on useless errands for so long before she catches on."

He could almost see the decision bouncing back and forth in her head. Everything weighed on her putting her hand in his. He needed her to trust him, and she needed him to find Asher.

Eventually, she huffed another breath. "Fine."

The moment her hand touched his, a jolt of fire shot through his veins, punching him square in the gut. Raine gasped and jerked back, but he locked his fingers around her hand before she slipped from his grasp. He held on tighter until his heart slowed and stopped bouncing around behind his ribs.

That jolt was new.

Raine recovered quicker, straightening her shoulders while masking her facial expressions just as he did with shadows.

"Get on with it, Hell boy."

He chuckled before closing his eyes to mist them from the parking lot.

A moment later, they materialized beside a weathered farmhouse on the other side of the country. The instant Raine opened her eyes, she yanked her hand from his and retreated, putting space between them.

"Where are we?" she asked, doing a three-sixty.

He didn't answer, the less she knew the better.

Surrounding them, mature cornfields swished in the night breeze. The farmhouse, set back from the main road, was one of many safe houses he'd acquired during his trips to the mortal realm. In case his destiny didn't go as planned, and Hell broke loose, literally.

The steel hatch on the outer edge of the barn resembled any other underground tornado shelter.

Lifting the latch, he swung open the door and motioned for Raine to enter. He expected her to argue, make him descend first in case he planned to trap her down there, but to his surprise, she didn't. She brushed past him, a little too eager.

At the entrance, Raine paused and lay her palm flat against the open door before closing her eyes.

Knew it.

An angel never changed its wings.

Well…some did, but that was beside the point.

He stood there, mesmerized by the powerful angel in front of him. Calling her out felt like a poor move on his behalf, even if it put him miles ahead in their game. He let this one slide.

After Raine finished, and descended into the bunker, he followed, latching the door closed from the inside. Lights flickered on as Raine entered the main living space.

At the bottom of the stairs, the bunker opened into a spacious area equipped with all the amenities he needed to survive if the apocalypse hit, and he found himself stranded for a long period of time in the mortal realm. Like, forever.

Raine halted on the opposite side of the rectangular table and peered around the room. "What's this place?"

"An abandoned tornado shelter." *Kind of.*

Sweeping his arm over the table, he pushed all the dust and unnecessary items he'd gathered over the years onto the floor. Housekeeping wasn't his forte.

"Really?"

Not anymore. "Mortals once used it to shelter from storms. I repurposed it when Blaine sent me to the mortal realm."

She didn't need to know why.

Raine unrolled a map on the table, pinning the corners down with cans of food he'd never eat. He flattened his palms on the desk. Fate had gone all out creating this world. So many fucking countries.

To track Asher in the mortal realm, he needed a better system than relying on his shadow ability. Even with Raine's gift, chasing the Fallen Azrael across this world could potentially take years.

Time he didn't have.

Raine would only tolerate him for a short period before she stabbed him in the heart for not recovering her sword quick enough. Even if he wanted to, which he didn't, he couldn't give her something he didn't have.

He lifted his gaze when Raine emptied the contents of her shopping bag over the map, before tossing the bag aside. "Does Blaine know about this place?"

Blaine didn't know a lot of things. But again, the less Raine knew, the better.

Ignoring her question, he held up a clear box of red pins. "What in the fiery Hell are these?"

"Tacks." She motioned to the items strewn over the table. "Plus, string, markers, tape, and shit like that. We can use them to mark where we've searched. This realm is bigger than you realize."

Raine was crazier than he thought.

"This isn't a craft competition, princess. We're tracking a Fallen."

She rolled her eyes at him. "I saw it on a mortal TV show. If it works for them, it'll work for us. They're far less intelligent."

Miles from what he had in mind. Was she

punishing him? Or pushing him until he broke?

Doing this the mortal way wasted time.

Leaning forward, he glared at Raine. "When I said I needed your help, what I meant was I wanted you to create a—"

"I don't do that anymore," she snapped.

His gaze locked with hers, searching for the truth. She'd said the same thing yesterday, but he didn't believe her, even though angels couldn't lie. Did Raine lose her powers when she came to the mortal realm? Did Fate revoke them as she had the Guardians?

Did Raine place her hand on the hatch out of habit rather than on purpose?

He gestured to the realm depicted by curvy lines and colors on the map spread out between them. "How do you suppose we find one Fallen in this entire realm?"

"Like mortals find criminals. We gather clues."

That was beyond ridiculous.

"No." He sneered, pushing off the table. "If I wanted to follow stupid mortal rules, I'd work alone. I wouldn't ask for your help."

"You *need* my help. There's a difference." She crossed her arms over her chest. "We do this my way or not at all."

In a split second, he ate up the distance between them, until he caged her in with her lower back pressed against the table. "You're in no position to bargain, princess."

Heat lit her violet eyes, making them darken. "Neither are you."

"Why would I bother working with you if you're going to pretend to be an ordinary Guardian?"

She held her ground.

Standing this close made his fingers twitch to touch her, to slide the zipper of her jacket all the way down and bare her shoulders. Once again, that subtle hint of sweetness drifted in the air. This angel stirred cravings in him he'd never experienced with anyone else, immortal or otherwise. But needing her pissed him off. Even if she pretended to be something else, she was still the angel most invested in recovering the Empryen. The only immortal who wanted it more than him. And that made her his weakness.

He needed the power back in his hands.

He inched closer, flattening his palms on the desk on either side of her hips. "Fine. We'll do this the mortal way." His front brushed hers, drawing a rumble from deep within his chest. "I would've thought you'd want it back sooner rather than later."

She flinched.

"I will get it back."

He leaned in, hovering at her full, peachy lips. Fire burned through his body. Eventually, she'd concede. He just needed patience. "You're so predictable."

A switch flipped in her eyes a split second before she slammed her forehead into his nose. Pain exploded through his head as blood burst from his nose.

"Surprise, asshole."

"Fuck," he groaned, staggering back.

Raine ripped a dagger from her thigh and held it against his throat, shoving his back to the wall. Now she had caged him in. The blade wouldn't kill him, but he bet she'd enjoy him bleeding out all over the floor.

"Raven may fall for your ploy, but I won't."

He sensed his eyes shift, the tiniest shimmer of

crimson reflected in her deep violet pupils, reminding him just how much she affected him. He fought for control. He'd worked too hard to lose now.

Losing was never an option.

Black blood gushed down his face, spilling between them, but neither of them acknowledged it. Pinned against the wall, with a dagger at his throat, he still had the strongest urge to fucking kiss her.

"Let's get one thing straight, traitor. The next time you try to kiss me, I'll hang you from the ceiling by your balls."

He gave a closed-lip smile. "Fine. I'll wait for you to kiss me."

She scoffed. "Which will never happen."

"We'll see, princess. We'll see."

Chapter FOURTEEN

With Slater out of sight, Raine wandered around the shelter examining everything he'd somehow acquired in the mortal realm. He likely hid in the bathroom washing away his tears, or the blood she drew and made no apology for. Served him right. He shouldn't have cornered her like that.

If he truly knew her, he would know better.

"We should start in the populated cities."

She turned her head as he strolled around the corner, somehow having lost his shirt between that room and this one. Now all those firm, taut muscles were on full display, ripped stomach, thick biceps. The smooth skin along his freshly shaven jaw called to her in an almost ancient way.

But his scars snagged her attention. She knew they existed but seeing them up close caught her breath. Black jagged lines marred his golden skin, extending from his shoulders, down his arms and around his torso. Based on the thickness, and the raised patches, someone must've tortured him with hellfire.

She swallowed the uneasy sensations sliding up her throat and focused back on the map. "Get blood on your shirt?"

He moved behind her, so close his heated breath swept along her nape. She clutched the edge of the table. Now wasn't the time to explore the awareness he stirred in her. She'd likely send his soul back to Hell and then her quest to reunite with the Empryen would fail.

"Something like that."

His voice rumbled through her middle.

She wouldn't let him intimidate her. Nor would she let him underestimate her ever again.

Moving to one side, she broke the uncomfortable intimacy of their position. When Slater redirected his attention to the map, she breathed a strange sigh of relief. Honestly, she'd rather not send his soul back to Hell. If she did, she'd never get her sword back and this realm would end.

It had nothing to do with not wanting to subject him to further torture while his soul regenerated.

Slater took one of the red pins from the box and pushed it into the map. "A mortal died here a few days ago with black swirls surrounding their pitch-black eyes." He repeated the process a few towns south. "This morning, another died here."

"Asher is heading south."

He nodded. "What I don't know is why."

Turning away from the desk, she ripped a Kiel from her belt and twirled it around her index finger. Why had Slater acquired this place? Being in the middle of a cornfield won points for location, but the setup inside the shelter made her suspicious. Even with her limited travel in the mortal realm, the furniture, the location, the craftsmanship, all lacked a mortal feel. Almost as though Slater had built it himself.

What was he hiding from?

She spun the Kiel faster around her finger, contemplating how much she should divulge to Slater about the Empryen. Trusting him was risky, yet they needed to work together to catch Asher. Unless she wanted their arrangement to last forever, she needed to at least give him a piece of the puzzle.

Hopefully, he'd do the same in return. A clue for a clue.

Rounding the table, she positioned herself across from him. No need to have a Fallen closer than necessary.

Using the Kiel, she stabbed the map. "There's a Raziel in the mortal realm that cleans up immortal messes. If Asher's running around killing mortals, this angel will know about it."

Slater braced his palms on the desk and pinned her with a hard stare. "That Raziel lives in the mortal realm?"

"Don't we all?" she grumbled.

He held her gaze for a heartbeat before she ripped the Kiel from the map and clipped it back on her belt. These days she couldn't waste Purah. "I suggest we pay him a visit first and then figure out our next move."

"How do you know he's still in the mortal realm?" He cocked a brow. "Maybe you just want to send me on a wild chase to spend more time together."

"Not likely."

Slater pushed away from the desk. "Oh, so now you want me to trust you?"

"Fine. You want to do one of those mortal trust exercises? Maybe share a few dirty secrets over gin? How about we start with how you got all those scars? Was it hellfire? Who did it? How long were you in the Pits?"

Slater's jaw tightened, eyes narrowed, and crimson

sparked in his pupils. Bingo. She hit a nerve. She didn't need a new buddy or BFF, as Tayla called them, her only focus was to recover the sword before the entire realm ceased to exist.

Slater was an obstacle to that mission.

"The last thing I want to do is spend more time with you than necessary. Let's just get this over with." She started toward the door. "Put on a shirt and mist us, Hell boy."

"I prefer not wearing one, princess."

"Well, I don't need to see all that." She motioned to the bulging muscles on his bare chest and arms.

In an instant, his anger vanished, replaced with the slightest smirk. "There you go again. Lying."

For the love of Fate. "Could your ego be any bigger?"

"Possibly."

She rolled her eyes as he chuckled on his way back to the bathroom. The sooner she rid herself of him, the better.

Chapter FIFTEEN

Guided by Raine's directions, Slater misted them to a covered parking garage. Just like last time he misted Raine, the second they materialized, she ripped her hand free and strode away from him.

He rather liked her rattled. When he caught her off guard, when he pushed her to the point of violence, it gave him the sweet satisfaction of knowing he caused it. Even more so when she pretended not to stare at his bare chest back in the bunker. Sooner or later, he'd wear her down.

And then she'd choose the path of least resistance.

He trailed behind Raine to the exit, scanning the garage. Clearly, she'd been here before, but when? It must've been before Fate revoked Raine's ability to mist.

A familiar sweet, not entirely unpleasant, smell lingered in the night air, but he couldn't place the scent. It niggled in the far recesses of his memory. This late at night, they were the only two in the garage apart from a few scattered parked cars.

Why in the fiery Hell did an angel hide out here?

"Where is the Raziel?"

Raine kept her pace. "Do you think he's stupid enough to allow Fallen to mist directly inside? We have to walk."

He caught up to her. "How do you know about the

Raziel?"

She side-eyed him.

Just when he thought he had cracked her impenetrable wall, he said something that made her fortify the barriers. In the Pits, visions of her were the only thing that kept his soul from wasting away. Not that she'd ever find out. If she discovered why their encounter had brewed for centuries, she'd never trust him.

Exiting the garage out onto the street, Raine steered them left along the deserted sidewalk until they reached a quaint bakery with a closed sign hanging in the window. No lights on inside, no sign of life, and definitely no sweet treats responsible for the smell he'd caught in the garage.

At the door, Raine placed her hand on the doorknob and lowered her head. A second later, a click disengaged the lock.

"You pick locks these days, too?" he asked, intrigued about his mischievous angel and her rebellious streak.

Fine. Technically, she wasn't his angel. *Yet*.

She glared at him over her shoulder. "Let me do the talking. Raziel don't like Fallen."

"Not all Raziel."

If they weren't in the middle of a mortal street, she'd probably stab him or punch him in the face again. Hell, she still might. He readied himself to mist before a sharp object slammed into his chest. Instead, Raine sneered at him before opening the door and striding into the bakery. He barely stopped the door from smacking him in the face as he followed.

Raine led him through the main shopfront, past the

counter to a back area, before stopping in front of another closed door. She touched the door and repeated the unlocking motions as though she'd been here more than once and knew exactly what she was doing.

"What? No secret knock?"

She ignored him. No fun at all.

Again, the lock disengaged, and she swung open the door to a flight of stairs. As they descended, he summoned shadows in one palm, but kept them concealed with his arm by his side so he didn't come off as a threat to the Raziel.

If the Raziel freaked out, Raine would stab him for sure.

At the bottom of the stairs, the room opened to a similar size as his bunker. No angel waited for them.

Glass jars filled with colored solutions lined the outer walls, with two couches in the center as though they were in a strange waiting room from another realm. He was about to ask Raine where they were when a prickle erupted at his nape. He spun as a Raziel materialized right behind him.

Tiny was an understatement. The angel barely reached Slater's shoulders.

The little guy gasped and staggered back. With silvery-white hair, glasses, and wearing a dark gray cardigan, the guy looked like he belonged tucked between the shelves of a dusty library.

Raine placed her palm on the Raziel's shoulder. "It's all right, Thatcher, he's with me."

He's with me.

Didn't those three little words send a blast of heat through his blood.

Thatcher's eyes widened at Raine. "How are you

here?"

Raine's shoulders sagged. "I have been for a while now."

"If you're not in the Heavens, who's protecting..." The Raziel's gaze darted between Slater and Raine.

Slater watched Raine like a hawk in case, for a rare moment, she let her guard down and revealed something she hadn't told him. She wouldn't, but a Fallen could hope.

That sounded weird, even in his head.

Raine motioned for the Raziel to sit. "That's why we're here. We need your help."

With a wary gaze at him, the Raziel gave a curt nod before parking his ass in an armchair. He might need help getting out of it. Raine sat across from the angel, but Slater remained standing, examining the jars along the wall, letting Raine take the lead.

This was her domain, not his.

"What can you tell me about the mortal found dead upstate last week?" Raine asked, straight to the point.

He admired that about her. How she never cared for bullshit, including his.

"I don't know of any mortal killing last week," Thatcher replied.

Slater paused with his hand on a jar. Something about this situation set off alarm bells. Angels couldn't lie. Had Raine deceived him and made them come here to cover for someone? Or something? Or was this Raziel hiding the truth?

He increased the shadows swirling inside his cupped palm.

"The mortal found with black lines beneath their skin? Killed by a fallen Azrael?" Raine pressed further.

"I'm sorry. I don't know what you're talking about. If a Fallen killed a mortal last week, I'd know. I would've assigned the cleanup or done it myself."

Usually, Slater was a good judge of character, especially when it concerned who to trust, but this angel stumped him. Mentally, he stretched out his senses, homing in on the Raziel's steady heartbeat, his calm inhale and exhale.

How could that be?

Slater faced the Raziel. "What about yesterday, when a mortal was found with the same symptoms?" he asked.

Thatcher removed his glasses and cleaned them with the hem of his cardigan before putting them back on. "I don't recall either of those instances."

He glanced at Raine, and her slight frown confirmed his own suspicions. Something was wrong. This Raziel was responsible for cleaning up immortal messes so mortals didn't discover their world. If that were the case, how did he miss two recent killings?

Unless he was shit at his job? But then why would Raine come here?

He lowered his voice, stepped closer, towering over the Raziel. "I thought you dealt with mortals killed by immortals? Do you often miss a few?"

That stirring in his gut intensified.

The Raziel cowered on the armchair, lifting his chin to maintain eye contact. "Never."

Slater raised his palm, facing it at the angel. Shadows swirled from the skin, looming in the air.

Raine shot to her feet at the same time the Raziel sank further into the armchair. Slater's shadows were faster. Lifting his arm, he locked the shadows around

Thatcher's neck, lifting him off the armchair to suspend in the air.

"Slater," Raine yelled.

He ignored her. An angel and a Fallen working together meant he'd always be the bad guy in these situations. He accepted that from the moment he requested her help. By now, he knew she'd never turn on one of her own, which meant that responsibility fell on his shoulders.

Not the first time he'd taken a shit deal.

As he inched closer to the Raziel, he curled his fingers, tightening the shadows around Thatcher's neck. "I'll ask you one final time. Who killed the mortals?"

The Raziel choked and spluttered. "I don't...know. I have...no memory of a..."

Slater stilled. He glanced left just as Raine threw a dagger at him. He tried to mist but something blocked his power. Damn it. At the last second, he sidestepped. The dagger shot past him and shattered a glass jar.

"What the fuck are you doing? He's the one lying," he snapped at Raine, still suspending the Raziel with shadows.

She ripped a dagger from her boot and aimed it at him. "Angels can't lie, dickface."

"Obviously, this one can. No memory of a Fallen killing two mortals? Not likely." He tilted his head and thought for a moment. "Unless..."

"Unless an Azrael wiped his memory," Raine finished, lowering the dagger by her side.

Look at that, they finished each other's sentence. Now their relationship was official. Well, in his eyes, perhaps, not hers. Yet.

An explosion thundered from above in the bakery,

rattling the roof. He and Raine peered at the ceiling at the same time.

"You expecting company?"

The Raziel shook his head.

Only one Azrael would need to wipe this angel's memories. And he bet it was the same one who just busted in on their party.

Slater released the shadows, dropping Thatcher back on the armchair. This time he summoned a stronger, more lethal set in both palms before turning to Raine. "Asher's covering his tracks."

"Why would he come back here?" Raine readied herself with a weapon in each hand.

He winked at her. "Let's go find out, princess."

Chapter SIXTEEN

Raine crept up the stairs closely behind Slater, a boot dagger in one hand and a Kiel in the other. If Asher came here to clean up his mess, he was more stupid than she anticipated. One Fallen was no match for her. Let alone her and Slater.

Halfway up, the door at the top of the stairs exploded. She threw up her arm to shield her face as bits of splintered wood ricocheted down the stairwell.

In an instant, Slater thrust his shadows in the air, concealing them in darkness.

"Back up," he whispered over his shoulder.

They had no option but to retreat down the stairs. In the confined stairwell, they had limited space to move, let alone fight. With steady steps, she snuck backward and ducked around the corner at the bottom. Heavy boots descended the stairs as not one but several immortals charged in.

Prickles erupted along her nape. Fallen.

When the first one reached the bottom, Slater thrust his shadows forward, snagging the Fallen around the neck and snapping it like a twig.

Kickass move, but it also blew their cover.

Four more Fallen barreled down the stairs, swords at the ready. With her weapons raised, she stepped free of Slater's shadows and engaged with the closest enemy. The loser didn't stand a chance. Before the

Fallen even noticed her, her dagger plunged through his chest, and he exploded into mist.

Three more Fallen bolted down the stairs, joining the others.

She quickly assessed their position while checking on Slater at the other side of the room in case he needed her to save him. He snapped necks faster than she unsheathed daggers. The Fallen wouldn't stay dead long, but the neck snaps put them out of commission until she stabbed them with her Purah dagger.

Slater's strong arms struck out in rapid, precise movements. He was almost as lethal as her. Though, she'd never admit that to him. His skill and the way his body moved with such deadly grace and speed made her knees weak.

And clearly, affected her brain.

Pain exploded in her skull as something hard slammed into the back of her head. She stumbled forward, hitting the back of the couch. In one swift move, she flipped over the backrest and landed on her feet facing the soon-to-be-dead Fallen. The Fallen jabbed a sword at her. She jumped backward, bumping into the coffee table. So much fucking furniture. As the Fallen launched over the back of the couch, Raine leaped forward and jabbed a dagger in the center of his chest.

Poof. One more toasted.

Thatcher screamed behind her. She spun just as a Fallen decapitated the Raziel. His eyes still wide and filled with terror as his head thudded on the floor.

"No!" she shouted.

Blood spurted from the Raziel's neck. His headless body jerked, then collapsed on the floor in a pool of blood. No immortal healed from that.

Any hope of recovering his memory vanished the instant that piece of shit Fallen sent Thatcher's soul back to the Heavens. Her only lead to Asher and finding the Empryen was gone. Now she was back to square one.

Fury exploded inside her. She palmed a dagger and sprang onto the coffee table, using it to launch at the Fallen, before tackling him to the floor. They wrestled, rolling back and forth as she tried to gain the upper hand. He overpowered her, pinning her arm holding the dagger to the floor.

This Fallen wouldn't win. No Fallen would win. She had to recover that sword at any cost.

She screamed a wild war cry right before slamming her fist under the Fallen's chin. His head flung backward, and she used the momentum to flip them, so she was on top, straddling him. As the Fallen moved to punch her, she jammed her dagger straight through his eye. He cried out, which only heightened her rage. Again and again, she stabbed, roaring as black blood and goo smattered her face.

Only when he passed out like a weakling, did she stab the dagger in his heart. Heaving in and out, she rolled off the Fallen and collapsed onto her back just as he convulsed then exploded into mist.

But the battle wasn't over yet.

Dagger in hand, she vaulted to her feet and engaged with the nearest Fallen. A sword swiped at her left. She ducked, sweeping her leg around, knocking the Fallen off her feet. A second Fallen lunged from her right, their sword narrowly missed Raine's side. She snatched a jar off the nearest shelf and threw it at the

Fallen's head. He ducked as the jar whizzed past, and Raine used the distraction to scoop a short sword off the ground and attack.

The two Fallen came at her. Back and forth she parried with them. Their swords clanged as she gained the upper hand only to have a Fallen push her back on the defense. When one was close enough, she balanced on one foot and side-kicked the asshole in the head. Bone snapped an instant before the Fallen collapsed.

As she twisted to face the second Fallen, her heel snapped, sending her stumbling backward. She flailed her arms but failed to right her balance. The world flipped. Her back hit the floor and the second Fallen attacked. Her one and only ever misstep. Towering over her, the Fallen raised a sword to plunge into her chest—

A dark shadow locked around the Fallen's neck, lifting his feet off the floor. The sword fell from his hand as his body jerked. Shadows snapped the Fallen's neck, twisting it at an unnatural angle before Slater flung him across the room. Glass shattered and the shelves collapsed in a heap on top of the Fallen.

Eerie stillness filled the room, and she breathed a relieved sigh. This battle was over, but they still had a long way to go before the end.

Slater stood over her. She glared at his outstretched hand. She didn't need his help, she could get up on her own. But…after saving her soul, the least she could do was not deflate his ego. And he proved a worthy comrade in this battle. Maybe he truly did want to work together.

She took his hand, letting him help her upright, but dropped it the second she stood. Each time they touched, a foreign tingle spread over her skin, becoming stronger and harder to ignore. Maybe her body repelled Fallen skin.

Stepping back, she kicked off her broken shoes and sighed at the loss. She went through heels like Aric went through daggers.

Slater leaned in, his gaze roaming her face. "You're hurt."

Using his thumb, he wiped something warm off her cheek, creating a curling sensation through her middle.

"It's…" She cleared her throat. "It's not my blood. They killed Thatcher."

Slater's thumb trailed along her jaw, making her breath hitch. Did he want another punch in the nose? Just before she did, he lowered his hand.

"If Asher sent those Fallen here to kill the Raziel, it means I was right. He's covering his tracks." He flipped a Kiel in his hand before offering it to her. "I fucking love watching you fight," he murmured.

His rich, smoky voice lowered as he encroached further into her space. Talk about a risk-taker. "We make a good team, you and I."

Agreed. But she'd never admit that to him. "I could still kick your ass."

"Perhaps."

For the love of Fate, this Fallen didn't know the meaning of personal space.

Her breath quickened. She'd blame it on the after-battle adrenaline coursing through her veins but that was a lie. Something about the black blood smattered on his face and the wildfire pulsing in his eyes, made her squeeze her thighs together.

Why did she keep letting him affect her like this?

Slater brushed his thumb over her lips, and she

Cassie Laelyn

couldn't decide whether to bite it or headbutt him.

"It baffles me why Fate called you Raine." His voice deepened further, while his fingers travelled along her neck down to her collarbone.

A foreign ache burned between her legs.

"You're too extraordinary to be named after ordinary water falling from the Heavens."

His molten gaze dipped to her mouth. Something squeezed her lungs.

"You're an untamed hurricane. A destructive tornado. A tsunami wreaking havoc across the realms." His fingers burned a path up under her chin, lifting it to meet his gaze. "You're a wicked, deadly storm."

Heaviness pressed against her chest.

Without crimson flaming in his eyes, she easily imagined he wasn't a Fallen, that he wasn't the enemy. That they weren't hunting the same thing.

Her heart thudded.

He was an extraordinary immortal. Almost her equal. But right now, he was an immortal who could release the tension building through her body. Usually, she didn't give a shit about such trivial needs. But he made her consider the possibility of letting go.

She leaned in. Slater met her halfway, his breath caressing her lips—

Lightning fast, he spun. Her back slammed against the wall, wedged between two shelves. Something immobilized her limbs. She fought against the invisible restraints.

Slater strode into the center of the room, kicking a fallen sword to the side with his boot. She zeroed in on the hand behind his back.

Bastard.

118

Faint, barely visible shadows extended from his palm. He pinned her against the wall with his stupid shadows.

She stretched her fingers, trying to grab the Kiel at her waist but couldn't reach it. All her other weapons lay scattered through the room. Just as she opened her mouth to give Slater a piece of her mind, a prickle at her nape signified the arrival of another Fallen.

A female Fallen descended the stairs, pulling up short when she spotted Slater. "What are you doing here?"

While keeping one hand behind his back, Slater scooped her dagger from the floor and flipped it casually in his hand. "I could ask you the same thing."

Relaxing a little eased the pressure against her throat and limbs, but the shadows still prevented her from moving. She'd kill him for this.

The female Fallen surveyed the room, so Raine did the same. It resembled a murder scene with icky Fallen blood and a fine layer of mist smattered over every surface.

"Did you do this? Why would you kill Fallen?"

Slater angled his body, forcing the female's focus away from where he had Raine pinned to the wall. She doubted the female could see through Slater's shadows anyhow.

"I have a better question, Peyton. Why did you send Fallen to kill a Raziel?"

Peyton? She'd heard that name before. Where?

"Unlike you, I'm hunting Asher and the Dumahel."

Hmm. They were all on the same mission. Why hadn't Slater mentioned Peyton to her? Was she the Fallen she'd seen at Blaine's mansion?

Slater waved his arm around the room. "Yet, they're not here." He flipped the dagger and pointed the tip at Peyton. "I don't take kindly to traitors."

If it wouldn't give away her position, she'd laugh. Slater didn't take kindly to traitors.

Pot. Kettle.

Peyton drew back. "Are you threatening me?"

A puny ball of magic swelled in the palm of Peyton's hand. Not the usual teal color of Raziel magic, more like a dark, inky version. As though ruining a beautiful painting by dipping it in dirty, stagnant water.

Slater barked a laugh and lowered the dagger to his side. With his shadows still pinning Raine, he couldn't fight Peyton. Clearly keeping Raine out of the way was his priority.

"Relax, Peyton. We both know you can't win against me with that weak magic."

For the love of Fate. Could his ego be any bigger?

"Why are you really here, Slater?"

He stabbed the dagger into the armrest. "I came here to question the Raziel, and then all these Fallen attacked."

Peyton studied him for a long moment before the ball of Raziel magic fizzled away. "I got a tip that Asher was here."

"And you brought a team of Fallen with you?"

She shrugged. "Blaine said I could use any resources I needed. Did the Raziel give you any information?"

Slater twisted the blade, digging it further into the fabric before yanking it out. "Nothing. Asher wiped his memory."

Peyton nodded. If Raine weren't watching so

closely, she would've missed the slight drop of the female's shoulders.

"Back to the drawing board, I guess." Peyton turned away and exited back up the stairs. "You coming?" she called out.

"Right behind you."

Slater followed, but before he disappeared up the stairwell, he glanced at her and winked. Pressure released around her limbs. She stumbled several steps before regaining her balance. Scooping a dagger off the ground, she bolted up the stairs and into the bakery just as Slater misted away.

Chapter SEVENTEEN

Raine landed barefoot on the grass outside the Guardian mansion with roughly thirty minutes of darkness left before the sunrise. That traitor had left her in the bakery, shoeless and without the ability to mist, meaning she'd flown non-stop just to make it back.

"Bastard," she grumbled, storming to the front door.

The next time she saw Slater, she'd tear off his wings feather by feather.

To think she'd almost kissed him. What an idiot.

He hadn't trapped her with shadows to conceal her presence when the other Fallen arrived. He likely did it so she didn't interrupt his side deal with Peyton. Whoever the Fate she was.

It seemed Slater made deals with anyone who benefited his agenda.

She paused and glared at the sky. Strewn with deep orange and blues, she hoped Fate looked down and witnessed all this mayhem. When Fate banished her and River here, she thought they'd retrieve the sword and return to the Heavens in no time. She never expected to stay for as long as they had.

Not by choice.

As she reached the gravel drive, she unfurled her exhausted wings and hovered over the coarse material to land on the front porch. Out of habit, she reached for her favorite dagger usually strapped to her hip but came up empty. Slater had taken it after the fight. He'd stolen it from her, knowing how much it would piss her off.

After she used it to tear off his wings, she'd stab him with it.

She yanked open the door, retracted her wings and headed straight up the stairs.

Aric strolled along the hall toward her. "Rough night?"

"Don't ask." Her fist curled tight. "Where's Raven?"

"Finishing up in the war room. You need to meet?"

"Yup. And someone summon Cole," she snapped, shoving past Aric to her room.

Inside, she changed clothes and grabbed a new pair of shoes. This time red croc-embossed with a four-inch heel—suitable for around the house. She ran her finger along the narrow heel, inspecting the craftsmanship. How could she make it stronger so it no longer broke when she fought? She studied her modifications to the tip. Instead of dipping only the cap in Purah, maybe she needed to coat the entire heel?

That might work. A task for tomorrow.

She slipped on the shoes, retied her ponytail, and took a deep breath to rid herself of Slater's toxic vibe, then headed to the war room.

Raven caught her gaze as she entered the room. "Did you find Asher?"

"No. But I did discover this hunt for the Fallen Azrael is bigger than we first thought."

Her hand reached for a chair tucked in under the table but stilled on the backrest. Sitting with the others wasn't wise, it led them to assume she'd finally accepted her role on the team as a Guardian. But that would never happen. Her destiny wasn't on the same path as theirs, in fact, hers curved off in an entirely different direction. The less they considered her family, the easier it would be when she wasn't.

Instead of pulling out the chair to sit, she backed up to the wall.

The remaining Guardians entered the room and took their seats around the table, but Cole still hadn't arrived. She needed a greater understanding of Azrael shadows to remain one step ahead of Slater.

EJ leaned back on his chair and peered at her over his shoulder. "This better be good, Rae. I'm missing breakfast for this impromptu get-together."

She waited until he turned around before slapping him upside the head.

"Ouch!"

"Don't be such a baby."

He glared back at her. "Don't be such a psycho."

She cocked a brow. "Elijah."

He scowled. Bingo. Of all the Guardians, he was the easiest to torment. Kind of like River only with better fashion sense.

When River and Cole entered the room, her shoulders relaxed, and she bent her knee to rest one heel against the wall.

Cole tossed a takeout bag into the middle of the table and offered a stack of napkins. "Breakfast."

"Do you need a pretty teapot and matching cups before we get started?" Aric asked the Azrael.

"Actually…" He considered the offer before biting into a bagel.

She rolled her eyes.

"Okay, Raine. Tell us why you called a meeting first thing in the morning," Raven said.

All gazes swung her way, something that still made her twitchy. She slipped a Kiel from her belt and twirled it around her index finger. "I met with Thatcher last night."

Raven tilted his head to one side. "Why does that name sound familiar?"

"He heads the Raziel crew tasked with cleaning up messes in the mortal realm. I wanted to question him about two recent mortal attacks, though, by the time I found him, an Azrael had wiped his memory."

"You think Asher did it?" Raven asked.

She paused the Kiel with her thumb. "Who else has a reason to cover their tracks?"

Raven pursed his lips, contemplating for a moment. "Did you bring the Raziel here?"

She spun the Kiel again, this time faster. She'd failed Thatcher. Another innocent soul caught in the crossfire since Fate banished her here. The Kiel whirled around her finger, faster and faster, a blur of sparkly silver. Heaviness pressed against her chest.

"Raine?"

She ceased the spinning, slicing a small cut in her thumb, before lifting her gaze to Raven. "Fallen raided the place and killed him. A Fallen named Peyton orchestrated their attack."

EJ threw his arms in the air, knocking over his soda. "Oh, this gets better and better."

River leaned forward. "What's your next step?"

"Find out if Slater is working with her."

"That wouldn't surprise me." EJ swiped a stack of napkins and sopped up the soda. "Where's the baldie

125

now?"

"He pissed off with Peyton. I've seen them both at Blaine's, so I'll check there first. I'm not sure what Slater's game is, but he knows more than he's letting on."

Aric grumbled, "That asshole is probably working both sides. He's got a hidden agenda. I can feel it."

Absolutely he did, but she kept her mouth shut. Until she figured out why Slater wanted to help her so badly, she'd keep that information to herself.

Too many secrets were at stake. For both of them.

Raven pushed away from the table to stand. "I'll let you run this how you see fit as long as you keep me informed every step of the way."

She nodded, thankful for the autonomy.

Raven pinned her with a hard stare, placing his palms flat on the table. "And let me know if Slater gives you any trouble. We're not exactly his biggest fans."

"Will do."

As the others filed out the room, she snagged Cole by the sleeve of his jacket. "You got a second?"

He nodded and held back.

She waited until the Guardians' footsteps faded down the stairs before addressing Cole. "How hard is it to erase memories?"

Cole frowned. "Like an Azrael erasing Thatcher's memories of those mortals? Or do you mean a tiny tinker here and there?"

As her pulse skipped, her fingers itched for the Kiel, but she didn't give in. Every angel had memory manipulation skills, but most could only change a short period of time or redirect a mortal to think what they saw was a dream or hallucination.

But only Azrael possessed the power to erase an immortal's memories.

When she didn't answer, Cole prompted her. "Please tell me you're not asking about permanent erasure."

Yup. "I wanna know how difficult it is for an Azrael to erase all memory of a particular immortal?"

Cole's steel-gray eyes narrowed. "Difficult. For Asher to manipulate every instance where he encountered Thatcher would've taken an incredible amount of power and concentration. It's possible, sure, but between you and me, I don't think Asher is powerful enough. He must've had help."

"Are you that powerful?"

He drew back. "Are you suggesting I'm aiding a Fallen?"

Just in case, she threw up a mental barrier so he couldn't climb into her head and find out how she planned to use memory-erasing power. "No. I'm trying to work out where angels sit on the power scale."

He studied her for a moment before answering. "Yes, I could do it. But there'd have to be a damn good reason. Messing with memories, no matter the motive, is dangerous. Erasing memories over a long period of time is even more so."

Perfect.

She only needed to know it was possible. When the time came to erase all her memories of an annoying, arrogant, self-obsessed Fallen and the unexplainable sensations he stirred inside her, Cole could do it.

She tipped her chin and turned to leave.

"That's it? That's what you wanted to know?"

"Yup."

Halfway to the door she paused, sensing a strange feeling inside her. Something wasn't right. It started as a slight prickle at her nape, progressing to a warm shiver down her spine, until a sizzling explosion tore through her middle.

Beside her, Cole stiffened. "A Fallen is on the property."

Not just any Fallen. "Slater."

Chapter EIGHTEEN

Slater landed in the forest surrounding the Guardian mansion and waited. How long would it take for one of the Guardians to realize he'd crashed their party? Would they charge at him with swords raised?

Would Raine?

He'd abandoned her at the bakery, giving her plenty of motive to stab him, but he wasn't here to offer recompense. Part of him felt the need to explain. About Peyton or his sudden departure, he wasn't sure. Why though? They were enemies, even more so given he intended to use her abilities once they retrieved the sword. Not honorable actions on his behalf. Yet, he felt this underlying...loyalty or...whatever to Raine.

Confusing as hell.

Either way, after he'd satisfied Peyton's need for information earlier, he'd found himself here.

Why did he wait in the forest? Hesitation? Or a sick thirst for the pain he craved if Raine attacked him?

He flipped Raine's dagger in his hand. The Purah blade sizzled each time it touched his skin, reminding him again of his choice to become a Fallen. A choice he made so many centuries ago, yet the day was still perfectly clear in his mind. A bright, cloudless sky. Sweet blossoms lingering in the breeze. How Fate gave him no opportunity to change his mind or explain his actions when she summoned him. How she'd thrust

129

another deal upon him before she tossed him out of the Heavens like a piece of trash.

His only crime being he sided with Zath.

But not everything after his Fall went as planned. If it had, would he have found himself here, consorting with a Guardian who harbored as many secrets as him?

A Guardian who'd never want him?

Why did that even matter?

Sick of his own mind games, he strode from the trees toward the mansion. The frigid morning air burned his lungs, clearing his mind, keeping him sharp. He was here to return Raine's dagger. That was all. A peace offering. His actions had nothing to do with the niggling sensation in his gut to ensure she'd returned safely.

If she hadn't…

No, he didn't doubt her ability to handle herself and he wouldn't start now. He'd not only seen her in battle, but he'd heard stories of the devastation she'd caused since the moment she stepped foot in this realm. Each time he envisioned her tearing a Fallen to pieces, a dangerous thrill pulsed in his blood.

One day, that Fallen would be him. He never doubted it.

Partway down the drive, the front door opened, and two Guardians stormed onto the porch. Aric and Raven.

Disappointment weighed heavy on his chest.

"What the hell do you want, Slater?" Raven sneered, halting on the gravel drive.

How far did the Raziel spell extend past the house boundary? Could he make it to the front door?

Did Raine know he was here?

Aric stood beside Raven, flipping a dagger in his

hand. He'd had a few run-ins with the Guardian over the years, particularly last year when Aric's soulmate spent some time with Blaine.

In the Heavens, they'd gotten along. Nowadays, not so much.

"I came to ensure your princess made it home."

His jaw tightened at his own words. Raine didn't belong to them. She didn't belong to anyone. *Except me.* The stray thought equally confused and enthralled him.

Aric stilled the dagger and ran his finger along the flat surface of the blade. "How sweet of you. I'm sure she couldn't care less, but I'll pass on the message. Now, piss off."

The Guardians were so protective of her. Had she told them the real reason for her arrival in the mortal realm? Did they know her dirty little secret?

He slipped Raine's dagger from his belt and held it by the tip.

"Is that Raine's dagger?" Aric's voice lowered, rumbling with fury.

A smirk curled on his mouth. "Sure is."

Before he fully appreciated annoying Aric, the Guardian got right in his face and clutched the front of his shirt in his fist.

"What the fuck is your game, asshole?"

Nobody questioned his motives, especially Guardians on a power trip.

He shoved Aric's chest. "Get your hands off me before I break them."

"Like you could."

He glared into the Guardian's eyes, sensing his own spark with crimson.

"You're just another Fallen who failed to choose the right side when you had the chance. Stay the fuck away from Raine."

Aric shoved him backward, releasing his shirt.

"Or what?" He jutted out his chin, testing the hothead.

Would they protect Raine if they knew she deceived them?

Aric narrowed his gaze.

He sensed Raine a second before she strode out the door, followed by her brother. He almost pissed himself laughing. Each of the Guardians thought they needed to protect her, like actual bodyguards for a helpless princess. Raine could gut all of them into tiny pieces and eat them for lunch before they unsheathed their weapons.

She wouldn't even use a blade.

Raine halted on the bottom step. At least he now knew where the Raziel protection spell ended.

"If you think returning my dagger makes us BFFs, think again."

He stepped forward, but Aric growled, blocking his way. If it wouldn't result in a pointless fight with the Guardian, he'd roll his eyes. He didn't know why the hell he was here, but it wasn't to draw blood.

He tossed Raine her dagger. She caught it, pinched between two fingers.

Such a fucking turn on.

"Now, run along." Aric sneered.

He ignored the Guardian, focusing on Raine. "What? No thank you?"

Her gaze narrowed for the briefest moment before she turned to leave.

"Princess."

She spun, lightning fast. The dagger whizzed through the air toward him. He stopped the blade just as it sliced his shirt, right in line with his fucking heart.

He exhaled a silent breath at yet another near miss. One day he wouldn't be so lucky. Stabbing him for pleasure was one thing, but sending his soul back to the Pits? *No, thanks.*

Ignoring the quizzical look from Raven, he cocked a brow at Raine. "Missed again, princess. You need to improve your aim."

Her eyes narrowed into thin, icy slits, mentally shredding his soul.

They were the perfect pair. Dark and light. Strength and power.

Angel and Fallen.

Before she followed through with her earlier threat to gut him, he dangled the only thing she cared about. "I have a lead."

She crossed her arms. "Spit it out."

"Let me inside the house."

"No way," Raven snapped. "A Fallen can't pass the Raziel spell. And even if they could, I wouldn't let you in."

He cocked his head to one side. "I bet Raine knows how to bypass that problem."

If he thought she mentally shredded his soul earlier, now she bombed him with the fire of a thousand suns. She charged down the path and slammed her palm into his chest. He didn't move. Instead, he hardened, heat flashing through his veins, and made no apologies for his reaction.

She pinned the tip of a Kiel against the soft flesh

beneath his chin. "I'm done working with you. Find that traitorous Fallen on your own."

"It's no fun alone."

Aric huffed. "For fuck's sake. Skip the sick foreplay and end this asshole already."

Again, he ignored the Guardian. This sick foreplay, as Aric called it, was the best kind, one he not only enjoyed but craved.

"I know Peyton's next target." He lowered his voice. "Let me in, Raine."

The slight twitch in her left eye was the only indication he'd made a crack in the impenetrable barrier surrounding her inner self. Whether she wanted to admit it or not, she needed him. She wouldn't give up the Empryen to spite him.

And he needed her after they found it.

She could let him in or…nothing. She'd run out of options, and he knew it. Perhaps he even exploited her situation.

His smirk returned, but he remained silent. Since his time in the Infernal Pits, waiting became one of his many strengths. He could stand with Raine holding a weapon at his throat all day. To prove his point, he inched closer until the Kiel stung as it pierced his skin. Raine's gaze snapped to the tiny trickle of warmth sliding down his throat.

An urge to smash his lips against hers nearly knocked him on his ass. Bet she tasted like fire. Hot, wild, and dangerous all swirled into one heady, intoxicating combination. Her gaze lifted to his lips and the world around him blurred. If the Guardians weren't standing behind her with their weapons drawn, he'd take her mouth with his, slam her against the nearest wall and never come up for air.

Raven cleared his throat, breaking the spell. "Raine?"

Raine blinked twice before lowering the Kiel and stepping back. He wiped a hand over his throat, smearing black blood on his palm.

Raine turned to Raven. "If you invite him in, he can pass the barrier."

"Are you fucking kidding me?" Aric shouted. "We're not letting him inside."

Raine snatched the dagger from his hand and secured it in her thigh sheath. "A Raziel can reseal the spell again after he leaves."

"Raven, man, c'mon. You can't seriously consider letting him inside. This is our only safe place. Willow and Tayla are in there."

"I'm not here for them," Slater interrupted.

Aric glared at him. "What are you here for?"

Raine.

Aric and Raven looked at each other, silence reigning.

Raine would let him inside the mansion because she wanted the information.

He'd wear down her resistance one tiny chip at a time. Patience was the key when it came to his fiery princess.

A few moments later, Aric threw his hands in the air and stormed back inside the house. A victorious grin stretched Slater's cheeks.

Raven shoved a finger in his direction. "You make one wrong move and I'll send your soul back to Hell myself."

He nodded, unable to take his gaze off Raine, who kept her back to him.

Raven gestured to the door. "Come on in, Slater."

Chapter NINETEEN

Raine shuddered as Slater strolled past, his arm brushing hers in the slightest touch that set her soul blazing. Why did she keep trusting him? Not just by letting him inside the mansion but trusting him with her secrets. Eventually, she'd fall for his pathetic charm and ridiculous good looks, and he'd betray her. Because like every other Fallen, Slater likely had his own agenda.

No doubt, it involved controlling the Empryen.

In the living room, Slater took a seat on the couch, with Cole directly opposite him for shadow defense. Raven sat in the armchair, while EJ and Aric remained standing. Hailee braced her forearms on the banister overlooking the living room—far enough out of Slater's physical reach but still involved in the conversation. As a Dumahel, her dreamwalking powers were unique and useful for gathering clues.

Raine hung back by the stairs at the entrance to the living room, with her brother by her side.

"Tell us what you know," Raven said to Slater.

River discretely offered her a candy, but she shook her head, too intent on listening to the conversation.

"Just before Thatcher's soul left his body, he planted a single word in my mind."

Raine drew back. Why in the Heavens would the Raziel give Slater a clue and not her?

"What word?" Raven asked.

"Sarael."

Raven frowned, tilting his head slightly. "What did you say?"

"You heard me."

"What does it mean?" Hailee asked from her vantage point.

Raven twisted, peering up at her. "It's an old angelic word."

"Meaning 'Protector of the Heavens,'" EJ finished.

Slater relaxed into the couch as though he lived here. Smug shit. She mentally cursed herself for letting him in.

Thatcher thinking that word probably meant nothing, if he even thought it. She hadn't heard it. This was probably some elaborate ploy on Slater's behalf to gain access to the Guardian's sanctuary and she was stupid enough to enable it.

In the final seconds before death, Thatcher could've thought anything. The wrong word, the right word, a plea for help or a random memory. They'd never know. Unless...the Raziel was a traitor who'd worked with Asher. If that were the case, he'd plant a word in Slater's mind to send him on a wild hunt around the realms, buying Asher time.

No. The Raziel had known who she was. Even though she'd surprised him with her presence in the mortal realm, he wouldn't betray her. Nor would he betray Fate.

But until she knew for sure, she'd investigate every possible lead.

"I haven't heard the word in Hell." Slater propped his feet up on the coffee table. "I suppose it has something to do with the mortal realm."

"Have some respect," Aric snapped, kicking Slater's boots off the table.

EJ pulled a cell from his back pocket and tapped on the screen. "I'll do a search and see if it shows up on any mortal sites."

Raine slipped a Kiel from her belt and twirled it around her finger. As though he caught the motion out of the corner of his eye, Slater's gaze zeroed in on her action. Something in the intensity in his eyes told her he wanted her to spin it faster, hold it against his throat again, draw blood from his veins.

Forbidden desire sizzled in the air around her, quickening her breath. She needed to get a grip. Maybe she should satisfy his craving for blood and stab him in the heart. That would solve one of her problems.

"What other information do you have?" Raven asked.

She snarled at Slater.

He smirked, returning his attention to Raven. "What do you mean? That's all the information I have."

Raven glared at the Fallen. "We invited you inside our home, put everyone at risk, for a single word you could've told us in the driveway? How can we trust that the Raziel even gave it to you?"

Exactly.

Slater drummed his fingers on his thigh. "Seems a bit risky on your behalf."

Aric growled.

Oh, she'd take great pleasure in inflicting pain on Slater when this was all over.

Raine slipped the Kiel back in her belt and pushed off the wall. "Is the other Dumahel still with Asher?"

Slater straightened. "Certain of it."

She glanced at Hailee. "Can't you dreamwalk to your sister and find out where they are?"

"I've tried. She's blocking me."

Raven swore under his breath. "EJ, find anything?"

"Not yet, but never doubt my awesomeness. I'll duck upstairs and check the dark web. If there's a mortal connection, I'll find it."

EJ dashed from the living room and up the stairs.

Slater's words came back to her. *Why have a power if you never use it?* Waiting for EJ to find a mortal connection to the word wasted time. Staring at the Fallen in their living room didn't help either. Until they had a solid lead, she needed to stay busy.

While Raven, Aric, and Cole continued their interrogation of Slater for more unhelpful information, she slipped out of the room and headed downstairs to the basement.

Cool stone walls calmed and centered her as she descended. Her breathing steadied along with her heart rate. Being in the same room as Slater wasn't ideal, especially with him sneaking glances at her when he thought she wasn't aware. She was. Every time his gaze landed on her, a warm prickle erupted at the base of her neck. Not entirely uncomfortable, but distracting and annoying as Fate.

She rolled her eyes at the bottom of the stairs. River had followed her. He wasn't the quietest walker, and of late, he never left her alone.

At the door, she spun. "What?"

He exhaled a breath through his nose. "I'm worried about you, sis."

She could ask why but didn't bother. Not when she already knew the answer.

"He's a Fallen. Don't let him fool you."

She punched the combination and the lock disengaged with a heavy clunk. "Maybe I'm the one fooling him."

Shoving open the door, she strode inside the armory. Her sanctuary, one place Slater couldn't invade.

River waited by the threshold, holding open the door. "Not only that, he's also a Fallen currently inside the Guardian mansion because you told the boss how to manipulate the Raziel barrier spell."

When River didn't continue, she glanced over her shoulder at him. "And?"

His expression fell along with his shoulders. "The only one you're fooling is yourself. And you know it."

Whatever the Heavens that meant.

River spun and let the door swing closed behind him. When the lock reengaged, she exhaled a ragged breath, releasing the tension clawing at her shoulders. Her and River were always close, but he needed to remember that Fate tasked her with this mission, not him. He'd just suffer the consequences if she failed.

She reached for her satchel, unraveled the tie, and rolled her tools onto the workbench. A loud thud hit the door.

She shook her head. River probably forgot the code again.

Her brother didn't care for conflict. Every time they left things a little tense, he always returned a few minutes later to clear the air. Little did he know, nothing could break their sibling bond, not a tiff or difference of opinion, and definitely not a stupid good-looking Fallen.

Her brother had the kindest, most free-spirited soul she'd ever seen. One day, if Fate ever created a soulmate for River, they'd better be a worthy match, otherwise, her brother's heart wouldn't survive the heartbreak. And his soulmate wouldn't survive Raine's wrath.

At the door, she disengaged the lock and heaved it open. "You really need to learn the—"

Her words stalled.

Slater filled the doorway, his strong arms raised, bracing his hands on the threshold above the door, a lazy smile on his face.

He was so infuriating.

"How did you get down here?"

He shrugged one shoulder and leaned toward her, close enough she could break his nose.

Not a second later, Cole raced down the stairs, lethal shadows swirling from both palms. "Raven will chain you up in their Purah cell if you try that stunt again."

Slater snorted, without even sparing Cole a glance.

Cole motioned up the stairs. "Let's go, Slater."

Slater lowered his arms but made no attempt to turn around. He didn't expect her to…what? Invite him inside the armory for chit-chat and cup of tea?

No way.

He leaned to one side, peering past her into the armory. "You work your magic in there?"

I'll kill him.

Cole's gaze darted between them. "This is awkward."

She reached for a Kiel but froze when Slater's gaze shot to her hand. He wanted her to grab it. She wanted to stab him with it.

Bastard probably wanted that, too.

"A quick tour?" he asked, one brow lifted.

River's earlier warning came back. She wasn't fooling herself. She knew exactly what she was doing. By lulling Slater into a false sense of partnership, he'd never expect it when she sent his soul back to Hell after they retrieved the sword. He'd never see it coming.

She stepped to one side. "It's fine, Cole. Slater isn't stupid enough to try anything in a room full of Purah." She squared her shoulders. "And if he is, then the joke's on him."

"Good point." Satisfied with her answer, Cole jogged back up the stairs. "Send him up when he annoys you."

Too late.

She spun and returned to the workbench, hoping the door smacked Slater in the face before he made it inside.

It didn't.

As she removed each tool from the satchel, Slater explored the armory in silence. She kept one eye on him, pretending not to care, though, the strange flutters in her belly at his nearness wouldn't disappear.

Her hand reached for a dagger to pull it closer. One could never be too prepared.

File in hand, she smoothed it up and down the blade. The dagger didn't need sharpening, but it provided a distraction from Slater's burning gaze every time she sensed him glance at her.

"About the bakery..." He moved closer to the workbench.

If she didn't engage him in conversation, maybe

he'd get bored and leave. One could only hope.

Awareness tingled along her spine, swirling in her belly as he drew nearer.

"I…had to leave. Peyton can't know we're working together."

Her breath jammed in her throat.

He'd hidden her from that Fallen for her safety? *Dumbass*. She didn't need protection, his or anyone else's.

"Whatever."

He drew closer still, until his body heat and that intoxicating fire and brimstone scent muddled her senses. Her skin tingled, sending sparks through her blood.

She swallowed.

Why did she let him affect her? She was better than this. An immortal, particularly a Fallen, particularly *this* Fallen, shouldn't make her knees weak. Yet, in this moment, they twitched ever so slightly.

His warm breath caressed her ear. "Why do you act as though you don't care?"

A better question: why didn't she jab him in the side with her elbow? Or stab him with the dagger?

She steadied her voice. "Because I don't."

His lips brushed her ear. Why was he so damn irritating? Clearly, he had a death wish.

"Liar."

She dropped the file and spun.

He grunted, eyes flaring wide.

She twisted the dagger, digging it further into his flesh, scraping a rib. "I told you, I can't lie."

He held still, as though the dagger were a feather tickling his skin. "Perhaps not. But you've proven you can skirt around the truth. Especially when you don't want to admit something."

She twisted it again, relishing in his fleeting grimace until a strange unease stirred in her belly.

"You know what I think?" Slater curled his hand over hers and slid the dagger free.

She snatched it out of his grasp, pointing the tip at his face. "I'm sure you'll tell me."

Her breath hitched the moment his finger trailed up the side of her neck, over her fluttering pulse. If she were in her right mind, she'd snap it. Or slice it off.

"I think you won't let me kiss you because you're afraid."

Afraid? She scoffed. "I'm not afraid of anything."

He dipped his head. "You're afraid of me."

"Why would I be afraid of you?" She wiped the blade on his shoulder, smearing blood on his jacket.

His thumb grazed along her bottom lip. Something squeezed in her chest, making it hard to breathe.

"Because, princess, I'm the only crazy motherfucker who isn't afraid of you."

Fire ignited deep inside her, but she wouldn't give in to the sensations. Not this time. Not ever.

Forbidden lovers were forbidden for a reason.

Sooner or later, someone died.

"And one of these days, you'll see that."

Before she replied, Slater lowered his hand and stepped back. Cool air rushed between them, though it did nothing to simmer the flames burning in his deep brown eyes. Such intensity she'd only ever witnessed after battle, but they'd battled for nothing.

Hadn't they?

The pin pad outside the door pinged as someone

punched in the code. She shoved Slater further back and rounded the workbench to stand on the other side. If River caught them this close, he'd send Slater's soul back to the Pits before they recovered the Empryen.

Whether she liked it or not, she needed this Fallen.

His information, not him.

The lock disengaged and the door swung open. EJ stood at the threshold. "I got a hit."

Chapter TWENTY

Slater trailed behind Raine and EJ back up the stairs. Doubt they'd let him venture anywhere else in this oversized monstrosity. Fine by him. Being in the same room as his feisty princess was all he needed.

As he rounded the banister into the living room to join the other Guardians, Raine broke away from the group to stand on the far side of the room. That angel would excel as an Azrael. She'd perfected the art of blending into the background. If she had shadow abilities, she'd hide better than him.

He parked his ass on the same couch as earlier for two reasons. It gave Raven the illusion that he listened to whatever the Guardian said, and it kept Raine in his line of sight. Thinking of leaving her at the bakery last night twisted his insides into angry knots, but he'd had no choice. Better to seek forgiveness than for Peyton to discover his arrangement with Raine. Besides, he never doubted she'd arrive back at the Guardian mansion safe. Still, abandoning her didn't sit right with him.

He meant what he said earlier. He liked her rattled. But even more than that, he enjoyed being right. Despite what she said, he scared her. Not because of his power or because he was a Fallen, he scared her because they were alike in so many ways.

And now he knew how to win her over.

"What happened to your shirt?" Raven asked,

interrupting his mental celebration.

He peered at the bloodstain. "Raine stabbed me."

Raine 2. Slater 3.

Someone muffled a laugh. At that moment, Raine shifted slightly, speaking in hushed tones with her brother. By the scowl on her face, the topic wasn't a happy one.

"You clearly need a lesson in ducking." EJ handed Raven a tablet. "I found only one hit, and I'm not even sure it's credible."

Raven glanced at the tablet, then back at EJ. "What is it?"

"It's an old bookstore in New Orleans."

He held out his hand for the tablet. Raven narrowed his eyes before passing it to him. The picture was a satellite image of a narrow street flanked on both sides by old shopfronts he didn't recognize. Possibly because he'd never been to New Orleans. After Blaine released him from the Pits, he'd spent most of his time in Aralim setting up their operations. When Blaine insisted they also have a base in the mortal realm, in the dreary town of Summit Creek of all places, he relocated.

He'd seen bits and pieces of this realm before he Fell, escorting souls from here and there, but the realm had changed so much during his time in Hell. Plus, he'd never cared for sightseeing. Why bother?

He passed the tablet back to Raven. "Why would the Raziel think of an old mortal bookstore?"

EJ shrugged. "Dunno. New Orleans is famous for witches and scary shit, so it could be anything. Sarael appeared in a book that's supposably in that bookstore. That's all we've got. I can't find a direct link between the bookstore and the Heavens. Or Hell. So my guess is the book is written by a mortal."

Slater stood. "We'll go check it out."

"I'm not going anywhere with you." EJ screwed up his face.

"I wasn't talking to you."

He peered at Raine. Another field trip gave him another opportunity to chip away at her resistance. With the sword still missing, Peyton likely aiding Asher, Blaine breathing down his neck, and a dead Raziel, their time was running out fast. And he needed Raine to go with him willingly for his plan to work.

"Are you coming, princess?"

A Kiel whizzed toward him. He leaned to one side and plucked it from the air a second before it slammed into his shoulder. If she kept missing his heart on purpose, he might think she cared for him.

Wouldn't that cause a stir?

Her violet eyes darkened, narrowing into tiny slits. "I told you not to call me that."

He brushed his thumb along the glossy, smooth surface of the Kiel. "And I told you, I don't care."

Raine 2. Slater 4.

EJ backed away from him. "If I were you, I'd watch out. She's hella skilled at throwing those Kiel. Not that I'd lose any sleep if one stabbed you in the heart."

"She won't send my soul back to Hell. Not yet anyway."

"You're as crazy as she is," EJ muttered under his breath.

He most certainly was.

****

Outside on the drive, he waited for Raine. EJ had given him the coordinates of a back alley near the bookstore, so he could mist rather than fly. If it were just him going, EJ probably would've given him the wrong directions or made it difficult, but not while Raine was with him. The Guardians had adopted her as their own. They wouldn't risk her safety. Though, Raine was so much more than a Guardian.

How had she fooled them for so long?

It didn't matter. She didn't fool him.

Raine strode out of the Guardian mansion wearing slim-fitting leather pants with tall, shiny, black pumps making her legs extend to the Heavens. She wore an equally tight black top, and matching leather jacket to conceal her countless weapons. The only one visible was the sheath strapped to her thigh.

Since he'd stepped outside, she'd pulled her hair into a tight ponytail. Just once, he craved for her to leave it down, so he could tangle his fingers in the silky strands while he took her mouth.

"Are we misting or are you planning on staring at my hair all night?"

His gaze slipped down to meet hers. "Both?"

She rolled her eyes. "Let's get this over with. My patience is wearing thin, Hell boy."

He chuckled at her pet name.

He held out his hand and Raine slipped her hand in his. Not just heat, but a blazing fire flashed through his blood each time they touched. The sensation oddly familiar, as though he'd experienced it before. Like a powerful force connected the two of them. Had Fate created the connection? *Doubt it.* She'd kicked his ass out of the Heavens with a no-return policy. Yet, the tether weaving between him and Raine drew him in.

He'd heard of the power of soulmates and their unbreakable bond that spanned the ages. Aric and Willow's connection stood the test of time even after Willow's spell in Hell. But a soulmate bond between an angel and a Fallen? Unheard of. Even if, on the rare instance that occurred, Fate would've had to create the pairing before one soul Fell. If that were the case, surely, he would've sensed it when he was in the Heavens.

Raine cleared her throat. "Having performance anxiety?"

He shook off the thought of soulmates and refocused on Raine. "I don't know what that is, princess."

Fate wouldn't align his soul with Raine's for an unparalleled pairing. She probably concocted this mission as payback. A shiny toy he could never play with.

The sooner he found the sword, the sooner this ended, and the sooner he had his freedom.

Closing his eyes, he envisioned the location in his mind and misted them to New Orleans.

The second they materialized, Raine slipped her hand from his and stepped back.

"Where's the bookstore?"

He scanned the alley—trash cans overflowed with rubbish, two closed doors, a brick wall at one end, and an exit out onto a street at the other. Exactly the location EJ gave him.

"It should be the next street over, on the right."

Without a word, Raine took off in the direction.

Out on the main street, mortals bustled along the

sidewalk, singing and dancing to the music spilling from various bars and cafes. Mortals lived such simple yet vibrant lives, oblivious to the immortal war raging around them. He almost envied them.

Raine weaved through the sea of mortals, not letting the slightest thing distract her. Did his princess enjoy music? Or did she prefer dancing with sharp objects?

Passing a busy café, he swiped a sugary treat off a table, ignoring the mortal's protests, and shoved it in his mouth. Powdery goodness fluttered from his fingertips down the front of his shirt as flavors exploded in his mouth. Sweet, floral nectar straight from the Heavens. Never had he tasted something so delicious.

He caught up with Raine.

She did a double take. "What in the Heavens is all over your face?"

He sucked the icing and honey off his fingers. "I don't know, but I'm getting more of those before we leave."

Raine rolled her eyes.

They turned down the next street and he spotted the bookstore nestled between a gift shop and a voodoo shop. A closed sign hung in the door window.

He side-eyed Raine and she huffed a breath.

In front of the door, she placed her palm on the lock and closed her eyes. Her power amazed him. He'd met powerful angels before, but Raine was something else.

Why did she keep it a secret?

The lock disengaged with a soft clink, and Raine opened the door just wide enough for them to slip inside. Wall to wall books filled the store, piles on piles, overflowing on the shelves and strewn across the floor. He'd never seen so many in his entire existence. How would they find the right one?

He eyed the closest book, trailing his finger through a layer of dust coating the cover. "This mortal needs a lesson in cleaning."

"Bit hard to clean when he's dead."

He glanced up. Raine stood behind the counter, staring at something on the floor. Stepping over the books, he rounded the counter to find a dead mortal with the dark shadows beneath his skin. Azrael shadows.

"We're missing something. Why is Asher killing mortals?" He knelt beside the mortal, placing his hand on the chest. "His soul is gone. How long has he been dead?"

"Do I look like a doctor?"

He motioned to the dead body. "Can't you just—"

A flare erupted at his nape, a second before the floorboards above creaked. Raine peered at the ceiling.

They needed to get out of there.

He flicked open his palm, instantly calling his shadows, concealing him and Raine. Not caring if she fought him, he grabbed her hand and tugged her into a dimly lit corner. Every bit helped. Whoever was upstairs couldn't know they were there.

With his back flush against a wall, he wrapped his arms around Raine from behind, holding her tight against him. Her body tensed.

He lowered his head to her ear. "Relax, princess."

She didn't. Of course, she wouldn't. Did she even know how to relax? After this, she'd probably think of a thousand ways to chop off his balls.

The floorboards creaked again as someone descended the winding staircase. Even with only the streetlights spilling in the front windows, he recognized the immortal.

Peyton.

How in the fiery Hell did she keep beating him?

Oblivious to his presence, Peyton paused at the bottom, peering at someone else at the top of the stairs. "When will he meet me?"

"I'll set it up for tonight," the other voice answered.

Motherfucker. Ebony was here, too.

He tightened his arms around Raine and shuffled them farther into the corner, hiding behind a stack of books. He didn't need to see the females. He heard them just fine.

"At the cemetery?" Peyton asked.

"Yes. Now that we have the book and another Raziel, we can start."

A pause in the conversation made him edgy. Raine leaned to one side, trying to look around the books, but he pulled her back.

"Someone's here," Peyton murmured.

Light footsteps crept around the stacks heading in their direction. Raine's hand inched toward her belt, but he gripped her wrist. Throwing the first knife gave away their position and he wasn't ready for that. Instead, he intensified the shadows, making them darker, thicker, layering an ominous feeling around the edges to ward off anyone who wandered too close.

Shadows didn't obstruct their vision. Inside them, he and Raine had a clear view of the situation, but it didn't work in reverse. Although Ebony was half Azrael, she didn't possess shadow magic. And Peyton would have no idea.

Peyton paused at the end of their aisle, her gaze darting left and right, up and down. One tiny step at a time, he tucked him and Raine farther into the corner until books encased them from all sides.

Beneath his arms, Raine's heartbeat thumped. She wasn't scared or nervous. In fact, her strong, steady pulse told him she readied for battle, just like him. If Peyton or Ebony somehow discovered them, they'd have no choice but to fight. He hoped that wouldn't happen.

Blaine needed Ebony alive.

A soft meow diverted Peyton's attention as a tiny, ginger furball strutted out from between two stacks of books to rub its tail over Peyton's leg.

Peyton pushed the kitten away with her foot and sheathed her sword. "It's just a cat."

When Peyton disappeared out of sight, he relaxed.

"I'll be in touch with a time," Ebony said.

A moment later, the flare of awareness along his nape vanished.

He kept his shadows primed and his arms wrapped around Raine, partly in case Peyton or Ebony returned, but mostly because he enjoyed the benefits of his current position. Having Raine's body pressed against his was something he rather liked.

Raine tensed for an entirely different reason.

The floral smell of her hair, and the way the wispy strands tickled the side of his face every time he breathed in, heated his blood. His mouth watered to taste her. Were her lips sweet like he imagined? How would she feel beneath him?

Curling his fingers inward, he recalled the shadows. Slowly, he slid his hands across her stomach to her hips, where he waited, gauging her reaction. He preferred his balls in one piece and not dangling around her neck like a trophy.

When Raine's chest rose and fell in a soft moan, and she didn't reach for a dagger, he lowered his mouth to the sensitive junction between her neck and shoulder. Risky, sure, but he could no longer resist the temptation.

Her delicate skin was smooth and velvety beneath his lips, such a stark contrast to the hard, tough exterior she portrayed. He continued gentle kisses up her neck while his brave hands ventured to her belt. Raine sank into him. Her breath quickened when his fingers slipped behind her belt buckle.

She tasted just how he imagined. Better even. A heady mixture of summer rain and wild thunderstorms wreaking havoc along a coastline. A wicked storm. He craved every inch of her. Not that he'd admit that weakness to anyone, especially his feisty princess.

She'd behead him.

In the dimly lit mortal shop, surrounded by stacks of books and years of dust, he'd never experienced such raw possession for anything as he did right now for Raine. The desire to run his fingers through her hair became too much. While he trailed his lips along her warm skin, back down her shoulder, one hand reached for her ponytail. The soft, silky strands were heavenly twisted around his fingers.

Raine angled her head slightly, affording him better access.

She pressed her ass against his growing hardness sending him into a downright frenzy. Only Fate knew what was in store for the two of them, but they'd fought this attraction far too long. He needed to have her. Craved her. A vision of her kept his soul in one piece in the Pits, but it didn't hold a feather to her touch, her scent, the taste of her skin.

His kisses became more urgent as need and desire swarmed together. His fingers dug into her hip, holding her against him, as his other hand toyed with her belt buckle. A low, raspy rumble vibrated in his chest. To undo it, he needed both hands. His palms were talented, but not enough to unclasp a weapon belt single-handed.

Caught up in the rush to hear Raine scream his name, the sharp object digging into his thigh didn't register until it sliced muscle. His leg twitched. Thick warm, liquid oozed down the inside of his pants. He dropped his arms, releasing Raine.

She spun lightning fast and pinned a Kiel to his jugular. "I told you not to kiss me."

Her tone lacked the fury he'd expect from her actions. She wanted him to kiss her. In fact, once Peyton departed, he hadn't held her against her will. He'd progressed slow and steady, and she could've kicked his ass into another realm at any point.

But she didn't.

He eyed the cut in his pants. "Correction, princess. I said I wouldn't kiss you until you wanted me to." He inched forward, clearly incapable of learning any lesson when it came to Raine. "You fucking wanted me."

She glared at him, pressing the Kiel against his throat until it stung like his damn thigh.

"Admit it." He lowered his voice, leaning forward,

daring her to slice open his throat. Maybe then, this torture would end.

She wouldn't end him. He was sixty percent sure.

"I'd never fall for a Fallen."

Her words were like a cold blast of snow over his body.

He clutched her wrist and lowered the Kiel from his throat. Raine yanked her arm free to step back.

If only she knew. He'd done nothing but protect her even before she knew him. But it didn't matter. Eventually, his path would betray her in the worst possible way.

May as well face his destiny. Playing the bad guy came naturally, so he needed to embrace it.

Another set of claws dug into his pants, this time lower, much tinier stings and less wild. He eyed the kitten using his leg as an immortal scratching post. Bending, he removed the teeny claws and scooped the furball into his arms. It purred and snuggled against his chest.

At least someone appreciated his affection.

With the kitten cradled in his arms, he straightened. "Peyton is meeting Ebony tonight at the cemetery. I suggest we arrive before them."

Raine held his stare. For a fleeting moment, her eyes softened. Her gaze dipped to the decent slice in his thigh. "I'm…"

"Forget it, Raine. I misread your signals." He petted the kitten under the chin while its tiny purring chest vibrated against his forearm. "It won't happen again."

Chapter TWENTY-ONE

Raine sat beside Slater on the rooftop of a decrepit crypt in the rear corner of the cemetery, waiting for Peyton's meeting with the Dumahel. Inside the cemetery gates felt like a different realm. The air was stiller and a few degrees cooler, the moon seemed larger, heavier in the clear night sky, and strange magic weaved between the graves. Mortal beliefs and folklore stemmed from ancient truths, but she sensed this magic was different. More powerful. As though something inside the cemetery amplified the connection to every living thing.

She hugged one arm around her bent knee, and carved thin lines in the roof with a Kiel. The same one she sliced Slater's thigh with earlier that night.

A strange twinge intensified in her chest, thinking of the bookshop. Slater's touch had affected her more than she cared to admit. He was right, she had wanted him to kiss her, more even, but then she'd remembered who he was. *What* he was.

During her entire existence, she'd never trusted anyone, other than her brother and Fate. Putting her trust, even a small bit, in someone who so easily drew emotions from her that she struggled to understand scared her. What if he broke that trust? He'd told her he didn't have the sword, that Asher had stolen it, but why was Slater so desperate to help her?

Could she really trust someone when she didn't know their motivation? Let alone trust a Fallen. Bad enough she was stuck in this forsaken realm. If he betrayed her, she wasn't the only one who'd suffer the consequences. So would River.

"You okay there, Peaches?"

She clenched her fist around the Kiel and counted to ten so she didn't stab him again. "Peaches?" She wedged the Kiel into the roof. "First princess, and now...peaches? What, do you have a whole list of stupid names to call me?"

She scowled at him.

A slow, easy smirk curled on his mouth as he petted the furball snuggled in his lap. "I was talking to the kitten. But if you'd rather I call *you* Peaches, then I can think of another name for her."

She ignored his stupid comment. Obviously.

Relief or something far more dangerous bubbled in her belly. Not only did he steal the cat from the bookstore, but now he named it?

For the love of Fate, would this day ever end?

"Do you intend on babysitting the creature all night while I do the work?"

He pointed to a black box between them. "She'll be safe here in the gift box until we're finished."

She'd roll her eyes if she weren't so shocked.

Safe.

Slater wanted safety for a damn kitten, as though he had feelings or was capable of caring. When he spoke like that, like he was still an angel, it made her blood boil. He wasn't. According to the Guardians, Slater was once one of the most powerful Azrael in all the realms, until he gave it up for Hell, for Zath and his lies.

Would trust come more easily if he weren't a Fallen?

She pushed that thought aside. The answer didn't matter, because he was a Fallen, and always would be. No Fallen had ever returned to the Heavens. She didn't even know how likely the possibility. Fate did. It must be possible, right? Fate sent the Guardians to the mortal realm to save Blaine.

She twisted the Kiel in the roof and cursed herself for even considering the possibility. It didn't matter. Once she recovered the sword, she would fulfill her mission and River could return to the safety of the Heavens.

Slater would be a forgotten memory.

Purring rumbled in the still night air. "Will you shut that thing up? They're going to hear us."

Slater curled his lip in a snarl and covered the cat's pointy ears. "Be nice, princess."

For the love of Fate. Now, she rolled her eyes.

Once again, she focused on identifying the strange magic layered in the air and searching for Fallen. They didn't know when or where in the cemetery Peyton would meet with the Dumahel. Ancient crypts and gravesites stretched far and wide, some so high they reached for the Heavens. Stone crosses and angels sat atop the larger crypts, as though the monuments protected the grounds.

She let go of the Kiel and placed her palm flat on the roof. Some mortals believed in protection from a higher power, which was half right. Raziel cast spells over cemeteries and sanctuaries like these, as they did in churches and sacred spaces. But the protection was more for the dead, rather than the living. Beneath her palm, the soft tingle of Raziel magic hummed against her skin. A powerful Raziel cast this spell. Perhaps she sensed that magic?

A deeper, more intense sensation sparked in her blood. Starting at her nape, it trickled down her spine before centering in her middle. She side-eyed Slater. Did he sense it, too?

The moment their gazes collided, the world around them slipped away. As though they were the only two immortals in this realm. She'd experienced that…side effect from the first moment she saw him in the mortal realm. When he and other Fallen attacked the Guardian mansion searching for Hailee. Back then, it started as a small spark, intensifying each subsequent time she saw him until she could no longer deny its presence.

But she could ignore it.

The pang in her chest heightened until the pressure caved in around her lungs, making it hard to breathe. She turned away.

Fallen better storm this cemetery soon, otherwise her mind might drift to "what ifs." What if was such a mortal concept, so positive and hopeful. Fate created paths for all beings with the power of free will. A choice to divert from one path to another, but not Raine. She had only one path and it ended with placing the sword in its rightful place.

Slater wasn't in her future.

Clearly, the Fallen wanted to make them wait all night.

Slater cooed to the furball curled up in his arms, driving her mad. Why did he act so tender to a creature? Why did he…

"Why do you act as though you're still an angel?" How in the Heavens did that come out of her mouth? She'd thought it and next second, her damn mouth blurted it out.

Slater's fingers stilled under the kitten's chin.

She'd take the words back, but a selfish part of her longed for the answer. She'd heard from the Guardians that Slater had a daring, adventurous side back in the Heavens, but surely the second he Fell all that humanity vanished.

"I'm far from it," he replied, petting the kitten once more.

"You act as though you care what happens." *As though you care for me…*

Lifting the lid, he eased the kitten inside the gift box. "I do care, Raine. Just because I chose to Fall, doesn't mean it's a different me."

She scoffed. She'd heard Raven talk like that about Blaine, but she didn't believe it. How could one's soul be the same when full of darkness instead of light?

She pivoted to face him. "You're not the same. You're no longer an angel. You traded your soul for Zath. Crimson now lines the rim around your dark brown eyes. The same color that replaced your gray feathers. You now crave terror and destruction, on the constant mission to siphon mortal souls for Zath." She closed her fist around the Kiel, slicing the inside of her palm. "How can you say that you're still the same?"

He scrubbed a hand over his face. "When an angel Falls, they don't automatically drop their past at the gates and stroll through with a completely clean slate. That shit follows. Sure, I made a choice, but have you ever considered that maybe it was my path? Maybe my destiny was to Fall?" His gaze locked with hers and the intensity pulled her in like a magnet. "Would it make you feel better if I wished things were different? That I wished Fate dealt me a better hand? Just because I'm a Fallen, Raine, doesn't mean I'm not capable of feeling. That I don't have wants." That lazy smirk curled on his lips again. "Or needs."

She cocked a brow.

He chuckled and turned away, peering out over the cemetery, but his words stayed with her. She'd never considered that Fallen had feelings or emotions. Honestly, she never believed angels had them either. Fate rarely created soulmates for immortals. Though lately…

She eyed the sleepy kitten snuggled in the gift box, protected, warm, cared for. Perhaps even loved. Was she wrong? Had she misjudged Slater? She'd never even considered that he regretted Falling or that Fate paved that path for him. Fate did pave devastating paths.

She would know.

Who was she to cast stones? She'd made decisions she later regretted. Her latest, leaving the Empryen unprotected. Though, none as big or as permanent as Falling. But still, the intention was there.

Did she judge him too harshly? Did she punish him for following his destiny?

"Why do you want the sword?"

He stiffened beside her, wrapping an arm around his bent-up leg. "I told you, I need to find Asher."

"Oh, c'mon. As if you don't want it, too?" She jabbed the Kiel into the roof and wiped the blood off her palm.

He remained silent.

"The most powerful sword in the universe, capable of destroying realms in a single swipe and you're telling me, you only want Asher? Why is he so important?"

When he turned to face her, her breath stalled.

Crimson rimmed his eyes with dark clouds swirling in the center. "I never said I didn't want the Empryen. You can blame me all you want, princess, in the end, it won't matter. Asher stole the sword and I need to find him."

An invisible force punched her chest, slicing open her heart.

"Why? Tell me why you're helping me." The words came out barely above a whisper.

Slater tilted his head as though he heard something. "It doesn't matter. They're here."

The Heavens it didn't matter. Too many unanswered questions made her uneasy. How did Asher steal the sword? Why? Why did Slater want to find Asher more than the sword?

The entire situation didn't add up. According to the timeline of Hailee and Ebony's birth, Asher Fell just over twenty-five years ago. How in the Heavens did a Fallen steal the Empryen from underneath Fate's nose?

"Raine?"

Slater tapped her leg, snapping her to attention.

He nodded toward the center of the cemetery. "It's showtime."

Chapter TWENTY-TWO

After one final check on his new comrade nestled in the gift box, Slater unfurled his wings, crept to the edge of the roof and leaped to the ground to land beside Raine.

Her questions and curiosity still itched beneath his skin. Why did she want to know now? She was all too happy to inflict pain on him when they first met, and every encounter since, not caring why he did what he did. He'd hoped she'd someday soften that hard exterior, making his mission easier, but maybe things were better off as they were.

Eventually, she'd hate him anyway.

He'd lied to her. He needed to find Asher because that Fallen stole the Empryen. What Raine didn't know was that Asher stole it from him. He'd possessed the sword first.

Getting the sword back was his last chance for freedom.

His only chance.

He stayed a step behind Raine, expanding his senses, assessing their situation as they crept toward a crypt in the center of the cemetery. Why in the fiery Hell would Peyton meet Ebony in a damn cemetery? Why inside that crypt?

Raine's wings were at ease behind her. Majestic glossy black wings that seemed so foreign. It took him nearly a century to adjust to seeing his own wings as a different color. In the end, wings were wings, it didn't matter the color. His fated path drove him forward, not the final resting place of his soul, nor the color of his wings.

Raine paused and held up her palm for him to stop.

A wild thrill shot through his blood at her taking charge. It suited her.

At Raine's silent hand signal, they slipped around the corner and soundlessly moved toward an oversized crypt at the junction of three pathways. How she walked in those mile-high pumps he'd never know, but he thanked the universe for them. On her feet, they were hotter than Hell.

He opened his mind to speak to her but wasn't surprised when he slammed into a brick wall. She rarely let him peek beneath her hard exterior, let alone have access to her innermost private thoughts.

That made things too easy for him. His fiery princess preferred torture.

At the entrance to the crypt, he and Raine paused. She slipped a Kiel from her belt at the same time he summoned shadows. Seeing her wield those Purah weapons made him feel a little inadequate even though his shadows were just as lethal.

Raine stepped inside the crypt, but he snagged her jacket, jerking her back.

"What's the plan, princess?" he whispered.

Going inside without one was stupid. Reckless. So typical for him, but not Raine.

"Kill the Fallen, get the Empryen."

Not a bad plan. "Agreed. But we spare Ebony and Peyton."

She cocked her head. "Oh, how sweet. You have little Fallen friends."

He almost corrected her, but the less Raine knew, the better. All she needed to know was that Ebony and Peyton's souls stayed intact. Without Ebony, Blaine couldn't execute his final plan. And if Blaine didn't finish his plan, he could kiss his freedom goodbye.

He never cared for friends, not even in the Heavens, but he did keep acquaintances. Peyton was…slightly more than that. He'd trained her into the warrior she now was. Even though she gunned for his position as Blaine's second, he wouldn't inflict centuries of torture on her soul. His soul was dark, not heartless.

"I need them to finish this," he replied.

Raine rolled her eyes, sending a blast of heat to his dick. Her sass would end him before any dagger.

"I can't promise anything." She lifted her chin. "If it's between their souls and the Empryen, I'll choose the sword."

He nodded, expecting nothing less.

"Now, can we go?"

This time he led. He stalked down the narrow entrance, hands outstretched, shadows swirling around them, concealing their presence. The dirt beneath his boots softened their steps. Halfway down, his stomach flipped, a familiar prickle zipped through his limbs. He spun just as Raine shuddered.

Her eyes widened. "We went through a gateway."

Fuck. Stretching out his senses, he assessed the slightest change in the air quality, temperature, gravity, anything to determine where the gateway had transported them.

Raine scanned their surroundings, no doubt assessing the same things. "We're still in the mortal realm," she murmured, her hand trailing along the stone wall.

His shoulders sagged as relief flooded his body. It didn't matter where they were, as long as it wasn't Hell. If they'd entered Hell, Raine would become a Fallen before they found the sword.

Had Peyton known about this place all along? Or had Ebony or Asher discovered it?

And who created the gateway?

At his nod, Raine followed him farther down the tunnel, stopping when hushed voices drifted along the stone walls. He thickened the shadows surrounding them. The tunnel led to a large chamber with several exits. More gateways?

In the center, Peyton stood with her back to him in front of a large stone dais while a handful of Fallen lingered along the outskirts of the chamber. He inched closer until he spotted Ebony, on the far side of the dais across from Peyton.

Silently, he waved Raine closer. From their position, they could listen without revealing their location, but Peyton obstructed his view of the dais. He couldn't tell if the Empryen was there or not. Did Raine sense it?

Ebony flattened her palms on the stone, addressing Peyton. "Did you bring the angel?"

He retreated a step out of Ebony's line of sight even though she couldn't see through his shadows. Raine elbowed him in the back. He peered at her over his shoulder, blocking her path. She could glare at him all she wanted, he didn't give a shit. He'd keep her behind him.

Peyton waved her arm in the air. From one of the other tunnels, a Fallen strode into the chamber dragging an angel by chains around his neck. A memory slammed into his mind so hard and fast his knees buckled.

He braced his arm against the wall to remain upright.

Sulfur burned his nose, poisoning the air in his lungs until he thought they'd burn like his soul. A sword scraped along the sticky stone floor. His stomach rolled. Hellfire chains encircling his neck and wrists singed his skin, layering the air with burned flesh and death. So much death. Screams tortured his mind day and night until he no longer distinguished between one and the other.

A Devoid stalked forward, dark endless pits of nothingness filled his eyes, a blazing dagger held low and tight in his hand.

Slater lifted his head. He never cowered in the face of danger. He never cowered to anything.

Excruciating agony seared through his body the second the dagger sliced his chest. Pain consumed him. The Devoid continued, fueled by Zath's compulsion, cutting him over and over. Muscles seized in his back, arching his spine as the poison ate him from the inside.

Still, he kept his head high.

He wouldn't give Zath the satisfaction. Nor would he waver under the torture.

He'd made his choice. Followed his path. Someday, he'd land on the right side, but first he needed to endure the pain.

"Slater…"

An angel called his name, drawing his mind from the darkness. It soothed him, wrapped him in a cool, soft blanket. He focused on her angelic voice, pictured her in his mind as the Devoid sliced the blazing dagger over his ribs.

His princess.

He'd see her when this torture ended. Fate had given her word.

Slater keeled over at the waist, sucking in gulps of air as his mind returned to the present. A cool hand touched his shoulder, making him shudder.

Raine.

She'd never know the torture he'd endured to protect her secret.

He straightened, turning back to the chamber, swallowing the nausea in his throat. Now wasn't the time to tell her. Composing himself, he reinforced the shadows and pulled himself together.

You wimping out? Raine's voice broke through the smoky haze swirling in his mind.

If he didn't still sense crimson in his eyes, he'd turn around just to see her expression. To know she was real. Finally, she'd given him access to her mind, but he didn't need to remind her that he was a Fallen.

Just making sure you're keeping up, princess.

She punched him in the shoulder.

Focusing back on the chamber, he found the imprisoned angel kneeling beside Peyton. With chains forged in hellfire around his neck, the angel couldn't mist or use his powers.

What did they need an angel for?

Raine moved closer, her front brushing against his back as she leaned around him. Her breath caught. Did she recognize the angel?

He's a Raziel, she mentally whispered in his mind.

Realization dawned on him. He moved to retreat down the tunnel, but Raine shoved him to a stop, shaking her head.

"Where is the sword?" Peyton asked, drawing his attention back to the chamber.

He thickened the shadows as a precaution. If they knew Raine was here…

"My father will be here any moment," Ebony replied, rounding the dais to tower over the angel.

"Are you sure this will work?"

Ebony lifted the angel's chin so he met her gaze. "Yes. My father said once the Raziel activates the sword, he can use it to kill Blaine."

What the actual fuck? Did Raine plant the words in his mind or were they his?

Ebony continued, "Blaine made my father forsake me for twenty-five years, he deserves nothing less."

Everything now made sense. Asher's insistence for Blaine to involve him in decisions and how he disappeared with the Empryen right after the battle with the Guardians.

This mission quickly became one from Hell. Literally.

It seemed he wasn't the only one with an agenda. Asher wanted revenge on Blaine.

He couldn't blame the Fallen Azrael. Twenty-five years ago, Blaine marked Asher's twins and recently used them to dreamwalk with Fate. Only Blaine and Fate knew what happened in that dreamwalk, but he never doubted Blaine would execute his plan. If something went wrong, Blaine would've told him.

He couldn't let Asher kill Blaine.

That sword wouldn't send Blaine's soul to the Infernal Pits. It would end it. End-end. Not even an immortal as powerful as Blaine came back from that.

Raine moved closer until she stood beside him. *We need to stop Asher,* she whispered in his mind.

From what he knew, once activated, the sword was a one-use weapon. What if Asher figured out another way to activate it? He needed Blaine alive and kicking to gain his freedom. This all started with a deal, and he'd risk anything to ensure he fulfilled his end.

Agreed, princess.

From the corner of his eye, Raine slowly withdrew a dagger from her belt. In the other hand, she palmed a Kiel. Nothing scared his stormy princess, not even a chamber full of Fallen in possession of the most powerful sword in the universe.

On the opposite side of the room, dark shadows swirled in the air at the entrance of another tunnel, drawing his attention. A second later, Asher strode into the cave carrying a long, dark leather scabbard.

He recognized it immediately.

His pulse kicked. Beside him, Raine stiffened.

Finally, the Empryen would be in his hands once more, and soon he'd have the key to unlocking its full potential.

Asher approached the dais with long confident strides. He lifted the scabbard onto the stone but stopped midair. "Someone's here."

Fuck. Slater retreated a step, but Raine blocked him, nudging him forward. He loved her faith in his shadows, but now wasn't the time for cockiness.

Ebony frowned. "Only the Fallen you requested.

Plus, this Raziel." She motioned to the angel on his knees.

Asher scanned the chamber, peering down each tunnel, keeping the sword tight by his side. Any minute now, Asher would reach their tunnel. If only the Azrael loosened his grip on the Empryen, he could use shadows to snatch it, then mist him and Raine out of there. But if Asher saw them first...

Slater darkened his shadows, but too late. In a split second, Asher spun toward him.

The Fallen saw straight through them.

"Slater," Asher shouted.

It all happened at once. Asher fled down a nearby tunnel with the damn sword. Ebony ran after her father. Two Fallen released the Raziel to draw their weapons.

He glanced at Raine. "Fight or flee?"

She gave him a cold, wicked smile. "Fight."

Chapter TWENTY-THREE

Shit hit the fan. Big time.

That asshole Asher fled from the cave like a complete and utter coward. The Fallen she now knew as Peyton grabbed the chains around the Raziel's neck and pulled him to his feet, screaming at him.

As if that angel could unleash the powers of the Empryen.

Slater glanced at her. *Ready?*

She was more than ready to take these fuckers down.

At her curt nod, Slater charged forward, his dark shadows orbiting around his powerful body. For a split second, she admired his lethal grace. The way his strong arms twisted in wide circles, curling shadows before thrusting them forward at the Fallen.

No longer concealed by Slater's magic, a Fallen charged toward her, sword raised. She pinched the Kiel between her fingers and threw it at the Fallen's head, hitting him between the eyes. The Fallen stumbled but adrenaline maintained his pace.

She tightened the grip on her dagger, shifting the weight to her back leg, readying herself. The Fallen lunged. She ducked, slashing her dagger across the Fallen's mid-section, so deep his insides oozed out. The Fallen grunted, staggering forward. She took advantage of his incapacity and, in one swift move, spun, delivering a round-house kick to the Fallen's head. He smacked against the floor.

To her right, Slater engaged two more Fallen, expelling shadows with one hand and striking forward with a dagger in the other. Hang on. Fury bubbled under her skin when she did a double take. That asshat had her dagger. The one he returned to her at the Guardian mansion. Bastard. How dare he use—

A sword whizzed through the air. She ducked a second before it sliced off her head. Spinning around, she attacked another Fallen. He swiped the short sword at her, but she blocked every strike, each time pushing the Fallen back, quickly gaining the upper hand. When the Fallen hit the stone wall and had nowhere else to go, he panicked, thrusting the sword at her middle. She sidestepped, then stabbed his forearm, slicing to the bone. His sword clanked to the ground. Before he tried any more amateur moves, she used her favorite maneuver and kicked him in the balls.

The Fallen keeled over, roaring useless profanities at her.

The Raziel cried out. She ran toward the angel, but something snagged her ankle. The world flipped. Without time to unfurl her wings, she tucked her arms in tight and landed on her shoulder with a painful thud.

"Your soul is mine." The Fallen sneered.

He kicked her lower back, careening her a few feet in the air. She threw her arms up to protect her head before she smacked into a wall. Air punched from her lungs. Sharp pain sliced through her side. The fucking Fallen broke her ribs.

She'd trained her entire existence to take down the deadliest Fallen. She wouldn't let this one, or any other, take the Empryen from her.

If Asher knew another way to activate it and used it to kill Blaine, instead of its intended target, her mission would fail. Her brother would become mortal. This realm would end. And for shits and giggles, Fate would syphon the power from Raine's soul and imprison her in Tartirim for the remainder of eternity.

That couldn't happen. She wouldn't let it.

Inner strength and determination swelled inside her. Gritting her teeth, she peeled herself off the ground to face the Fallen. He smirked. Little did he know, he'd never win. She crooked her finger at him, and he took the bait. He charged toward her. She shifted her weight, steadied her breathing, slipped a Kiel from her belt, and zeroed in on her target. When the Fallen was within range, she threw the weapon. It shot through the air and slammed straight into the Fallen's heart before he knew what happened.

His eyes went wide, and his body shuddered right before he exploded into mist, sending his scummy soul back to Hell.

She inhaled as deep as her semi-healed broken ribs allowed, turning as Slater bolted down the same tunnel Asher used. Movement to her left snagged her attention. Peyton shoved the Raziel to the ground, grabbed an ancient-looking book off the dais and fled down a different tunnel.

Follow Peyton or Asher?

At some point, she had to trust Slater. He'd catch Asher and recover the sword. But if he didn't, they needed Plan B—Peyton and the book.

She swore to herself before racing after the Fallen. The Raziel scrambled out of her way as she sprinted past. Rounding the corner into the tunnel—

A dagger thrust forward. She leaped to one side. Peyton swiped again, pushing Raine farther down the tunnel.

"I never expected Slater to lower himself to work with a Guardian."

Technically, he didn't, but she wasn't in the mood to engage in chit-chat. Word fights weren't her thing.

Peyton lunged. Raine spun to one side and elbowed the Fallen in the back. Peyton grunted. The next time she struck with her dagger, Raine was ready. She twisted, caught Peyton's wrist, and disarmed the Fallen in a single move.

Peyton staggered back and Raine didn't stop. She tossed the dagger on the floor, shoved Peyton against the wall, and slammed her forearm across the Fallen's throat. The all-important book dropped to the ground.

Peyton coughed and spluttered, scratching at Raine's arm to free herself.

"Where did Asher go?" Raine snarled.

Peyton spat right in her face. The fuck she did.

Raine shoved harder against Peyton's windpipe. "I'm not in the mood for this shit. Tell me where Asher went."

"Or…what?"

From her belt, Raine grabbed her last Kiel and stabbed it in the Fallen's side. Peyton screamed as Purah burned her flesh, seeping into her blood.

She dragged the Kiel lower. "Where did he go?"

Peyton lifted her knee, but Raine twisted her thigh to block the move. She eased the pressure on Peyton's throat just enough for the Fallen to speak. "You have two more seconds before I slice off your fingers one by one."

"You crazy bitch."

She angled her body slightly to gain a better grip.

"Raine." Slater's voice thundered down the tunnel.

She turned her head to him as he prowled toward them from the opposite end of the tunnel like a deadly predator in the night. His crimson eyes blazed in the darkness.

Resistance against her arm vanished, causing her to stumble forward, slamming her elbow into the wall. Peyton misted away.

"What the fuck?" she screamed at Slater. "She got away because of you."

A low, deep sound rumbled from his chest. "And I told you not to hurt them."

For the love of Fate, was he serious?

When he neared, she shoved him in the chest with every ounce of the frustration and anger exploding inside her. He didn't budge, just stood there, staring down at her with a dangerous fire in his eyes.

"No, you told me not to *end* them," she snapped. "Which side are you on, Slater? Because if you're playing both, I'll fucking end *you*."

Muscles tightened in his rigid jaw.

Intensity and raw heat sparked between them. How dare he stop her from doing her job. From fulfilling her destiny.

"She was our best chance of finding the sword and you blew it."

His flaming gaze dipped to her mouth. "We'll find another."

Her heart pounded.

Slater leaned down, hovering a hair's breadth from

her lips. He wouldn't kiss her. He'd vowed not to until she gave in, which she wouldn't. *Couldn't.* If she conceded, he might use their attraction against her. He'd stop her from fulfilling her mission.

He'd destroy her destiny.

She turned away, but Slater snagged her jacket. She stilled as though suspended in time, staring down the dark tunnel. Once again, she found herself at a junction. Another diversion in her path. But for the first time, she had no clue which direction to choose—punch Slater in the face for his protectiveness bullshit or...

Why would she think of kissing him?

Tingles danced over her skin, warming her blood. No, more than that. Slater's intense heat stroked every cell in her body, sparking it with a magnetic energy she'd never experienced. Bone-deep need consumed her. It burned through her veins, firing inside her.

Only one choice would make it stop.

She spun. Without breaking free of his grasp, she closed the space between them and smashed her lips against his. Slater's hand gripped the back of her neck, holding her in place, angling her head to deepen the kiss. He moaned into her mouth, sending a wild thrill through her blood.

Kissing Slater was nothing like she imagined, full of heat, possessiveness, and something far more dangerous. A sensation that blasted her soul with light.

Their kiss was anything but gentle. Tongues collided, fighting for dominance. He devoured her as though she were the key to unlocking his soul's potential. But more than that, this kiss proved they had a connection. That Fate tied them together somehow and for some reason she needed to figure out why.

But now wasn't the time to decipher her choices or her path, nor the obstacles in her way. This moment was about Slater's tongue stroking hers, his body pressing her against the dirty tunnel wall.

This moment was only about expelling the forbidden lust exploding between them.

Slater dipped his hands under her thighs and lifted her with ease, wrapping her legs around his waist. He groaned, pressing their bodies so tight, they became one.

Still, she didn't stop kissing him.

Out of instinct, or perhaps self-preservation, her hand reached for a weapon, but stopped. She wanted this. She'd instigated their kiss. Instead of stabbing him, she dug her nails into the base of his skull. He moaned, pressing his hips forward, hard against the sweet spot between her legs. Sparks lit her blood—

Slater jerked. He staggered to one side, dropping her legs.

Her feet hit the ground and she stumbled before righting her balance. "What the—"

Peyton stood behind Slater, a dagger in her hand tipped with black Fallen blood. Not just any dagger.

Raine's dagger.

"No," she shouted.

She slipped a knife from her boot and threw it at the Fallen. Peyton misted. The dagger slammed into the tunnel wall before clunking to the ground.

Slater grunted, unsteady on his feet. His eyes wide with terror as he clawed at his shirt. He toppled back, tripping over his own feet, and smacked the ground.

She rushed to him, crouching beside him and tore open his shirt. Bright white light pulsed from his chest, dangerously close to his heart.

Purah.

From her dagger. Peyton stabbed Slater using Raine's own dagger.

She slapped his cheek. "Get up, Hell boy. It's just a scratch."

He gurgled, coughing up blood.

She smacked his cheek again. "Get yourself together. We had a deal. You can't renege."

His deep brown eyes gave her a knowing look. One she was all too familiar with. Every Fallen she ever killed had the same expression right before Purah reached their heart. The second they accepted their fate. The moment before their soul exploded to mist.

Slater.

He had less than a second before that happened to him.

If she didn't save him...

Wild rage came from somewhere deep inside her. She needed to save him. She wouldn't let Slater's soul return to the Pits. Not now. Not ev—

Not before they completed their mission.

Closing her eyes, she willed her true form. The part of her she hid from every immortal in this realm. The part of her Fate forbade her from using.

Damn the consequences.

Now, she called upon the magic. Embraced it. Unwrapped each thread of power as it swelled and bloomed inside her, exploding from her fingertips.

Chapter TWENTY-FOUR

Agony seared through his veins. The burn so intense it consumed every cell until he thought his body would explode. Liquid bubbled up his throat, filling his lungs, making it impossible to breathe.

He opened his eyes.

His fiery princess scowled down at him. For the first time since his vision of her countless centuries ago, he saw true fear in her luminous violet eyes. But not just fear, a familiar look also simmered beneath the surface.

Annoyance. He'd seen that one plenty of times.

If he weren't about to return to the Pits, he'd laugh. Clearly, his slow and agonizing death annoyed the hell out of his princess.

Blood gurgled in his throat.

Purah thrummed so close to his heart, he had seconds before it destroyed his soul. With his remaining strength, he raised his hand to touch her face, but his arm never lifted off the ground.

He'd failed.

His soul would return to the Pits. No one would come for him. By the time Blaine realized, Asher would've figured out how to activate the Empryen and used it to kill Blaine.

He'd never get his freedom.

He'd never experience another moment with Raine.

A ball of brilliant teal light exploded beside him.

Raine pressed her hands on his chest, closing her eyes. Her brows creased.

He reached for her wrists. She couldn't do this. Revealing her true form put her in danger. He wouldn't let her. He'd promised Fate he'd protect her secret, not allow herself to become a beacon for every Fallen in this realm.

Excruciating fire scorched the muscles surrounding his heart. Something hotter, more intense, competed against it. Raine pushed harder, cracking his sternum.

He fought against her hold.

She swatted away his hand. "Stop moving, dumbass."

When he chuckled, blood bubbled up his throat. He coughed again.

Thumping energy pulsed from her palms. Steady, strong beats until it exploded with bright light, illuminating the tunnel.

All he could do was stare in awe.

In his final moments, she'd tried to save him. He'd never forget that.

Another wave of intense light burst in his chest, colliding with the Purah, fighting for control of his black heart. Raine pushed even harder. He tried to roll away, to stop her, but she straddled him, pinning him to the ground.

As perspiration beaded her brows, his eyes slid closed.

Heavenly magic streamed through his blood, fast and pure, healing wounds, repairing damage to organs and tissue. Slowly, it gained control. The Purah surrounding his heart fizzled, fighting against Raine's magic, but it was no match. Eventually, the Purah vanished in a final blast of light.

Heaviness lifted from his chest. He inhaled a tentative breath before opening his eyes. He was alive. She'd saved him.

Raine sat back on her haunches, her eyes still simmering with teal sparks.

Never had he seen something so mesmerizing. So beautiful.

He swallowed, moistening his throat. "I thought...you didn't do that...anymore?"

She punched him square in the jaw.

His head snapped to the side. "Oww."

"That's for getting yourself stabbed."

Not for kissing her? *Interesting.*

He rubbed his throbbing cheek. "Won't happen again, princess."

"Heard that before," she snarked, climbing off him to stand.

He peeled himself off the ground, a little groggy, or perhaps high on magic. "You healed me."

She grunted. "Who else will look after that stupid cat?"

He snorted, not fooled at all by her badass attitude. She liked Peaches.

Raine snatched the book off the ground and returned to the main chamber as though saving his soul was as normal as unfurling her wings. He took a moment to compose himself and brushed the dirt from his pants. No point bothering about his shirt. He needed a new one. Though knowing Raine had torn it apart gave him a thrill. The last few minutes felt like a dream. One second, he had his mouth on Raine's, the next,

Peyton stabbed a Purah dagger in his back. She just rocketed to the top of his kill list.

He held back at the entrance to the chamber, watching Raine with the leather-bound text in her hand. He'd heard stories of her magic, legends. But seeing it firsthand and experiencing the moment she neutralized the Purah poisoning his system blew his mind.

Should he worry? Were there side effects? Would her magic linger in his blood? Were Raine's actions temporary?

Questions he should figure out, but not now.

The kidnapped Raziel stammered to himself, drawing his attention.

Raine crouched beside the Raziel. "When did they take you?"

The Raziel's eyes widened. "You're…her."

"Answer me."

The Raziel's gaze darted past Raine to where he stood. "You're working with them?"

A growl rumbled low in his chest. He was so sick of others judging Raine for working with him simply because they were an angel and a Fallen. They made the perfect team. Especially now that she'd shown him her magic worked in the mortal realm.

Raine pinched the Raziel's chin, redirecting his gaze to her. "When did the Fallen take you?"

"Two nights ago. They were fast. I didn't have a chance to mist."

Raine glanced over her shoulder at Slater, a knowing look in her eyes. Peyton had been one step ahead of him the entire time.

The Raziel lowered his voice. "The Fallen thought I could activate the Empryen."

"You're safe now." Raine straightened and turned to him. "Release the chains."

Holding out his hands, he summoned his shadows. They grew and thickened, curling in the air before he shot them at the chains. The collar around the Raziel's throat snapped. The Raziel stumbled. Slater repeated the process for the cuffs on the Raziel's wrists.

Raine tossed him the leather book as she helped the Raziel to stand. He flipped through the pages until he came to one with a picture of an angel kneeling on the ground, head bowed, the Empryen grasped in their hands with the tip in the dirt. A strange sense of foreboding twisted in his blood.

He held up the image to the Raziel. "Why did the Fallen have this book?"

The Raziel's gaze darted between him and Raine. Raine gave a curt nod to answer.

"It speaks of the Sarael and this chamber."

Finally, they had a solid clue.

Raine placed her palm on the Raziel's shoulder. "Mist back to the Heavens but never speak of this. Do you understand?"

The Raziel opened his mouth to argue, but when Raine narrowed her eyes, he nodded and misted.

For a moment, Raine stared at a spot in the dirt where the Raziel had crouched. "Asher now knows we're after him. After that blast of magic, he'll be able to track me."

He pursed his lips. "He doesn't know who you are."

"Not yet. But our time is running out."

"The sword's no use to Asher in its current state."

She turned to him, hard lines on her face. "Which

is why he's kidnapping innocent angels, probably because of something in that book." She circled the chamber, scooping up her weapons off the floor. "Since that stupid Fallen came back to finish you, they know you're working with me."

He should warn Blaine. But what would he say? He couldn't tell Blaine Asher had the Empryen, and he certainly couldn't tell him that because Raine healed him Asher could track her. He watched Raine as she redid her hair, pulling it into a tight ponytail.

He also couldn't return to Hell and leave her unprotected. Not now.

Raine held out her hand. "Mist us to the Guardians."

Familiar warmth zapped through him when he curled his fingers around hers, only this time, it bloomed a soft ball of heavenly light in the center of his chest.

He gasped, jerking back his hand.

Raine frowned. "What?"

"Did you…"

He couldn't say it. Couldn't even think it. He stood there stunned, staring at her, sensing every slight sensation in his body, in his blood.

In his soul.

Emotion swirled around his insides like a tornado colliding with his dark shadows. Light swept through them, cleansing them.

Was Raine…? Surely not.

"Did you hit your head?" Raine snapped.

No, he didn't hit his head. A Fallen had almost stabbed him in the heart using Raine's dagger. Purah had been seconds away from sending his soul back to Hell. Then Raine saved him.

She connected herself with him.

Chapter TWENTY-FIVE

In one quick stride, Slater cupped her face in his hands and crushed his mouth against hers. Her tongue collided with his, craving his wild, fiery taste. He kissed her with so much intensity it felt as though he was afraid to ever let go. A fierce sensation overtook her body. She wanted his scent, his body, plastered all over her.

She wanted everything he gave her.

Breathing heavy, he drew back and searched her eyes, as though silently seeking her permission. Unspoken words passed between them. She sensed his gratitude and his desire. But a stronger, more powerful emotion swelled inside her with such clarity she couldn't ignore it. His intense dark eyes told her he felt it, too.

When she smashed her lips against his, a raspy moan rumbled from him. She surrendered to the sensations, to his touch, and the warmth blooming within her. A strange thread expanded deep in her chest, building and strengthening until it consumed her. She gasped as the invisible light burst from her, shooting into Slater.

Residual magic? Or something worse?

Whatever it was, it made Slater kiss her harder, with a fevered intensity that rivaled any battlefield. Lifting her, he locked her legs around his waist and misted them not to the Guardian mansion, but his bunker.

She nipped at the sensitive junction at his neck while he unlocked the door and carried her inside. With a sweep of his arm, he cleared the table before setting her down on the edge.

Breathing heavy, he hovered at her lips. "Raine?"

Again, silent words rushed between them. And again, she couldn't ignore them. Nothing had ever felt so powerful, all-consuming.

She grabbed his shirt and tugged him between her legs. "Stop talking."

If they spoke, they'd break the spell. Then all the reasons why they shouldn't do this would come front and center. They'd played with this fire for too long. They needed to get it out of their systems so they could focus on recovering the sword before Asher did something stupid.

He tore off her clothes in a desperation that only excited her further.

Slater ripped off his shirt before returning between her bare thighs, his crimson eyes blazing. This time instead of repulsing her, those tiny flames thrilled her.

She hooked her hands around his neck and pulled him to her lips. He kissed her, this time slower, while his hands roamed along her sides. When the ache threatened to shred her soul, Slater drew back, giving her a wicked grin.

"Tell me what you want, Raine."

Heat flashed through her blood. She wanted the ache to stop, and she wanted him to end it.

"Make me scream to the Heavens."

The intensity in his flaming eyes promised more

191

than that. She sensed he could make her scream to all the realms in the universe.

He dragged a nearby chair over to sit between her legs and placed his hands on her inner thighs, spreading them further apart. She didn't think, not about what was happening, or what it would mean later, just braced one hand behind her and offered herself to him. His wild gaze held hers as he lowered his mouth to her. Breath punched from her lungs with a ridiculous moan.

He devoured her, sending her ache into a frenzy. She gripped his hair, her nails digging into his skull as he lapped and stroked, taking her to new heights. Higher and higher she soared as waves of heat flashed through her blood, a coil clenching low in her belly. Her thighs squeezed around his head holding him in place. Given the deep, throaty sounds he made, she doubted he wanted to move. When he angled his head to look up at her from between her legs, his eyes burning with crimson flames, that coil of bliss exploded within her. Her head fell back. Tiny stars burst before her eyes. Still, he didn't relent, not even when she cried out, shuddering beneath his touch.

As the last of her tremors eased, Slater drew back to stand, kicking the chair behind him, sending it skidding across the room. Her breath punched in and out, her mind floating on a foreign plane between the Heavens and the mortal realm. Splaying her palms on his defined pecs, she smoothed them over his shoulders while her pulse steadied. He dipped his head to nip at her neck, his hardness pressed against her middle, reigniting the heat simmering in her core. The sensations so intense they frightened her.

Before Slater, she'd never cared for sex. Why,

when her whole purpose was to protect the Empryen? In the mortal realm, fighting released an equal amount of tension, if not more.

Yet here, now, Slater delivered the most explosive wash of euphoria she'd ever experienced, and he'd barely touched her.

Standing between her bare legs, with intense possession in his eyes, flicked an internal switch. He'd never hidden his desire, but only now did she stop and consider her own. She craved his touch, hungered for it. But...

He straightened, no doubt sensing her mood shift. "Raine?"

She swallowed. What did she say? Could she give herself to a Fallen? Go against everything she believed?

Could she trust him? Surrendering her body to him felt...significant, as though in doing so, she also gave him her...

"I...can't..."

"Can't what?" His fingers brushed up and down her sides, waiting for her reply.

He was different from the other Fallen. He'd protected her when the Fallen attacked the bakery and again back in the chamber. Then, driven by an all-consuming need she still didn't understand, she'd unleashed her magic to save him. Even though she knew the consequences of using that much magic in the mortal realm.

Yet, somehow, Slater knew her, the real her, and he'd kept that secret.

Fate had created Raine to forge the deadliest weapon in the universe. She possessed power beyond an immortal's comprehension. Magic she'd kept hidden for centuries.

Curling a finger beneath her chin, he lifted her gaze to his. Deep grooves lined his forehead.

He was right with what he said back at the Guardian mansion. He did scare her. Not because he didn't fear her. This Fallen terrified her because when they were together, she forgot he was a Fallen. She forgot her destiny.

And that was more dangerous than any sword.

"I can't do this."

Slater turned to leave, but she snagged his arm.

He leaned down, placing a gentle kiss on her head. "You don't need to explain, Raine."

But the heaviness constricting her heart told her she should. Shouldn't she? He deserved an explanation, or at least to know he'd done nothing wrong. Before she formulated the words, Slater slipped free of her hold, gathered his shirt, and disappeared into the other room.

When she heard the shower turn on a few seconds later, she collapsed on the table and stared at the concrete ceiling.

Chapter TWENTY-SIX

He'd never recover from this.

Just when he thought kissing his fiery princess was enough, he went and tasted her. Massive mistake. She was heavenly, everything he remembered from that realm. Every magical taste, sound, and touch combined into one beautiful angel he suddenly had the urge to claim as his.

Tiny cells beneath his skin sparked with wild static. Wild was an understatement. A soft simmer of her magic thrummed through his blood.

When she'd healed him, something primal ignited deep within, securing his soul to hers. But he'd only ever heard of that happening between...soulmates. How was Raine his soulmate? Fate had no control over Fallen, nor did she create soulmates for them. Though...he was once an angel...

He shook his head and stepped out of the shower.

All this time, he'd waited for Raine so he could fulfil his bargain and gain his freedom. But being with her threatened to destroy all he'd worked to achieve. With one taste, he wanted to touch her, devour her, have her beneath him clawing his back.

How fucked up was that?

He was clearly delusional. She'd never fully give herself to him. He was a Fallen, the creatures of Hell she despised. She'd made that clear.

Raine 3. Slater 4.

After wiping condensation off the mirror, he inspected the swollen bite mark on his neck. A crazed thrill heated his blood at the memory of her teeth in his flesh. Clearly, cold showers didn't work.

Pulling on his pants, he made his way back to the main room and found Raine dressed, bending over the map rolled out on the table. *Speaking of cold showers.*

He rounded the table to stand across from her. "Find anything, princess?"

She stiffened. He braced for a Kiel to shoot toward him, but she refrained.

He smirked. That right there was progress.

"You told the truth," she murmured.

"Again, you'll have to be more specific. Told the truth about what?"

She glanced up at him through thick, long lashes. Something in his chest tightened, so badly he wanted to reach out and touch her.

"Asher has the sword."

He frowned. "I told you he has the sword."

"I didn't believe you. In the back of my mind, I suspected you were playing me. That you had the sword all along and were just gaining my trust."

A sour taste seeped up his throat. He hadn't lied about the sword, but he hadn't told the whole truth either. The accuracy of her assumption made his stomach churn.

He'd do anything for his freedom, or so he thought.

When he didn't reply, Raine redirected her attention back to the map. What was she looking for?

"Are those scars from hellfire?"

Her question came out of nowhere.

He inhaled a deep breath as he peered at the angry black scars marring his bare chest, as though expecting them to heal one day.

Her voice softened. A side of her he rarely saw. "How bad is it?"

He tilted his head, focusing on her violet eyes, anything to keep his mind in the present.

Something in her tone puzzled him. Remorse? Regret? Sympathy? He couldn't be sure, but her mood had mellowed while he was in the shower.

"Why the curiosity? I thought every Fallen deserved torture?"

A pained expression flashed across her face as her hands curled around the edge of the table. "I've never considered the ramifications. Does a Fallen's soul leave the Pits once it regenerates?"

"Unless someone frees them earlier."

"Like Blaine did for you?"

He narrowed his eyes. He'd never told her that, someone else must have. Why did she care now? "Something like that."

"That's why you stay with him. Out of obligation."

He flattened his palms on the table, leaning in. "Stop looking for reasons to make me a good guy, princess. I've done things even you couldn't stomach. I don't want to be good, and I never will be."

She rounded the table to stand before him. "I disagree."

Weird sensations stirred in his belly when she leaned in to softly kiss a scar on his chest. Her magic ignited deep inside him. This angel had such a hold on him that it scared the shit out of him. Easily, he imagined a future with her once he had his freedom.

But then reality set in, and he remembered all the reasons why they'd never work.

He was a Fallen. She was a powerful angel destined for greatness.

Their two worlds would never align.

He drew back, putting space between them. "How long will your magic last inside me?"

She shrugged.

"Raine?"

She paced the room for a moment before turning to face him. "I dunno. I've…never done that before."

"What do you mean? You've used your magic before. I know you have."

Her hands flung to her hips. "I've never healed an immortal. Let alone a…"

A Fallen.

She didn't say it, but he knew what she intended.

He thought for a moment. "But you knew you could."

"Lucky guess."

He wasn't so sure. "If you don't heal with your magic, what do you use it for?"

She flipped a Kiel, and it landed upright with the point stuck in the table. It glittered under the hanging light with a subtle teal he'd never noticed until now. "I fuse a hint of magic into each weapon, tuning it to the owner. I thought my magic…well, I never knew it healed."

Realization dawned on him as he put all the pieces together. "That's why the Guardians are so fucking lethal. Their weapons are an extension of their souls."

She nodded again.

"What about the Empryen?"

She narrowed her eyes. "What about it? I thought you didn't want it?"

He lifted one shoulder as though he didn't care. "Just curious. Who did you tune it to?"

She swiped the Kiel and twirled it around her index finger, something she did when nervous. No, not nervous, rattled.

"Me."

Muscles in his jaw clenched. "Say again?"

She lifted her gaze to his, staring him down from across the room. "I forged the Empryen for me."

That put one hell of a kink in his plan.

Why did Fate need him to bring the sword to Raine when it was hers in the first place?

Chapter TWENTY-SEVEN

After a quick detour back to the cemetery to collect Slater's new pet, because Fate forbid if he left the thing unattended for more than a few hours, they materialized in front of the Guardian mansion as the sun rose over the mountains. This realm had its moments. The Heavens didn't have sunrises like here. Well, it probably did, but she'd never experienced a sunset or sunrise during her time there, only continual night.

One thing she didn't miss.

Slater lowered his zipper a touch and cooed at the tiny creature nestled inside his leather jacket. It purred like a miniature version of EJ's car. A kickass Fallen brought to his knees by a kitten.

She thought watching romantic comedies lowered her badass reputation. With a furball sidekick, Slater had no hope. He might as well throw on a cardigan and take Cole out for afternoon tea.

She strode ahead of Slater. "Is that thing going to tag along everywhere?"

He chuckled, his boots crunching the gravel as he kept pace. "Be nice, princess. You'll hurt Peaches' feelings."

She rolled her eyes.

At the front door, she paused with her hand on the knob. Raven had summoned a Raziel to renew the spell preventing Fallen from entering the house, but her magic was far superior. She overrode it with one small manipulation.

Now, Slater was the only Fallen who could enter.

He came up behind her, ever so slightly his hand brushed over her hip. If only she didn't like it. She could easily surrender to his touch, his mouth on her, the way he made her blood ignite with a single look.

But too many lives were at stake for her to fail.

Inhaling a deep breath, she opened the door and strode into the mansion.

Raven halted at the bottom of the stairs. "Raine." He glared at Slater behind her, narrowing his eyes. "I see someone invited you back in."

For once, Slater used common sense and remained silent. Raven was more forgiving than Aric. Thank the Heavens he hadn't come down the stairs—

Shit.

The only one more overprotective than Aric was her brother.

River jogged down the stairs so fast he almost collided with Raven at the bottom. His gaze shot between Slater and her, then landed on the kitten sticking her head out of Slater's jacket. "You moving in?"

Slater tickled the furball under the chin. "Maybe. This is Peaches."

Usually nothing fazed her brother, but she sensed his confusion and worry through their bond.

Sis? The word appeared in her mind.

It's fine. She snapped back, slamming her mental walls closed.

"Update me so he can leave." Raven motioned for them to follow into the living room. "How did it go at the bookstore?"

Raven sat, but she refrained from joining him. Not because she had an aversion to seats, but because everything felt so out of whack. Uncomfortable. Foreign.

She sensed Slater's gaze on her, burning a path along her body, tracing where his lips had earlier. She shifted and moved to the side table, leaning against it.

Aric and EJ soon joined them, along with Hailee.

She filled the Guardians in on the events in New Orleans followed by the cemetery, leaving out the parts where Slater had kissed her, where Peyton had stabbed him, and the following clusterfuck back in the bunker. Though, Aric's stare gave her the impression he knew exactly what happened and wasn't happy.

That made two of them.

"We're back to square one," Raven stated when she'd finished.

Slater moved closer to her. She took one step in the opposite direction. The Guardians would kill Slater if she confirmed what happened between them. She wasn't ready for that yet.

Hailee straightened in the chair. "I still can't connect with Ebony, she keeps blocking me."

Blocking...

Hailee needed something that broke through her sister's barrier. Something strong and powerful enough not only to untie the spell, but connect Hailee with her sister no matter which realm they were in.

She thought for a moment. How could she create a spell without telling Hailee what it would do?

Raven stood. "I'll contact Cole so he can track the signatures from the cave."

She side-eyed Slater. Why hadn't he done that? Were his shadows not as powerful as Cole's? From what she knew, Slater had the most powerful tracking magic until he Fell. Did his magic lessen as a Fallen?

She'd seen his shadows. Nothing compared to them.

Was she wrong to trust him in the cave? Was she wrong to heal him?

She needed answers, but this wasn't the place. She needed to lure him somewhere private where he couldn't avoid her when she tortured them out of him.

"Let me know what Cole finds," she announced as she walked from the living room. "I'll be in the armory."

At the top of the stairs, she smiled to herself when she sensed Slater following.

She needed to forge a weapon for Hailee and elicit answers from Slater. Two immortals, one dagger.

After punching the code on the door, she strode into the armory, not bothering to hold it open for Slater. With any luck, it smacked him in the face.

It didn't. Slater slipped into the armory just in time.

Straightaway, she fired up the two chambers before grabbing her satchel and unrolling the tools. Slater crouched and placed the kitten on the floor. It scurried off, exploring the space.

She ignored Slater as he rounded the workbench to stand opposite her, silently watching her work. Lulling him into a false sense of security made it easier for him to slip up when she demanded answers.

Using a small pail, she collected Purah from the basin, taking it back to the workbench. She summoned her magic. This was why she'd insisted on a lock on the door. So the Guardians didn't waltz in and discover her secret.

They couldn't know her true form.

Magic swelled inside her, spilling from her hands and onto the workbench, coating the surface in bright teal light. She grabbed the pail, poured the Purah onto the workbench and got to work.

Swirling her hands through the shimmering heavenly water, she weaved her magic, connecting it to every tiny molecule in the Purah, threading them together. She closed her eyes, allowing the magic to consume her.

Nothing gave her a bigger thrill than wielding her powers.

Her hands operated without command. Envisioning her intended weapon, she kneaded, massaged, and spun the Purah into shape, never once opening her eyes, never breaking contact with the magic.

Although Slater remained silent, she felt his heated gaze roam over her skin.

When she finished, she opened her eyes. A small Purah charm in the shape of a wing lay in her hand. In this state, the charm was too fragile, only held together by threads of magic. Before Hailee used it, she needed to strengthen it. Easing the charm onto a long-handled shovel, she slid it into the cooling chamber.

When she turned back to the workbench, Slater stood right in front of her.

"Your magic is…beautiful. Strong and fierce, like you." His fingers trailed along her jaw. "Why don't you let others see it?"

She moved to walk past him, but he blocked her. Technically, she allowed him to block her. If she wanted him to, she'd make him move.

But this time…she didn't.

He dipped his head. "Why do you hide who you are? Is it because Fallen can sense your magic?"

She shook her head.

Sure, large bursts of magic, as she'd used in the cemetery, made it easier for Fallen to find her, but she could deal with them. Combined with Fate's threat to revoke River's immortality, it should've been enough to warn her from telling anyone. Ever.

The longer she spent in the mortal realm, another more dangerous threat presented itself. If the Guardians found out, if they knew she wasn't one of them, they'd resent her for hiding her true self. Or worse, they'd accept her into their makeshift family here in the mortal realm.

They'd want her to stay.

Fate banished the Guardians to the mortal realm too, but they managed to somewhat make the most of their time. They'd formed a…family. Something River craved.

Because of Fate, she'd spent her entire existence just…existing. River never questioned their mission, trusted Fate to guide them. But she'd left out certain details. River was her one and only weakness. Fate knew that. If her brother discovered her true mission, he'd stop her, and she'd fail.

"No one can know," she whispered.

Slater hovered closer, his deep brown eyes searching hers. "Why, Raine? You can trust me."

Slater calling her princess wasn't so absurd. She wasn't a princess, but she'd felt like one locked in a tower her entire existence protecting a sword until the time was right to fulfill her destiny.

A vow she intended to keep…until…

"I…" Her gaze lifted to Slater's.

Pressure intensified in her chest as that invisible connection drew her in, subconsciously pulling her to him. Blood whooshed in her ears. His fingers intwined with hers, sending a burst of light through her soul.

Realization stuck her like a bullet to the heart.

River wasn't her only weakness.

Slater…

She jerked her hand free and staggered back.

To think she'd almost confided in him. She almost trusted him.

Shaking her head, she cleared the fog and focused on the task. She needed to ask him questions, not the other way around. "Why didn't you track the souls at the cave?"

Slater sighed as he straightened. "I can't track Ebony when she's cloaked."

Hailee had said the same. "What about Asher?"

"He's cloaked, too."

She narrowed her eyes. "Funny how the most powerful tracker can't locate two souls when needed."

He matched her hard stare. "Funny how the most powerful angel refuses to use her magic around others."

They both harbored secrets. Was that why she felt so…drawn to him? So…connected?

So…*bonded*?

No, that feeling was adrenaline as a result of the earlier battle. Not an imaginary connection she shared with the Fallen standing too close to her.

He reached behind to twist her ponytail around his fist. He didn't give up, did he?

Her breath stalled. Why did she let him affect her?

Desire sparked low and hot in her belly, and suddenly she couldn't stop thinking about how amazing he felt between her legs. Her gaze darted to the workbench. Maybe if she gave in just once to whatever simmered between them, the spark would fizzle, and they could refocus on the mission.

Clearly, he sensed her change in mood because he lowered his mouth to her ear. "How long will the charm take?"

Wet lips trailed down her neck to her shoulder, igniting annoying flutters in her stomach.

She angled her head, giving him better access. "Long enough."

Their connection was a distraction she needed to rid herself of before something stupid happened. Mainly, before he made her question her destiny again.

"What should we do while we wait?"

Shivers danced along her arms at his low, rumbly tone.

Slater was the first immortal she'd ever healed. The first immortal she'd ever...considered saving. Why now? Why him?

For centuries, Fate had kept her powers hidden. But she didn't need to hide from him. He knew the real her and that felt...liberating.

She'd witnessed the makeshift bond with each resident in the household, the love and loyalty they possessed for one another. That same look now burned in Slater's gaze. She let him draw her in because for some unknown reason, she did trust him. Otherwise, she wouldn't have permitted him inside the mansion. She wouldn't have agreed to their arrangement.

She wouldn't have used her magic to heal him.

Slater cupped her face between his rough palms, hovering at her lips. "Tell me what you want, Raine."

For once, she could experience truly living while she still had time. And when they recovered the Empryen, she'd save Slater one final time.

"You. Just this once," she whispered.

His eyes lit with desire. "The Guardians will know. They'll sense it."

She held his gaze, not wanting to turn back now. "Let them."

When he leaned down, she raised on her toes to meet him halfway, crushing her mouth to his. Like earlier, her magic swelled inside her, threading tiny spells, curling them in the air between her and Slater. A small ball of light glowed from Slater's chest in the same spot she'd healed him.

He growled, taking her mouth in a searing kiss. In an instant, he stripped off her clothes and tossed them behind him. She clawed at his shirt and unbuckled his pants before he lifted her. Heat enveloped her, sending her senses on a wild thrill ride. With her legs wrapped around his waist, she rocked along his hardness as burning pressure consumed her.

He carried her to the workbench, lowering her back to the surface. Hovering above her, his eyes peered deep into her soul, once again stirring emotions she couldn't identify. This time she welcomed them all.

Dipping his head, his mouth explored her neck, her shoulders, over the hard peaks of her breasts. Goosebumps sprouted along her legs, colliding with the tingling sensations building in her core.

She embraced every sensation. If they only did this

once, she wanted to savor his touch, his gentle strokes, every second of the magic pulsing between their naked bodies.

She curled her fingers around the nape of his neck, scraping her nails along his flesh. Slater groaned, nipping her skin, sending a blast of fire through her veins.

"Slater…"

For the love of Fate, now she whimpered. What a loser.

When Slater lifted his head, she braced for a cocky grin. Instead, she found something far more troubling. The gaze locked on hers held nothing but…awe.

What the Fate?

Holding her gaze, he reached between them and angled himself at her entrance. The moment their bodies combined into one, a coil snapped inside her soul. Like a dagger slamming into the target, her blood exploded with vibrations, humming with so much intensity it brought tears to her eyes.

Why did she think this was a good idea?

Somehow, without her knowledge, Slater had slipped inside her soul, unraveling her defenses. The dangerous, forbidden aspect of their relationship lured her in a way she couldn't comprehend, nor explain, but now she suspected their connection was more than that. The way she sensed him before he appeared, how her magic stirred when he neared. How a tether of heavenly light streamed from her soul to his.

Tight spirals of pleasure curled low in her belly, expanding and magnifying as Slater rocked inside her. He worshiped her with his mouth and body, and for the first time in her existence, she surrendered.

She scored his back with her nails, making him thrust harder. Sweat glistened his defined pecs, sliding against her breasts. Her back burned, rubbing against the hard surface of the workbench, creating delicious sensations that left her teetering on the edge.

When their kisses became too fierce, Slater locked his mouth on her neck, biting down hard as she flew off the cliff. Pinpricks of light exploded before her eyes. Slater moaned, shuddering inside her.

Mine.

The single word appeared in her mind. Planted there from her or Slater, she didn't know. That invisible thread between them brightened, filling not just her soul with light, but also streaming that light from her to Slater.

Her breath stalled.

All the signs were there, but up until now, she'd refused to acknowledge them.

Slater was her…soulmate.

How the Fate did that happen? Could she screw up this mission even more?

Once their breathing settled, Slater leaned over her, bracing his palms on the workbench, searching her eyes. She unhooked her legs from around his back and flopped them over the edge of the workbench, unable to move even though she should roll out from beneath him.

She should kick his ass out the damn door.

He cupped one side of her face. "We're good together."

She cocked a brow and almost…smiled. Almost. "If you say so."

His chuckle rumbled in her belly. "Oh, princess.

210

Admit that you want me."

"Never."

She couldn't allow herself to want him. Nothing good came from wanting something she couldn't have. A connection that would eventually end.

He kissed her slow and deep, sharpening the pain near her heart. "One day you will."

And that scared her the most.

Slater eased out of her, and she cursed at her flash of disappointment. Sex and desire hung heavy in the humid air, mixing with Slater's fire and brimstone scent, coating her skin. Peeling herself off the workbench, she watched him dress. Such a powerful, perfectly sculpted immortal. An immortal she considered as equally lethal as her.

Had Fate tied their souls together because he was a Fallen? Was he part of her destiny?

He caught her ogling and cocked his head to one side. "Like what you see?"

She composed herself, never lowering herself to flirting as though stuck in one of those romantic comedies. Not now, not ever. "Get over yourself, Hell bo—"

Someone punched the combination on the door. *Shit.*

Slater tossed her clothes and she caught them, scrambling to dress before the door opened.

Chapter TWENTY-EIGHT

Raine barely finished dressing when River strolled into the armory.

Raine's brother paused just inside the door, his gaze darting between him and Raine. "What you doin'?"

He almost laughed at River's poor attempt to pretend he didn't sense Slater had just bonded with his sister. Their scent was all over each other. And if River was somehow oblivious to all that, surely, he smelled the heady scent of sex lingering in the air.

He didn't want to hide what had happened between him and Raine. But he sensed she wasn't ready. Even now, her rapid pulse thrummed through his blood, warning him not to overstep.

Raine slid the long-handled tray inside the chamber and removed the item she'd crafted before they'd…distracted each other with more enjoyable activities.

"I forged a charm." She placed the tray on the workbench, right where he'd just made her fall apart beneath him.

Her pulse kicked up. She gave him a sideways glance, clearly remembering the same moment. Heat flashed through their bond.

Maybe he was right? Perhaps Fate had tied their souls together, which explained his vision of her while he was in the Pits. Fate sure liked to create cryptic as Hell paths, so it wouldn't surprise him. All this time he'd assumed the vision connected Raine to the sword, but what if it connected her to him?

Raine dangled a Purah feather from her fingers, holding it up for River. "It's for Hailee."

Slater eyed the charm. Now wasn't the time for making jewelry. They needed to find Asher. "Why make the Dumahel a charm?"

She narrowed her violet eyes. "So she can do what you can't."

Without waiting for his reply, Raine strode out the armory, leaving him with River.

Talk about awkward.

River cleared his throat.

"Something to say, River?"

The angel glared at him. "You can't stay here."

"In the armory or the Guardian house?"

When River didn't answer, he turned away and searched for Peaches. Poor kitten had gotten quite the peep show earlier, more than she bargained for. After a thorough search, he found her asleep, tucked behind a stone basin. He scooped her off the floor and headed to the door, but River snagged his shirt.

"You'll destroy her destiny. All she's trained for."

He yanked his arm free. "What if I don't? What if Raine's path includes me?"

River screwed up his face, as though the idea was so absurd, he couldn't believe Slater said it aloud.

Why in the fiery Hell were he and Raine such a ridiculous pairing? Sure, they fought on opposite sides of this war, but they wouldn't forever. Once he and Raine recovered the Empryen, Fate would grant him his freedom. How she'd do that, he didn't know nor care. He assumed she'd somehow sever his link to Zath, granting him the freedom to stay in the mortal realm, neutral territory. Fate was the queen of the universe. If anyone had the power to fulfill that deal, it'd be her.

The Guardians permanently resided in the mortal realm, so why couldn't he?

Maybe then, he could be with Raine.

"Whatever you're doing, stop it. I don't want Raine getting hurt."

He almost laughed. What Raine needed, what she deserved, was an equal. Not a half-assed angel who fell to their knees at Fate's every command. Sure, he wasn't an angel, but soon, he'd answer to no one. He'd chosen his own path. And when it came to being Raine's equal, he was up for the challenge.

He'd fight beside her. He'd defend her. He wouldn't try to control her.

He pinned River with a hard stare, his blood boiling. "Raine can make her own choices. Never forget that."

Before River played the protective brother card again, Slater strode out of the armory.

Avoiding the other Guardians, he carried Peaches out the front door so she could do her business on the grass. Raine would lose her shit if the kitty pissed in the armory.

He lowered the kitten on the lawn by his—

Someone shoved him in the back. He stumbled forward, jumping over Peaches so he didn't squash her.

Shadows swirling, he spun, prepared to fight.

"What the fuck is your game?" Aric snarled at him. *Not this again.*

He would've bet his left wing on Raven picking a fight with him sooner or later. Not every day the Guardian had a Fallen inside his home. But no, Aric prowled around him, a dagger gripped in his hand.

The hothead was always quick to retaliate. Especially when it concerned Willow. But this time the Guardian was out of line. Besides, Willow chose her own path. In fact, while she was in the mortal realm, he trained the Ariel so she could defend herself. Aric should thank him.

He thickened the shadows curling from one palm. "What are you talking about?"

"Raine, you dumb fuck."

"You know what? I'm sick of everyone thinking it's their right to get involved in her business."

Aric lunged at him. He misted, reappearing behind the Guardian.

"Coward." Aric snarled.

He clenched his jaw. He wasn't a coward. He'd survived Falling from the Heavens and centuries of subsequent torture in the Pits. He'd fought for his path, made a deal that secured his freedom, and did unspeakable acts to ensure it.

One Guardian was no match for him.

He stalked forward, right up in Aric's face. "What happens between Raine and me is none of your business."

"Like hell it isn't." Aric shoved his chest. "I see the way you look at her. Stay the hell away."

That just pissed him off. Aric, or any other immortal for that matter, had no right to tell Raine who she could be with. If they wanted to release sexual tension, they would.

If they wanted to tie themselves together for eternity. They fucking would.

He leaned forward, narrowing his eyes. "Or what?"

Aric swiped his dagger. He leaped back, the blade narrowly missing his side. Aric swiped again, nicking his arm.

Fine. If Aric wanted a fight, he'd get it.

Withdrawing his shadows, he swung his fist at Aric, punching the Guardian in the jaw, splitting his lip. Aric spat blood on the grass and growled.

Slater widened his stance, readying himself. He could resummon his shadows and end this quicker, but he sensed Aric needed to see him fight like an immortal. Like males.

The Guardians needed to see how serious he was about Raine.

Hang on.

Serious about Raine?

Yes. He was, about time everyone knew it.

Aric punched him in the ribs. He grunted and swung, connecting with Aric's jaw again. Blood spurted from the reopened cut on his lip.

Whatever their future held, he'd just bonded with his soulmate. This fight was more than a Fallen and an angel. Right now, he fought Aric for his honor. For their respect.

He didn't need their blessing. Raine didn't belong to them. They didn't even know her true self. He did.

Aric swung a right hook and Slater blocked it, returning the punch from the left. Back and forth, they parried, attacking, defending, connecting, missing. Blood covered their knuckles, smeared their faces, but still they kept swinging.

With no end in sight, Slater unfurled his wings in one swift rush and struck his talons at Aric's throat, halting a hairbreadth away from the flesh.

Aric stilled, a dagger raised midair. His eyes went wide, darting between Slater and the talon about to rip through his throat.

Striking Aric with Fallen venom would seriously piss off Raine. She'd retaliate. If that happened, she wouldn't help him find the Empryen, or she'd do it without him.

He couldn't let that happen. Besides, he'd fought Aric to prove himself as Raine's equal. Poisoning the Guardian undid all he'd just worked to achieve.

Plus, he sensed Raine cared for the Guardians, in her own way.

He lowered his wing, withdrawing it to his side.

"The deal's off. Find Asher on your own." The Guardian glared at him before heading back to the mansion. "Don't bother coming back, asshole."

Newsflash, he wasn't going anywhere. He still had a mission to finish. To hell with the other Guardians, Raine decided her own fate, and soon, so would he.

He fanned his wings, releasing the built-up tension in his shoulders, cracking his neck left and right. Tingles spread along the inside of one wing, as though the individual feathers reacted to the morning sunlight. Impossible. Since becoming a Fallen, the sun's rays no longer healed him. His soul no longer harnessed its power.

The tingle swelled, spreading over his wing. Curiosity got the better of him. He curled the wing inward and lifted his arm, peering at the feathers beneath.

He froze.

Tucked under his arm, amongst the dark crimson splayed over his wings, were two single gray feathers.

Holy fuck.

He staggered back. It couldn't be.

An invisible force squeezed his chest as he stared at the overwhelming evidence.

How had his feathers changed? When? Did it happen when he acknowledged his connection to Raine? Or when they had sex? Had he somehow upset the power of the universe by choosing an angel over a Fallen?

Reaching across his body, he brushed his fingers along the now unfamiliar feathers. They tingled, spreading warmth up his arm into his chest, right to the spot where...

Raine.

Dread filled his belly like a tornado of black emotion, swirling until it consumed everything inside him. To stop the Purah from entering his heart, Raine had flooded his veins with her magic.

She was powerful. But was she *that* powerful?

He'd sensed Raine's magic inside him when they kissed, and again in the armory. Even now, he sensed her power expanding, consuming every cell, repelling his darkness. He'd assumed it was their twisted soulmate bond. But what if...

Fuck.

Raine's magic hadn't just healed his wound.

It healed his soul.

He glared at the Heavens, hoping Fate looked down on him. "What the fuck have you done?"

Fate had vowed to grant him freedom. Healing his

soul wasn't part of their bargain. He didn't want to return to the Heavens under Fate's command once again. He didn't want to ever go back.

He wanted to choose his own path.

His blood raged.

He should've known better than to make a deal with Fate. Had she planned this all along? Had Fate tricked him into connecting with Raine, so they sealed their bond? So Raine healed his soul?

If Fate succeeded, she could recall him to the Heavens without notice.

If that happened, he kissed his freedom goodbye.

Chapter TWENTY-NINE

Raine found Hailee with the other soulmates in the entertainment room, sitting on the couch with a pile of snacks scattered over the coffee table. Sweet buttery popcorn filled the air. Some movie played on the big screen.

She recognized the whimsical music and shuddered, another romantic comedy.

All she needed after her episode lusting after Slater.

Tayla waved her over. "Come join us."

She'd rather go on a field trip to Hell than watch another movie where the female lead disowned her badass reputation for love. *Gag.* "I need Hailee."

Someone paused the movie. Thank Fate.

Hailee stood. "Is something wrong?"

How did she answer that?

Raine dangled the Purah charm. "This will break the cloaking spell so you can dreamwalk to your twin." She jiggled the charm for Hailee to take it. "Where's your bracelet?"

Hailee rounded the couch to Raine and held out her wrist while Raine secured the charm.

"Try connecting with your sister."

Hailee frowned. "Now?"

"Yup." Raine held out her hand. "And you're taking me with you."

Aric barged through the door so hard it slammed against the wall. "Raine."

"Not now."

"Yes, now."

She scowled at the Guardian. "What's so critical that you have to speak with me right this instant? I'm busy."

EJ and Raven trailed into the room after Aric. For the love of Fate, she couldn't do anything around here without them all up in her face.

"Are we having a movie session and I missed the invite?" EJ asked on his way to the bar.

Raine withdrew a Kiel and slid it onto her forefinger. "Fine. Since you're all here. I forged a charm to break through the Dumahel's cloaking spell." She addressed EJ. "Your soulmate was about to dreamwalk us before you idiots barged into the room."

EJ stilled with his hand around the neck of a vodka bottle. "It's not exactly safe while Ebony is with their father."

Safe? Nothing was safe anymore. Not her mission in the mortal realm, not her secret, and now not even her soul was safe because she'd hitched it to a damn Fallen.

She needed to find the Empryen and finish this before she made any more stupid decisions.

She threw her hands in the air. "You have a better idea?"

His mouth twisted to one side as he tapped a finger on the bottle.

Hailee softened her voice. "We need to try. Blaine is hunting Asher. What if Ebony is caught in the crossfire?"

"You keep protecting her, Hails. But what if she's working with Blaine? Or your father?"

"She's my sister. Until I know that for sure, I have to at least try."

When EJ gave a conceded sigh, Hailee sat on the closest couch and patted the space beside her for Raine. "We'll be fine. Raine's coming with me. Plus, I have my Purah ring. I proved I can use it."

The pride beaming from EJ's expression almost made her gag.

Raine sat and linked her hand in Hailee's.

Aric rounded the couch. "Why are you still helping that asshole?"

She glared up at Aric. "I'm getting the sword." She frowned, scanning the room. "Who's watching Slater? I wouldn't let him wander around the mansion."

"He bailed."

Slater left…without telling her?

Why? More to the point, why did that bother her? Just because she'd sealed a bond with him didn't mean he answered to her, or they resembled the sappy couple currently paused on the TV. Their connection was…convenient. They had a mutual understanding. Besides, it wouldn't last. Everything would end once she recovered the sword.

Until then, Slater could come and go as he pleased.

Yet, the sharp sting in the center of her chest made her second guess that thought.

Aric's gaze darted past her toward Raven, then back. "Listen, there's something you should know about Slater—"

"Now's not the time." She cut off Aric, not even sparing him a glance. Whatever he wanted to tell her about Slater could wait. She squeezed Hailee's hand. "Let's do this."

At Hailee's nod, Raine closed her eyes.

Light dispersed through her soul, swirling around the darkness behind her closed lids. Weightlessness filled her body, starting at the tips of her toes, blooming up her spine before detaching her soul, and floating her through the ether. A bright ball of light hovered next to her, and she kept a tight grasp on the tether connecting her to Hailee.

What happened if she let go? Would her soul float in the nothingness for eternity? Or would it return to her corporal form on the couch in the Guardian mansion?

When the sensations faded, reuniting her soul to solid form, she opened her eyes. Immediately, she recognized the place. Hailee had dreamwalked them to the chamber where she and Slater fought the Fallen.

Ebony, Hailee's twin, spun, gaping at them. "What the hell? How did you connect with me?"

Raine didn't bother with small talk. In an instant, she dropped Hailee's hand, grabbed Ebony by the front of the shirt and shoved her against the stone wall. "Where's the sword?"

Ebony twisted her mouth into an ugly snarl. "You're the Guardian working with Slater."

"No shit. And your evil BFF stabbed him." She snatched a Kiel from her belt and pinned the tip against the Dumahel's throat. "Where's the sword?"

Ebony struggled against Raine's hold. "I'm not telling you anything. I have as much right to that sword as any other."

She growled, lifting Ebony's feet off the ground. This Fallen didn't deserve to live. She should rot in the

Pits for all of eternity. "The Empryen belongs to me, and I want it back."

Hailee squawked, clawing at Raine's arm, trying to pull her back. "Stop, you're hurting her."

Defiance darkened Ebony's eyes. She leaned in, pricking her own throat with the Kiel. "You saved that Raziel, but we'll just get another. You won't stop us."

Raine laughed. Actually, laughed.

"You have no idea what you've gotten yourself into. You have no clue how to activate the Empryen."

With a final shove against the wall, she released the delusional Dumahel.

Ebony stumbled before righting her balance. "A Raziel can activate the sword."

Raine laughed again. Why did Fate create such stupid immortals?

The time for hiding was over. She'd had enough of chasing superior immortals, trying to recover something that belonged to her and only her. Fate destined Raine to forge the Empryen and told her to activate it when the time came.

That time was now.

If they wouldn't hand over the sword, she'd make them come for her.

She pinned the Dumahel with a lethal stare, pointing the tip of a Kiel in her direction. "Correction. Only *one* Raziel can activate the Empryen, and that Raziel is me."

Chapter THIRTY

Slater burst through the gateway to Aralim, his boots slamming the loose dirt as he stormed through the forest until he reached Blaine's lair in Hell. Outside the entrance, he scowled at the nearest Fallen guarding the mansion. No one would attack them here. The Guardians had already pulled that stunt and wouldn't return anytime soon.

They'd gotten what they wanted.

Asher wouldn't show his face again until he was ready to kill Blaine. And he couldn't do that without Raine.

Fuck.

"Dagger." He sneered at the nearest Fallen, holding out his palm.

The Fallen didn't bat an eyelid, handing over the weapon. They weren't stupid enough to challenge him or question his command. Another advantage of being Blaine's second.

Dagger in hand, he threw open the door and stormed inside.

Twisted plots and plans scrambled his head. Asher wanted the sword to kill Blaine. Fate wanted Raine to have it. And to gain his freedom, he needed Raine to activate it.

All plans centered on a Raziel who had hidden her true form in the mortal realm. But now that Raziel had thrown everything into a spin by fucking healing him.

Raine 4. Slater 4.

If he didn't hurry up and find the sword and somehow convince Raine to activate it before his soul fully healed, Fate could recall his ass to the Heavens.

It became a race to see who got the sword *and* Raine first.

How quickly would Raine's magic heal him? How long before he could no longer stay in this realm? How long before Fate regained control over his soul?

He tightened his grip on the dagger. Slowing down the healing process, or better yet, stopping it was the priority.

On his way to the second floor, he shoved past Fallen mingling inside the mansion. Without his wings unfurled, they had no idea what had just happened to him. But soon, they'd sense the change.

All those centuries in the Pits, plotting how to win over his fiery princess, how to gain her trust, had turned around and bitten him in the ass.

Or the wings, same difference.

He ducked into a spare room on the top floor, searching for a mirror. Thankfully, he hadn't run into Blaine. How the hell would he explain this to Blaine? How he'd become…

Compromised.

The only word that came to mind.

He'd fucking compromised himself by being with Raine. She was powerful, yet he never expected her to heal his soul.

How was that even possible?

"Fuck!"

In front of the mirror, he unfurled his wings,

punching twin holes in the walls. Who cared about a shitty wall when his soul was at stake?

Peering in the mirror, he eyed the compromised feathers. Two silvery-gray Azrael feathers. The exact color of his wings before he Fell.

An invisible force slammed into his chest.

Being in Hell wouldn't fix this problem or it would take too long. He needed a faster solution before the heavenly light cleansed his entire soul.

Using the mirror to guide him, he positioned the dagger and dug into the base of the first feather. Fire burned through his wing. Gritting his teeth, he continued. He inserted the blade further into his flesh, slicing through tissue and muscle, until it hit bone. Twisting the blade, he circled the base of the feather, digging it out as one would a pesky weed.

These two feathers were poisonous weeds in his garden. If he left them, they would multiply and eventually send his soul packing straight back to the Heavens.

Blood oozed from the wound. He dug further. Deep beneath the quill, he severed the last connecting tendon with a satisfying snap. The feather tumbled to the floor, landing in the pool of blood at his feet.

He tossed the dagger in the basin. Black dots flashed in his vision. His body swayed. He steadied himself with a hand on the vanity and inhaled slow, deep breaths, calming his heart rate.

He couldn't stop until he'd removed both.

When the dizziness settled, he straightened. Grabbing the dagger once more, he repeated the process for the second feather, gouging a deep hole around the base. After it fluttered from his wing, his legs gave way, dropping his ass onto the stone floor. Black Fallen blood pooled beside him. At least the color of his blood hadn't changed.

With any luck, he removed the feathers before they caused any real damage.

He needed to be more careful around Raine. If she healed him again, the magic would eventually reach his soul and become permanent.

He sat there for what felt like hours with his back against the wall, his eyes closed. How had this mission turned so shit?

In the beginning, he pursued Raine because her Raziel abilities led to his freedom. But now…everything had changed. Since the moment he first saw her in the forest surrounding the Guardian mansion, something stirred deep within him. He thought getting under her skin would be simple, yet, during the past few months, she'd somehow squirmed her way into his…heart without him even realizing.

That backfired.

His fiery princess kept him sane in the Pits, but outside, in the mortal realm, she made him crazy. Now, he didn't know which way was up, right or wrong. Was he still on the correct path or had he diverted?

After composing himself, he willed his wings to return inside his back, grabbed the two compromised feathers and headed downstairs to the living room. Standing before the lit hearth, he tossed the feathers into the flames. The second the flames took hold, sharp pain cut through his chest in the spot Raine had healed him.

How was any of this possible?

He'd never heard of Fallen wings reverting to their

original form, ever. In fact, he'd only experienced the reverse—his angel wings turning to crimson when he Fell. But Fate banished the Guardians to the mortal realm to save Blaine. Before now, he'd considered that idea ridiculous. A failed mission that exiled the Guardians from the Heavens for eternity.

Now, he wasn't so sure.

The evidence before him said otherwise.

"I'm surprised to see you here."

He spun as Blaine strolled into the living room.

"Aren't you meant to be tracking a certain Azrael?"

He shot a quick glance at the flames just as the feathers turned to ash. *Whew*. Close call.

Moving away from the hearth, he collapsed into a repaired couch. "Peyton fucking stabbed me."

Back in the cavern, he'd wanted to end Peyton for calling Raine a bitch, but he'd hesitated. Then she'd fucking stabbed him in the back, literally. Raine was right. His loyalty was as confused as him.

Blaine sat in the armchair. A glass of bourbon materialized in his hand. "Nothing you didn't heal from, I gather."

If Raine hadn't been there…He shut down that thought quickly.

"She's working with Asher."

Blaine sipped his bourbon. "I presumed as much."

His head lolled onto the backrest as weariness seeped into his bones. He could fight battles all day but digging out feathers from his own wings was another level. Fire burned at the wound site as though it refused to heal, even though he was in Hell.

He suspected they wouldn't heal. And that

knowledge concerned him more than how they appeared in the first place.

"Thanks for the heads-up," he said.

Blaine smirked. "Don't sulk. You're more than capable of dealing with a traitorous Fallen, even one with Peyton's skills. After all, you trained her."

True.

Blaine materialized a bourbon on the table in front of him, and Slater reached forward to grab it. He took a sip and grimaced as the liquor travelled down his throat. Mortal bourbon was so much better than whatever the hell this was.

He should just return to his bunker or Blaine's mansion in the mortal realm. At least he'd have decent bourbon.

But for some reason, he kept his ass on the couch.

A niggling feeling in his gut, not a result of the disgusting drink, told him Blaine knew more than he let on, and it was time he shared it.

He straightened and pivoted to face Blaine. "What do you know about the Empryen?"

Blaine shot back his drink and slid the empty glass on the coffee table, acting not at all surprised by his question.

He watched him, gauging every slight twitch in his expression. How much did Blaine know? Did he know Asher had the sword? Did he suspect Slater had teamed up with Raine to get it back?

Did Fate tell him her plan when Blaine dreamwalked?

Eventually, Blaine relaxed in the armchair, crossing his ankle on his knee. "Let me tell you a story."

"Not this again." He groaned. "I'm gonna need better bourbon."

A fresh glass appeared on the coffee table, and he snatched it.

"The Empryen resides in its own realm, guarded by the powerful Raziel who created it. Fate compelled the Raziel to hide away like a fairy princess, guarding a sword only a select few knew existed." He paused. "The Empryen is the only weapon capable of killing an immortal permanently."

He knew all that. Blaine had told him the story when they were both in the Heavens. Back then, he'd shrugged off the information. Why did he need to know about a powerful sword? Had Blaine known Fate would offer him the deal?

This time, he listened more intently.

Plus, it wasn't bad having cushions for his tired ass.

Blaine continued, "One day, a powerful angel will use the sword to ignite a final battle between the Heavens and Hell. The Sarael."

He sat up straighter. "Did you say, Sarael?"

Blaine nodded. "The Protector of the Heavens."

His jaw dropped. Holy shit.

Was Raine the Sarael? Was that why Fate compelled her to create the sword? Did Raine know?

Blaine pointed his glass at Slater. "Word on the streets of Hell is the Empryen is missing."

Blaine clearly knew more about the Empryen than Fate had told him, which shouldn't surprise him. His first mistake was trusting Fate to make this mission easy for him. His second was trusting her word.

He should've known she'd only give him half the

story.

Blaine and he had known each other forever. Even though he craved his soul's freedom, to remove himself from beneath Zath's rule, he owed Blaine. The Fallen had freed him from the Pits and granted him a position of power by his side.

He could trust Blaine.

"Asher has the sword."

Blaine looked at him over the rim of his glass. "I wonder how he got his hands on it. Given it's meant to be hidden away in the Heavens."

He took a long sip of his own drink, using the time to figure out how much to reveal. "He wants to use it to kill you, you know that don't you?"

Blaine waved a hand through the air, dismissing Slater's concern. "The sword is useless without the Raziel to activate it. Eventually, Asher will become desperate and make a mistake."

What if Asher figured out he needed Raine?

Why didn't Blaine tell him?

He pivoted to face Blaine. "Why me? Why did you pull me from the Pits?"

Over the years since, he'd wondered, but it hadn't mattered. Blaine freed him from centuries of torture and all he'd requested in return was hunting down the Dumahel twins. At the time, he'd considered the request so easy he questioned Blaine's negotiation skills.

But since the twins turned twenty-five, everything had fallen apart. When he materialized at the Guardian mansion a few months ago to negotiate for the other Dumahel, he'd seen Raine for the first time. Seeing her in the flesh had ignited something hot and almost lethal in his blood. Back then, he didn't know why. But now, the reason was so obvious he almost laughed.

"Did I ever tell you about—"

He groaned again. "Oh, for fuck's sake, don't tell me another story."

Blaine slapped a palm over his chest and gasped. "You don't like my stories?"

Some days he wondered how no one shoved a Purah dagger in Blaine's heart.

"Give me the short version," he said, sipping the too smoky bourbon.

Blaine exhaled an exaggerated sigh. "Very well. But just so you know, I'm a little offended." Blaine thought for a moment. "Remember when I told you that your shadow powers were stronger, more powerful than a regular Azrael? Remember what it felt like to harness that power?"

He nodded. Blaine had told him that when they were in the Heavens. They'd often experimented, seeing how far Slater could push the power.

"Most angels believe Fate creates each faction equally, with the same amount of magic and power. Besides the Guardians, of course." He shrugged one shoulder. "But every now and then, she shows off and creates a rare immortal. An angel with far more potential than they, or anyone else, realizes."

Again, he knew all that. Blaine had convinced him he was one of those immortals, but he'd never believed it. Sure, back in the Heavens, he'd felt wasted, yearned for something greater.

But it still didn't explain why.

Blaine continued, "Even less often, Fate creates a soulmate pair."

He nearly choked on the bourbon.

Raine.

"Imagine the result when these two rare angels join their souls and unite their powers on the same side."

Acid burned through his middle. Unite their powers? Surely, Blaine didn't plan for him to bring Raine to Hell to join his army?

No fucking way.

Muscles in his jaw tightened as he clenched his teeth.

Why would Blaine need Raine's powers as well? Unless… "You knew Asher stole the Empryen. That's why you tasked me with hunting him down." A thought sprung a hot, furious coil in his gut. "You know Raine's my soulmate."

"Don't forget where your loyalty lies, Slater." Blaine leveled his gaze. "Bring your soulmate and the sword to me."

Chapter THIRTY-ONE

Hailee stared at Raine. She said nothing, just stared.

EJ sank into the seat next to Hailee, reaching for her hands. "Did it work?"

Hailee turned to face her soulmate. "Yeah. But..." She glanced back at Raine, frowning.

She couldn't blame the Dumahel, after all, Raine had just dropped the bomb of the century right in her lap. The time had come for her to embrace every part of her true self. No longer would she hide behind Fate's threats. She was a Guardian of sorts, just not in the way these immortals thought. She guarded a sword. The Empryen.

She wasn't part of Fate's elite personal guard, sent here to save one of their own. No. Fate sent her here to save this realm and everyone in it.

"Hails?" EJ prompted.

"It's not my place to say," Hailee murmured.

Raine stood, unsheathing the Kiel from her belt. While she was in the dreamwalk, her brother had joined everyone in the entertainment room. He stood beside Aric with a slight frown on his face.

He knew. Her stomach twisted with what she was about to say.

Would Fate punish River? She'd kept the secret since arriving in the mortal realm. But only now did she realize she couldn't finish it without help from the immortals surrounding her.

She glanced to Raven. His expression was always hard to read, even more so now. Although Aric was the hot-tempered, overprotective Guardian, Raven was more grounded. He said few words yet always managed to preempt the situation before it arose. Did he suspect her secret?

"Raine, what happened?" Raven stepped forward, his head tilted to the side as he studied her.

She spun the Kiel around her index finger.

Now or never.

She eyed her brother and caught his discreet nod.

The Guardians could help her find the Empryen. They could help her finish this.

No longer would she need to hide her true form. River could enjoy his time here, rather than harboring her secret. He'd always had so much faith in Raven to lead them. Now, she needed to trust her brother and everyone else in this household.

If she could trust Slater, then trusting the Guardians should be a walk in the clouds.

That didn't mean she'd suddenly turned into a chick-flick girly-girl. It just meant, maybe for once, she'd embrace...friendship. She grimaced. Even the word felt weird in her mind.

Pausing the Kiel with her thumb, she lifted her chin. "I'm not a Guardian."

There, she'd said it.

She waited a few moments for Fate to zap her with lightning or for a massive crater to open in the floor and suck her into Hell.

Nothing happened.

She continued, "Fate sent me to the mortal realm to retrieve the Empryen."

Raven frowned. "It's been missing that long?"

"Yes and no. I'm not sure when it went missing in mortal time, or how it happened."

"I thought a Raziel guarded the Empryen."

Her gaze darted to River. A soft smile lifted his face as though he'd found peace. He'd also never been so damn quiet.

She inhaled a deep breath and addressed everyone in the room. "I'm the Raziel."

Again, she waited for lightning to strike or for her soul to burst into flames. Which, again, it didn't.

"I need a frickin' drink," EJ muttered under his breath as he moved behind the bar.

Raven settled into an armchair. "How about you start from the beginning?"

A martini glass with sloshing clear liquid appeared in front of her, courtesy of EJ. She accepted it, grateful for the distraction. That Guardian annoyed her sometimes, but he sure made good cocktails.

After the initial sip loosened her shoulders, she placed the drink down and sat on the edge of the couch beside Hailee. "Fate created me to forge a weapon unlike any other. One capable of annihilating an entire realm in a single strike."

"The Empryen," Aric said.

She nodded. "I guarded it for centuries, millennia even. I don't know exactly how long in mortal years. Then one day, it disappeared. Fate summoned me to her sanctuary. As you can imagine, I didn't take the news well."

EJ snorted. "Shocking."

She side-eyed him. He ducked behind the bar. "Chicken."

He poked his head around the side. "Can you blame me?"

A soft smile warmed her cheeks. "Anyway, Fate sent River and me here to find it." Her fingers curled around the soft edge of the couch. "While here, Fate granted me permission to forge Purah weapons for you all. But I channeled a small amount of Raziel power into each one just to piss her off."

An almost proud smile twinkled in Aric's eyes. "That's why the blades are so fucking good. They're powered by Raziel magic."

Raven leaned forward, his forearms along his thighs. "Why didn't you tell us?"

"Fate forbade it. If I told anyone, River would suffer the consequences, not me."

She left out the part about Fate revoking River's immortality. That only created more questions she couldn't answer.

Raven swore under his breath. He pivoted to River. "So, you're both Raziel?"

"Yeah, boss."

"How did such a powerful weapon disappear from the Heavens?"

She'd like the answer to that also. "I've been asking myself that same question for the past three years. One second I had the sword, then the next thing I remember, I stood outside Fate's sanctuary."

"Unless…" Raven thought for a moment. "Unless someone removed the memory."

"An Azrael." Aric sneered.

She shook her head. "Azrael replace memories

with shadows. I can't see any. Besides River and I, only Fate, and possibly Gabe, knew the location of the realm."

After handing out the last drink, EJ perched on the armrest beside Hailee with his own glass. "Slater must have it. Otherwise, why would Fate send me that vision?"

"I thought the same at first, but he doesn't. Asher does."

Hailee stiffened beside her. "Hasn't he caused enough damage already?"

"There's more." Her nails dug into her thigh. "He wants to use it to kill Blaine."

"Say what?" EJ squawked at the same time Hailee gasped.

"Asher wants revenge because of what Blaine did to you and your sister." She sighed, grabbing her drink. "That's why I don't do attachments."

Aric snorted. "Too late for that."

She glared at him. Clearly, word travelled fast.

"Can you use Raziel magic to recover the memories, if an immortal did remove them?" Raven asked.

"Not that I'm aware."

She'd thought non-stop about the time leading up to arriving at Fate's sanctuary, trying to figure out how an immortal stole the sword from right under her watch. But each time, she hit a black wall of nothingness. They must've removed the memories.

Unless…someone messed with time. Powers both Fate and Gabe possessed.

It just didn't make sense.

Every spell had a loophole, one that could undo the

magic and reset it. Figuring it out was the hard part. Given Fate sent her to the mortal realm, she didn't have access to other Raziel in the Heavens. The select few she found here, like Thatcher, weren't powerful enough or willing to risk defying their almighty queen.

"You sure Slater doesn't have anything to do with this? Don't you think it's strange he came to us for help to find Asher, who conveniently stole the Empryen? Then he squirmed his way inside the mansion, among other things." Aric held her gaze, testing her limited self-control when it came to dumbass comments.

She clenched her jaw so she didn't throw a damn dagger at his head. "What's your issue with Slater? He chose the wrong side in this war, but you of all immortals should know a thing or two about regrets."

That shut Aric's mouth.

But she didn't stop. "Yes, I think Slater has his own agenda when it comes to the Empryen, but to date, he's shared every lead with me. And twice now, he's stabbed a Fallen about to end me."

Aric tilted his head. "He did?"

She nodded.

No need to add that she returned the favor by saving him with her magic. For the love of Fate, she'd never used her Raziel magic to conjure a protection seal around an immortal's heart so Purah couldn't penetrate it. But in that moment, she couldn't cause him more pain and torture. Slater had endured enough. And maybe, just maybe, she'd…miss having him around.

"We can't rule out Slater's involvement." Raven slid his glass on the nearest table and stood. "I'll summon Gabe. I think it's about time he gave us answers."

She withdrew her boot dagger, balancing it in her palm. "The Empryen is useless without me to activate it."

"That's my main concern," Raven replied, his tone softer. "What does Fate want you to do once you recover it?"

"Take it to its rightful place."

"Back in the Heavens?" Raven asked.

She glanced at her brother. Heaviness again pressed on her chest.

Instead of speaking, she nodded.

When she recovered the sword, she'd complete her destiny. That was all they needed to know.

Chapter THIRTY-TWO

Slater materialized in the forest surrounding Blaine's place in the mortal realm. He'd stayed in Hell as long as he could, until the tug in his chest became unbearable. All he thought of was Raine. Her platinum blonde hair tangled around his fingers, her violet eyes radiating in the darkness, the pointy heels she wore when she kicked a Fallen's ass.

She didn't need him to fight for her, yet he wanted that honor.

Standing between the giant pines, he unfurled his wings and peeked underneath his arm. The compromised feathers had regrown.

"Fuck."

Not just those two feathers. They'd somehow multiplied. Now, he had a goddamn handful. At this rate, the gray feathers would consume his entire wing by the end of the week.

How in the hell would he hide them?

At what point would Fate regain control over his soul?

He could pretend all he wanted, but he already knew the answer. *Soon.* He felt it. The steady stream of heavenly light filling his soul, the bone-deep pull drawing him to Raine, both intensified with every passing moment. Even in Hell, it refused to sever between them. He sensed her anger, her frustration, her confusion. And in fleeting moments, her desire for him.

He could fight it until this realm ended in a fiery explosion, but it wouldn't change a thing.

Raine was his soulmate.

He didn't understand it, but he couldn't deny it any longer. Fate had always weaved her magic in mysterious ways, and a Fallen with an angel soulmate was more proof.

All he knew was soon, likely when the gray feathers replaced all the crimson, Fate would recall his soul to the Heavens. Would she punish him? Would she imprison him in Tartirim? Or would she look past his betrayal because he'd done the one thing she commanded: protect the Empryen and deliver it to Raine.

But there was another path. Before the heavenly light consumed his entire soul, he needed to convince Raine to activate the sword. Then, and only then, would he have the bargaining power to gain his freedom. Fate couldn't go back on her word. He just needed to complete his end of their arrangement before she won.

To make matters worse, now he also had the problem of Blaine questioning his loyalty. Blaine wanted Raine and the Empryen. He understood why. Such power was alluring for any immortal. A few times, he'd even considered it for himself. But at some point, the scales tipped. His loyalty swayed, not to Fate, but to…Raine.

He wanted her, with or without the Empryen. And that was plain crazy.

Now he understood why immortals referred to the soulmate bond as unbreakable.

It screwed with their minds and souls.

Tucking his wings behind his back, he strode from the forest to the mansion, but pulled up short a few feet from the porch. A wild, stormy scent punched him deep in the gut.

Raine.

She was here.

A thrill heated his blood at the thought of seeing her again, but he needed to keep his head in the game. If she used her magic on him again, it would speed up his healing, which careened him closer to an unwanted reunion with Fate. For now, Raine couldn't know. Not until she activated the Empryen, and he faced off with her almighty queen.

Then again, he'd left the Guardian mansion without saying goodbye. Maybe that pissed her off so much that she came here to plunge a Purah dagger into his heart.

That seemed like an easier fucking option.

Drawing his wings inside his back, he strode along the porch and entered the mansion, not bothering to announce his arrival. Raine lounged on a couch with her legs stretched out, feet on the coffee table, crossed at the ankles.

She barely spared him a glance. "Where you been, Hell boy?"

"Did you miss me, princess?" He closed the door with the back of his boot. "I see you've been busy overriding cloaking spells."

"The place looks a whole lot better without the abandoned castle vibe."

She shifted slightly and her violet gaze locked with his. That damn tug lit tiny pinpricks of heavenly light through their connection, all but dragging him into the living room.

"We had an arrangement and you bailed."

He crossed to the hall table and poured himself a bourbon, taking a long sip while he considered what to tell her. Asher still had the sword. Raine still expected him to help her recover it. Blaine wanted it. But he needed it first.

"I had some things to take care of in Hell."

Not really, but he couldn't exactly tell her he fled there to cut out traitorous gray feathers that appeared after she'd healed him.

Raine stood, spinning a Kiel around her index finger, sending a surge of heat through every cell in his damn body. Her obsession with sharp pointy objects was the biggest fucking turn on.

How in the fiery Hell would he keep his distance from her?

She jutted out her chin. "Next time you wanna run to Hell, make sure you take that damn cat with you."

He snorted. "Peaches?"

As though the ginger kitten responded to her name, she skidded into the living room and scrambled up a drape to hang at the top like a crazed monkey.

Warmth bloomed inside his chest. "You brought Peaches here?"

She continually surprised him.

"I considered dropping it off at an animal shelter. But...whatever."

She said the words as though they weren't a big deal, but they were.

Placing the bourbon on the nearest surface, he crossed to stand before her, so close her stormy scent invaded his every breath. He trailed a finger along the

245

side of her jaw. "C'mon, princess, admit it. You like her."

She scoffed. "Hardly."

"Why else would you bring her here? Unless..." He bent slightly, searching her eyes for hidden answers. "You did it for me."

She cocked a brow. "Why would I do anything for you?"

Clearly, she enjoyed skirting the truth. He ached to hear her say it, for her to admit she not just cared for Peaches, but that she had feelings for him. That what he felt wasn't one-sided. Being with her, choosing her, was a huge fucking risk.

But it felt right. As though this was his path all along.

"Admit it, my stormy Raine. We're bonded now, don't forget. I can sense your emotions. You like having your soul connected to mine."

Her eyes narrowed. "I don't need anyone."

His mouth kicked up at the corner as he held back his smirk. He'd backed her into a tight spot with only two ways out. She either admitted her attraction to him or she lied.

Given she couldn't lie...

"I know you don't need anyone. You never did and never will. I don't want you to need me, princess." He brushed his thumb along her lower lip. Her breath hitched and wicked satisfaction zipped through his veins. "I want you to *want* me."

What the hell happened to keeping his distance?

"Tell me, Raine. Tell me you don't want me," he murmured against her ear.

She responded beneath his touch. He caught the

skip in her heart rate, the scent of her arousal.

When it came to his fiery princess, restraint exploded like the fires in Hell.

As his lips whispered along her neck, her palm shifted, reaching for the dagger strapped to her thigh. Before he knew it, she unsheathed the blade and held it against his throat.

"I'm here because we have unfinished business." Her breath was heavy, and her tone lacked her usual snark.

She pressed the long edge of the blade against his throat. Not deterred, he trailed his tongue up to her ear to suck on the fleshy lobe. Raine moaned.

"You're so fucking violent," he said, angling his chin to give her blade better access.

"Pot. Kettle."

A warm droplet trickled down his throat. Raine scraped the tip of the blade on the outside of his skin, following the blood.

"Are we finished talking? 'Cause you pinning a knife to my throat makes me wanna tear off your clothes and fuck you until we both can't walk."

"Is that all you ever think about?"

He drew back, losing himself in her deep violet eyes.

"Fucking you? No. I also think about how sweet you taste on my tongue. How I want to lick every inch of your body. How I want you to brand me with that blade for the entire universe to see."

The heat behind her gaze burned brighter than the damn sun.

She could deny it all she wanted, avoid saying how she truly felt. She didn't need to tell him. He saw right through her mask. In this moment, not just lust smoldered in her eyes, but want.

She wanted him.

The blade fell to the floor. "You win."

She smashed her mouth against his. He took all her need, desire, and want, swirled it around his soul and delivered it back through their kiss. Raine moaned, pressing against his hardness.

Want was so much more powerful than need. By wanting him, she'd chosen him. She let her guard down and showed him beyond her walls, and it made him wild. Never did he consider ever finding a soulmate. Let alone one so fiercely independent and lethal, never one so goddamn beautiful.

A ferocious need to have her naked consumed him. His palms slid down her waist to grip her ass, lifting her legs—

Raziel magic burst through their bond, exploding into his soul. The small cut at his neck tingled as it healed.

He froze.

Reality smacked him like a sucker punch to the gut. Raine used her magic to heal his cut. But little did she know, in doing so, she healed his soul.

Dread choked his desire, extinguishing the fire.

He couldn't risk it. His entire plan went up in smoke if she continued to use her magic on him.

Gently, he lowered her legs back to the floor and drew back. Their heavy breaths collided in the sliver of space separating their lips.

He stood there for a moment, until his pulse calmed, and his brain functioned as much as it could around Raine. "We should…ah, figure out where Asher is."

Her brows drew together as she processed his words, and he hoped like hell she didn't draw any conclusion other than the timing was shit. He'd worked so damn hard to get to this point, the last thing he wanted was for her to retreat.

The moment her expression hardened, an invisible fist squeezed the life from his heart. In an instant, her emotions shut down and she rebuilt that brick wall.

Fuck.

Raine stabbing him with the Purah dagger would be less painful.

Chapter THIRTY-THREE

A hot and bubbling sensation consumed her body, until she no longer knew what to trust. Slater wanted her to want him, which she had, then he'd all but pushed her away.

When she focused on the tingles colliding in the tether connecting their souls, she felt...Sorrow? Regret? Desire?

Who the Fate knew anymore?

Trusting their bond got her nowhere. Trusting him to guide her in whatever this was between them was pointless. Besides, once she recovered the sword, none of this would matter.

Centuries of determination had made hardening her emotions easy, slipping back into battle mode, and locking away those unhelpful feelings in a spelled box at the far recess of her mind.

The process never failed.

Stepping back, she wiped the blood off her dagger on the sleeve of Slater's T-shirt.

Fire sparked in his eyes. "So fucking hot."

"I've killed Fallen for calling me less." She slipped the dagger back into the sheath strapped to her thigh.

"Yet, here I am, with my soul intact."

He laughed, but the tone was different, less...his usually cocky self. Was he as conflicted as her?

I want you to want me.

His earlier words rattled her more than she'd admit. She'd never wanted for anything, let alone anyone. No, that wasn't true. A handful of times she'd wanted a different destiny than the one Fate paved for her. She wanted to be like the others, carefree, living their existence, on a mission without an expiration date. She wanted to not have the fate of this realm precariously balanced on her shoulders. Billions of mortals depended on her fulfilling a near-impossible destiny.

Everything relied on her delivering the Empryen to its rightful place.

If she didn't, if someone else got their hands on it…she couldn't finish that thought.

The ginger furball strutted past her, brushing its tail on her leg, its purr a loud rumble in the silence.

"Raine?"

She lifted her gaze to his. He called her by her name. Not princess, or any other ridiculous pet name he came up with.

Maybe she'd misread the feelings through their bond?

He remained quiet for so long she began to wonder if he'd asked her a question. Around him, her pulse was erratic. It beat faster, stronger, deeper, whooshing in her ears. She couldn't explain it.

River worried that Slater would betray her, but perhaps all she'd done was betray herself? Little by little, she'd let down her guard around this Fallen until, when he skipped off to Hell, she'd mourned his absence.

Was that the want he spoke of?

If only she knew how to show him.

Of all the pairings in the universe, Fate gave her

the most forbidden. For a reason? A Fallen and an angel. It sounded more like the start of a mortal joke.

Why was she even concerning herself with this? Just because Fate tied their souls together didn't mean their destinies would ever align.

Redirecting her thoughts, she focused on the mission. "Did you find any leads while you were in Hell?"

He opened his mouth as though to say something but changed his mind at the last second. Instead, he grabbed a glass and collapsed on the couch. The cat leaped onto his lap, clearly desperate for affection.

"Blaine agreed to provide reinforcements to hunt down Asher. They're on the way."

She rounded the couch to face him. "Here?"

He nodded.

The last thing she wanted to deal with was more Fallen. A few weeks ago, she'd threatened to end their arrangement if Slater pulled this stunt. But that was before...everything happened. Now that Asher likely knew she was the only Raziel who could activate the Empryen, they needed to prepare for an inevitable battle.

Asher would come for her. She'd bet her wings on it.

"When will they arrive?"

Slater's lips parted as he tilted his head slightly, giving her the same look as earlier. Wonder? Confusion?

Why did it cause flutters in her belly?

"What?" she snapped.

"I...nothing." He shook his head, focusing once again on the stupid kitten. "I didn't expect you to take it so well."

Where was EJ and his cocktails when she needed him?

"We need all the help we can get. I'm not stupid enough to deny that when the fate of this realm is at stake."

That look again. What the Fate did it mean?

He was so damn infuriating.

"They'll arrive at nightfall. Blaine summoned them when I left." He propped his boots on the coffee table and stretched out his long legs. The cat snuggled into his lap. "How is the fate of this realm connected to the Empryen?"

Sitting on the edge of the opposite couch, she fiddled with a Kiel on her belt. "The Empryen is not just one of a kind. It's a weapon forged with a combination of my Raziel magic and Fate's, with one specific purpose. If it's used for anything else, it could have devastating effects."

He petted the cat under its chin. "Such as?"

She slipped the Kiel from her belt and spun it around her finger, the Purah shimmering in the light. If Fate wanted to strike her down, she would've done it by now. "Anything from permanently killing an immortal to destroying an entire realm."

Slater's gaze snapped to hers. She didn't fill the silence with senseless small talk, nor did she feel the need to pace the room. In fact, she also no longer had the urge to spin the Kiel on her finger. All at once, the realm around them seemed to grind to a halt.

Talking about the Empryen with Slater felt different. Her shoulders didn't stiffen with tension, she didn't worry that he'd ask a question she couldn't answer in case Fate followed through with her many threats. It didn't feel unfamiliar and foreign. In fact, he spoke of the sword as though he already knew all the details.

How?

He frustrated her to no end, but beneath that annoyance was…respect. How fucked up was that? She respected a damn Fallen.

Served herself right for gaining him as a soulmate.

After a long moment, Slater finally spoke. "Why did Fate want you to create the sword, Raine?"

Raine.

Every time his tone softened, and he called her by her name, an ancient tug pulled inside her chest. It intensified, blooming within her until she had difficulty inhaling.

What bullshit. The Guardian soulmates had turned her life into a sappy romance. They believed in happily ever afters because they didn't know the horrors that bled behind the scenes. She did. Those horrors were all she'd ever known.

Everything she'd ever fought to prevent.

She wanted to trust Slater with the truth, yearned to confide in someone, but something told her if he knew, he'd try to stop her.

She broke eye contact and resumed spinning the Kiel. "All that matters is I need it back."

Slater didn't push for an answer, and she refrained from saying anything further that could bite her in the ass. Regardless of the puzzling looks he gave her, and the gaping hole she felt when he wasn't there, their arrangement would eventually end.

As would their soulmate bond.

Chapter THIRTY-FOUR

Blaine had told him half the story. His own fault. He only ever asked Blaine for the shortened version, so he didn't subject himself to hours of Blaine's rambling. That Fallen could spin tales like no other. In hindsight, when it came to the Empryen, he should've sucked it up and listened.

Raine forged a sword using a blend of Fate's magic and her own. The idea blew his mind. A sword with the potential to obliterate an entire realm? How was that even possible?

Did Fate intend to use it? Of course, she did, otherwise why command Raine to make it? What seemed more farfetched was that Fate commissioned a powerful weapon and then handed it over to him, a soon-to-be-Fallen. All she'd said to him was he needed to deliver the sword to Raine when the time was right.

Was Fate insane? *Possibly.*

He'd waited for a sign, guidance of some sort, but given that he'd severed his link to the Heavens when he Fell, it never came. Over the centuries, he became…complacent and then Asher fucking stole it.

He studied Raine while the Kiel spinning on her finger distracted her. Purah caught in the light from a nearby lamp, reflecting a kaleidoscope of colors over her black clothing. Delicate and lethal. The way she'd avoided his questions told him she knew more about the

Empryen, or perhaps her own instructions from Fate.

They were in this together. Why not tell him everything? Just when he'd broken through her walls, she reinforced them.

If only he'd known her in the Heavens. Back then was she this withdrawn? Had she always remained so guarded? Or did the mask she wear harden over the years in the mortal realm?

What made her so…cynical?

Until now, he'd thought patience was the key with her. That eventually she'd trust him enough with the full story, not the one she chose to give him, but they no longer had the luxury of time. Every second without the sword was a step closer to his soul fully healing.

He needed answers.

Opening his mind, he zeroed in on Raine. A small tendril of invisible power weaved from his mind to hers, seeking a glimpse of her inner thoughts. Anything that told him this was the right path. Something to confirm Fate hadn't set him up to fail at the hands of Raine.

He snuck through the first layer, extending his power through the outer barrier as gently as he could so she didn't notice. Not his finest moment. Regardless of what others thought, he wouldn't usually resort to slipping into her mind for the answers she didn't verbalize. Even he had morals. But whatever information she withheld from him was clearly important, and he needed to know.

For centuries, Blaine and Fate had kept him in the dark, using him as their pawn. That ended now.

Concentrating harder, he weaved his power through a tiny gap in the inner layer of her mind, entering a…dark room. Swirls of ominous silvery shadows erupted before him, not Azrael shadows, something different. They curled inside the room in Raine's mind, striking at him as his power neared one corner, drawn to it for some reason. He fought against them, catching flashes of a bright white flame in the center of the shadows, but he couldn't focus on the blurry image. Each time his power advanced, the shadows struck him like a viper, protecting the flame.

Or hid it?

Power pulsed through his middle as he poured more into Raine's mind. Just a glimpse was all he needed—

Raine cried out. White shadows snagged his power so fast it severed the connection with a painful snap. His head slammed into the back of the couch from the invisible impact.

Raine pressed the heel of her hands against her temples. He shoved Peaches aside and rushed to her, wrapping an arm around her shoulders. "Raine…"

In an instant, as though the pain vanished, she straightened, lowering her hands. "What in the Fate was that?"

A sour taste seeped into his mouth. Lying to her was even lower than what he'd just done. "There's…something hidden in your mind."

Her eyes widened for the briefest second before she shoved him in the chest, and stood. "You did that?"

Yes. No. Shit.

He had no excuse. He'd craved answers so badly, he'd resorted to hurting her. Was whatever Raine hid from him worth it?

The answer was clear. *No.*

"I…fuck." He exhaled a breath and dragged a hand over his smooth skull. "I feel like we're always one step behind Asher and it's frustrating the hell out of me. I needed to know if you knew more about the Empryen than what you told me."

"So, you just helped yourself to my memories?" Raine pinned him with a hard, angry glare.

That sour taste travelled into his throat, creating a giant lump.

Raine hadn't erected her walls to keep him out. He'd fucked that up all on his own. "I'm…sorry."

She held his gaze for a moment, her nostrils flaring before she turned away to pace the room. "You could've asked."

The slight tremor in her voice sliced deeper and sharper through his chest than any dagger.

He could've. *Should've.* His determination to beat Fate before his soul healed had twisted his morals. Perhaps, despite what he thought, he never had any.

Raine paused on the opposite side of the room with her back to him. "It's been there since Fate told me about the missing sword. The memory's linked to the Empryen, I know it. But I can't access it."

"Have you tried an Ariel?" When she turned to face him, frowning, he continued, "Ariel have regeneration powers. You live with one, remember?"

She rolled her eyes at him, shooting a blast of heat through his veins. He said earlier her sass would kill him, and he meant it. The more time they spent together, the more he couldn't exist without it or her.

"I tried to access it with my magic, given my powers are linked with the sword."

"Hang on." He held up his hand. *Raine's magic…*

"You forged the Empryen with your magic."

Raine threw her hands up. "Were you not listening?"

As though on cue, her Raziel magic warmed the spot in his chest where she'd healed him, swirling through the connection between their souls.

Why didn't he think of it earlier?

"If the sword is half your magic, I can use the connection to track it. It's inside me."

Her deep violet eyes narrowed at him. "What did you say?"

He crossed the room to stand before her. "When you healed me in the cave, your magic somehow attached itself to me. I can use that connection to track the sword."

Her chin lifted just enough to tell him the news didn't surprise her. In fact, if he didn't know better, he'd swear she planned for her magic to remain inside him.

"Do it." In one swift movement, she ripped a Kiel from her belt and pinned it to the soft flesh beneath his chin. "But if you try that party trick in my mind again, I'll slice you into tiny pieces and feed it to your damn cat."

He couldn't hold back his smile. "There she is. My fiery princess is back. I worried you'd mellowed while I was in Hell."

Her eyes darkened, but it didn't scare him. This side of Raine made him feel more at ease than when she did sweet gestures like caring for Peaches. That freaked him the hell out.

As Raine lowered the weapon from his neck, he stepped back and held out his hands, summoning his magic. Smoky, dark gray shadows curled from his palms, swirling in the air, thickening and expanding. He widened his stance, planting his weight as he bowed his head, chanting Raine's name in his mind. A spark ignited deep in his chest, bursting through his blood until it blended with the shadows extending from his hands.

Raine sucked in a breath. Knowing she wasn't in any danger, he didn't lift his head to see her expression. Instead, he poured all his concentration into building his weapon.

Few Azrael had shadow tracking powers like him.

Blackness overtook his vision as his mind followed the shadows into the ether, searching for Raine's magic. A bright teal light, only he could see, streamed from his palm. It shot through the darkness at an unnatural speed. His knees trembled under the intensity of the power pulsing through his body.

A soft hand rested on his shoulder. Steady streams of heavenly light filtered from Raine into him through their connection, amplifying his shadows.

The teal light collided with the source of its magic. He jolted from the impact.

Slowly, the blackness cleared, revealing the Empryen's location. Thick forest, tall ancient pines, a woodsy scent lingered in the air. The place seemed familiar. In his mind, he pivoted, scanning the surroundings.

Ice replaced the light warming his blood. Just ahead, through the thicket of trees was…

He snapped closed his palms, ceasing the shadows in an instant. Blinking a few times, the room came back into focus. They were out of time.

Raine lowered her hand. "Where's the Empryen?"

"The Guardian mansion."

Raine's expression hardened, sliding into her familiar battle mode. "They're coming for me."

Chapter THIRTY-FIVE

Impending battle charged the air inside Blaine's mansion, so thick it consumed her veins, sizzling around her body. One by one, Fallen misted to the property and filed into the living room. The scene before her was ridiculous. Here she was, standing in a living room full of Fallen, preparing to battle not against them, but beside them.

Who would've thought?

Fate, probably.

So far, Fate hadn't struck Raine down with lightning or recalled her soul to the Heavens, which meant only one thing. Raine was on the right path.

Her destiny.

Earlier, she called Raven to update him with the latest information, so they could prepare for Asher's arrival, if he wasn't already hiding in the forest.

This was it. The day she got her sword back.

From the far end of the room, she watched Slater with a mixture of respect and something else she couldn't quite put her finger on. But the warm feeling spread through her chest. He took charge of their mission, instructing Fallen with natural leadership. Even though he maintained a stoic expression, the thrumming through her veins revealed his true emotions. Adrenaline, a touch of unease, and a shit load of determination.

Slater didn't just want to find Asher and help her recover the sword. He thought this was his destiny.

Was it?

Had Fate intended for their destinies to intertwine at the end?

Shifting her weight, she bent one leg up to brace her foot on the wall behind her. Slater snagged her gaze from across the room, causing a fierce knot to tighten in her belly. He didn't say anything or whisper sarcastic comments in her mind even though she'd kept her walls lowered for him. His intense look communicated everything words couldn't.

This was their toughest battle.

More than their souls were at stake.

One of them might not make it back.

For the first time in her existence, trepidation swirled under a thick layer of unpacked emotions. Up until this point, Asher had always been one step ahead of them. In battle, so many things could go wrong. Immortals she…cared about could get hurt.

There, she'd said it. She cared about Slater.

He could break out the streamers.

But now wasn't the time to doubt his fighting skills, she'd had no reason to before. He'd proven his lethal ability again and again. This time would be no different.

How in the Heavens did she end up here? Not just fighting with a Fallen, but…caring for one.

Another Fallen said something to Slater, diverting his attention and she'd never been so thankful for an interruption. Pushing aside the unhelpful and confusing thoughts, she focused on the task at hand.

The cell phone in her hand vibrated with an

incoming message.

Raven: *Ready.*

One simple word. *Ready.*

But was she?

She slipped the phone back into her pocket and pushed off the wall. "The Guardians are in place," she announced to the room.

Slater gave her a curt nod. His gaze roamed over the twenty or so Fallen standing before him, all waiting for his instruction. "You know what to do. Keep an eye out for Fallen not currently in this room that might've defected. And no one, I mean no one, touches Asher. He's mine." His voice lowered to a deep growl. "And remember, no one targets a Guardian. If you deviate from this truce, I'll personally hold you down as Raine removes your soul piece by piece until you beg me to send you to the Pits. Understood?"

A smirk lifted her lips as murmurs of agreement echoed through the room.

If it weren't already clear, this was proof. Slater was her soulmate.

He motioned to the front door. "Let's do this."

In a mass exodus, she trailed behind the Fallen as they marched out the front door to mist to the Guardian mansion.

Outside on the gravel, Slater slipped his hand in hers. "Are you ready, princess?"

He'd squirmed his way into her heart, made her feel things she never expected, and now stood beside her to fight for her destiny. "Yes. It's my path."

A shadow flashed over his eyes, darkening the color. "As you are mine."

Although he didn't say it, his tone and intention

were clear. He thought she was his destiny. Funny how she'd thought the same.

That tightness in her chest returned, making it hard to breathe.

Before he said anymore, she slipped her hand free and unstrapped the sheath on her left calf. "Here..." She offered the dagger to him.

Frowning, he peered at the black handle extending from the leather sheath. He slid the dagger free, inspecting both sides, balancing it in his hand to test the weight.

He didn't need to test it. The weight and size were perfect.

His gaze lifted to hers. "This isn't yours, is it?"

"No."

He held her stare, searching her eyes. Once more, unsaid words bounced between them. Words that choked in her throat.

His puzzled expression softened. "You made this for me?"

Yup. She'd forged it right after he disappeared from the Guardian mansion on his field trip to Hell. Though, she'd had no intention of giving it to him. Like most weapons she made, an all-consuming urge overtook her thoughts and drove her actions until the finished dagger lay on the workbench before her.

But the way he demanded the Fallen respect her, how he protected and defended her in the face of her enemy. How his eyes saw past her shields deep into her soul...Well, if he risked his soul and reputation for her, he may as well have a decent weapon to aid his shadows.

She shrugged one shoulder. "It doesn't mean

anything."

He threw his head back and laughed. "Oh, princess. It means you like me."

"I didn't say that."

He strapped the sheath around his thigh. Luckily, she made it extra wide. In an instant, he closed the space between them and took her face in his strong, rough hands. Despite the pre-battle adrenaline firing through her blood, her body sank into his embrace.

"You don't need to say it, Raine. I feel it."

He kissed her as though he drew his energy and life force directly from her soul. Wild tremors zapped through her middle, swirling around in her body until her blood sizzled.

Too soon, he drew back, his hands still cradling her face. "Thank you."

She reached for a Kiel as her skin prickled from the gratitude. Thank you meant she did something because she cared, and she didn't. Well, she *hadn't* until…

She sighed.

Who was she kidding? She'd fooled herself all along.

He kissed her forehead, lingering for a long moment as though breathing in her scent and locking it away in the furthest cage of his memory.

When he pulled back, a furrowed brow and the hard set of his jaw replaced any lingering amusement. "I know you can fight your own battles. Hell, that's one of the things I fucking love about you. But promise me you won't take stupid risks when we find Asher."

Her heart thudded. *Love?* Was that what she felt streaming through their connection?

Slater dipped his head, searching her eyes.

"Promise me, Raine. Make it back to me."

She swallowed. How the Fate didn't she realize? To mask how rattled she felt, she opted for sarcasm. "Why? Would you miss me?"

A smirk curled the corner of his mouth. "Something like that."

Words failed to pass the growing lump in her throat.

She wanted to tell him that she hoped for the same. Not just that she'd make it back, but so would he. That they'd make it back together, but all that seemed unnecessary. After their mission, after she retrieved the Empryen, their connection would end. His illusion of her, of what they shared, would vanish once she transported the sword to its destination.

Slater lowered his hands and took half a step back. "Let's go kill some motherfucking traitors."

Pushing past the churning in her stomach, she placed her palm in his. "Now you're talking."

****

Slater misted her to the far east of the Guardian property. The other Fallen scattered themselves throughout the estate and Slater relayed their coordinates to her. Once in position, she opened her mind to the Guardians and conveyed the information. EJ and Hailee were on the rooftop overlooking the perimeter, Aric checked in from the rear of the estate, her brother positioned himself in a tree to her right, bow nocked ready to fire. Willow guarded the rear entrance to the mansion while Tayla guarded the front. Pride swelled in her chest, knowing that if it came down to it, the soulmates could handle themselves in a battle.

Her gaze slid to Raven standing out in the open, in

the center of the manicured lawn with a sword at ease by his side, as though he not only challenged Asher to face him but invited him.

Pity that asshat Fallen and his Dumahel daughter weren't here.

She took the pre-battle time to concentrate on her breathing, steadying her pulse, clearing her head. An action made difficult with Slater still holding her hand, but she was reluctant to let it go. For some reason, letting go of his hand felt symbolic, as though if she allowed those fingers to slip from hers, she'd lose him, too.

She wasn't ready for that.

"Fucking Hell," Slater groaned.

She side-eyed him. "What?"

Slater let go of her hand. Something splintered in her chest.

"Blaine's here."

On cue, Blaine materialized beside his brother on the lawn.

"Why is he here? I thought he sent Fallen to help us. Did you know he'd join us?"

Slater didn't speak for a long moment. When he did, bitterness and betrayal tainted his tone. "Everyone wants the Empryen, princess."

Hot tension coiled inside her. Of course, Blaine wanted the sword, probably for the same reason Fate did. But she never once thought he'd fight Asher for it.

Was he here to steal it from the Guardians?

Ice skated down her spine as she turned to Slater. He didn't look at her, not once, but he didn't need to. His rigid stance, the hardness in his jaw, how his hands clenched and unclenched, told her all she needed to know.

He expected Blaine to come. Surely, Slater hadn't planned to double-cross her.

Had he?

Her gaze darted between Blaine and Slater, trying to decipher the situation. Her fingers tightened around the Kiel at her waist, unclipping it from her belt.

No. The things Slater said to her were real, she'd sensed the truth through their connection. Had it all been a lie?

Her pulse quickened. As she opened her mouth to ask him, the air rippled a few paces in front of where Raven and Blaine stood. A split second later, Asher materialized, followed by Ebony. One by one, more Fallen materialized, surrounding Raven and Blaine.

Hundreds of Fallen. So many she lost count.

"We're severely outnumbered," Slater muttered.

Had he thought recovering the Empryen would be easy? Asher wouldn't just hand it over.

Angling her ear, she tuned into the conversation on the lawn.

"It's one thing to materialize uninvited. It's another to invade my property with an army of Fallen." Raven scowled.

Beside her, Slater snorted.

She crept around the back of a tree to get a better view. She couldn't see the Empryen, but its presence hummed in her blood.

"Raine," Slater said, warning her.

She shot him a dark look. His mouth tightened right before he misted to her side.

Damn it. All the Fallen blocked her view of Asher. Peering up, she gripped a sturdy branch above her head and flipped herself into the tree, climbing farther before crouching on the highest branch.

"Just when I thought you couldn't get any hotter," Slater said from the ground.

From her position in the tree, she spotted the dark leather sheath strapped around Asher's waist. A black handle protruded from the top. She recognized the sword.

It didn't take a genius to know Asher wouldn't leave it lying around where someone else could steal it.

"I've come for the Raziel they call Raine," Asher said to Raven. The bastard slipped his hand over the hilt of the Empryen as though it belonged to him.

Blaine cocked his head, looking left and right, before turning to Raven. "I don't know who he's referring to. How 'bout you, brother?"

Raven shrugged his shoulder.

Asher prowled forward, ignoring Blaine to address Raven. "There's no need for bloodshed. Give me the Raziel and the Guardians will walk away from this unscathed."

Blaine threw his head back and laughed.

Raven narrowed his eyes. Although his twin short swords still hung parallel to his body, she knew Raven was ready to attack. Not many immortals rivaled him, and those who did, were on the same side tonight.

"You've got three seconds to hand over the Empryen and mist the hell off my property before I send your soul to the Infernal Pits." Raven rolled his shoulders. "One…"

Blaine smirked. "Three."

From out of nowhere, a fireball shot toward Asher.

Chapter THIRTY-SIX

Everything happened so fast. Blaine summoned a hellfire ball and shot it at Asher. Asher misted, reappearing a few steps away. All at once, battle cries rang out as every immortal in the vicinity drew their weapons and attacked.

What the hell did Asher hope to achieve? Fighting the Guardians wouldn't activate the Empryen, it only resulted in the Guardians, or Blaine, ending him. Unless Asher was under the delusion that to prevent all the bloodshed, Raine would go willingly.

He scoffed.

If that were the case, clearly Asher didn't know Raine.

Holding out his palms, he called forth his shadows, readying them in case Asher's followers decided to attack him and Raine. He peered up at her perched on the branch, her gaze glued to the battle below, a dagger gripped in her hand. The wise move was to wait this out. Let the Guardians and Blaine annihilate Asher, then at the last second, mist in and reclaim the sword. But the pre-battle buzz firing through his connection with Raine told him she had no intention of sitting back and watching this unfold. Not when her sword was at stake.

His respect for her skyrocketed, even if her eagerness to fight irritated the hell out of him. He'd wanted a female that wouldn't break when he touched her.

Fate had delivered.

Raine flipped the dagger in her hand.

"Princess," he warned. If she engaged too early, things would get messy.

But of course, she didn't listen. Without a word, she leaped from the tree, barely landing before she bolted through the forest, heading straight for the battle.

"Fuck," he grunted.

Torn between the driving need to protect her and wanting that damn sword, he waited less than a second before sprinting after her.

Fallen allies and Guardians spilled from the forest and sky, engaging Asher's army. He weaved through the trees, following Raine's path, keeping her in sight. At the tree line, he engaged his first traitorous Fallen. The Fallen's eyes widened as he recognized him, but Slater didn't hold back. Using his shadows, he snapped his neck in one swift strike. The Fallen thudded to the ground. Every cell in his body protested him taking out one of his own, especially one he knew. But in times of war, loyalty was everything, and that Fallen had chosen the wrong side.

Glancing up, he caught sight of Raine. Stepping over the Fallen body, he raced forward, dodging swords left and right. His shadows disarmed enemies, tossing their weapons aside before he snapped their necks. They'd heal, but it would take a few hours. By that time, the Guardians would've sent the souls back to Hell.

All around him, grunts and cries echoed in the night. Swords clanged. To his left, Blaine's fireballs shot in every direction, taking out enemies in a fiery explosion of ash and Fallen blood. But for each Fallen they defeated, more materialized. The enemies still outnumbered them.

How many had Asher fucking recruited?

Behind Blaine, Raven engaged in a sword fight with two Fallen. Caught in the moonlight, Raven's twin swords pinwheeled in the air, slicing Fallen in a blur of precision and power. Raven and Blaine were a lethal force as they slayed enemies, surrounding themselves with a pile of bodies and ash.

He paused for a second to scan the yard. Blood and black Fallen residue darkened the moonlit grass. Headless bodies littered the ground where the Guardians had lacked the patience or the time to finish off the job. He understood why Fate created the warriors as her personal guards. Once, he'd wished to join their elite ranks. With their skill and his shadows, he'd be unstoppable, but Fate had other plans.

A Fallen charged at him, striking with a sword at his head. He ducked. A flaming arrow whizzed past his shoulder, slamming through the Fallen's forehead. The sword hit the ground a second before the Fallen. Spinning around, he caught River now positioned on the rooftop, another flaming arrow already nocked in his bow. The Guardian gave a curt nod before firing the weapon at another enemy.

The situation was so bizarre. Fighting with angels to take down Fallen when, technically, he still was one. Though, he sensed the change was imminent. This battle felt...strange, but right.

More like fucked up.

Someone rammed into his back. He stumbled

forward, spun, and regained his balance as a Guardian tripped backward over the lifeless Fallen on the ground with the arrow lodged in his head. An enemy Fallen lunged forward to strike Aric. Slater didn't hesitate. He flung a shadow at the enemy, flipping the sword out of the Fallen's hand, disarming him. The Fallen dove for the sword. Recovered, Aric launched off the ground and stabbed the enemy through the back. The Fallen didn't even see it coming.

Aric turned to face him. Black blood smeared his face and dripped from his twin daggers. "Thanks, man."

He tipped his chin at the Guardian.

Regardless of what happened next, in this battle, they were allies.

Aric wiped his daggers clean on the thigh of his combat pants. "This is a fucking nightmare. There are so many."

He grunted in agreement.

So many. More than he and Raine had anticipated.

"Where are the others?" he asked.

Aric tipped his chin toward the mansion. "River's on the roof with Hailee spotting for him. Raven and EJ are in the middle somewhere. Willow's at the front entrance with Tayla. Whatever Fallen remain on our side are holding them back at the rear. I lost sight of Raine."

They needed a better strategy. "Instead of fighting enemy Fallen, we need to target Asher. He has the Empryen."

Aric peered toward the carnage strewn across the lawn. "Where is the scumbag?"

He searched the bloodbath, hoping someone intercepted Raine before she made it to Asher. Swords still clanged, mingling with battle cries of fury and pain. He spotted Raine in the chaos, weaving through the thicket of bodies in a whirl of speed and grace, striking her dagger into the hearts of Fallen within her reach. In her wake, she left a path of exploded mist.

He squinted, looking past her, anticipating her target. Found him.

He pointed in the direction. "Raine's heading to Asher. We can't let that asshole take her."

Aric glanced at him. "Agreed."

At that moment, Asher whipped around and spotted Raine. The fucking bastard smiled as though all his plans had fallen into place. Like hell they had.

Slater made a deal with Fate to deliver the Empryen to Raine and nothing, absolutely nothing, would stop him.

He needed to reach Asher first.

Following Raine's path wouldn't work. To beat her to Asher, he needed to come from the other side or mist there. Given the chaos with swords flying everywhere, misting was too risky. He might materialize in front of a damn blade that took his head off. Flying sent him into the path of River's flaming arrows or Blaine's fireballs lighting up the sky.

The safest option was on foot.

He turned to Aric. "I'll go west and come up behind Asher."

Aric nodded. "I'll cut through the middle behind Raine." Aric pinned him with a ferocious stare. "Take that asshole down."

Something swelled inside his chest, expanding his lungs. Sure, he never thought he'd team up with the Guardians to battle his own kind, but more than that, he never thought the Guardians would team up with *him*. He'd all but blackmailed Raine to help him find the Empryen to secure his freedom. She'd only agreed out of loyalty to Fate and her own mission.

With Aric it was different. The Guardian willingly joined forces with him.

Before he thought too much into it, he tipped his chin at Aric. The Guardian raced into the madness, daggers slashing at anything in his path.

Raising his hands, he projected the shadows, cloaking himself in darkness, allowing the sounds and roars surrounding him to fade away. With the other, he palmed the blade Raine made for him. The Purah tingled in his palm, the weight and size perfect. He gripped his fingers around the leather-bound hilt, channeling Raine's energy, allowing it to flow through him.

He focused his mind on one target. Asher.

Closing his eyes, he sucked in the energy from the battle, fueling his rage and his thirst for freedom. His thirst for the existence promised to him by Fate.

His thirst to avenge Raine.

Blending with the night, he sprinted around the outskirts of the main battle, keeping Asher in his sights. Nothing stood in his way. Not Fallen, not weapons, not the mass of bodies strewn over the ground. He annihilated every damn thing in his path.

Others here wanted the Empryen.

But in this moment, he wanted it the most.

Chapter THIRTY-SEVEN

Raine plowed through Fallen as though they were nothing but leaves fluttering in the wind. Never did she lose sight of her sword. Never did she lose focus.

That asshole chose the wrong immortal to mess with.

Asher stood proud and tall in the center of the battle, protected by his measly shadows, like he was a pretentious king.

She didn't have time for this shit, nor the patience.

Summoning her magic, she raised her palms to the Heavens. Raziel power streamed through her veins, filling her with intense light. The magic consumed every cell in her body until her skin hummed with energy, pulsing in a teal glow.

She slowed her step, prowling forward.

Asher's eyes widened.

Had he never seen a Raziel? Did he not know of her power?

Fool on him.

Enemies no longer attacked her. They either realized they needed her alive or the power spilling from her scared them shitless.

Teal magic dripped from her fingertips as though made from molten lava. It hit the ground, luminating the earth by her feet. She zeroed in on Asher through a teal lens as the magic overtook her vision.

He withdrew the Empryen from its sheath and raised the tip to the Heavens. "Activate the sword and this all ends."

Liar. This wouldn't end until that sword was back in her hands.

She laughed at the absurd demand. Consumed with magic, her own voice sounded foreign to her ears. Only once before had she let the power engulf her.

When she forged the Empryen.

In the corner of her eye, a shadow weaved through the enemy, racing toward Asher.

Slater.

His name broke through the magic haze overtaking her mind.

He wants the Empryen. The random thought entered her head as though her magic spoke to her, conflicting with the connection she had with him.

Protect the sword.

Asher swiped his free hand, snapping shadows around her feet, anchoring her in place.

Rage filled her. Curling her hand, she weaved a ball of magic and threw it at the ground. The shadows exploded. Asher grunted, staggering back.

This ended now.

She dipped her chin and narrowed her eyes, focusing on the Empryen. She called its magic. The sword vibrated in Asher's hand.

Slater's shadow neared, approaching Asher from behind.

Asher gripped the sword with both hands, holding tighter as it wobbled and pulsed with her power. She crouched, increasing the magic, building it in her palms. With a cry, she thrust her open palms against the ground. All at once, her magic exploded, blasting in a wide circle, with her at the epicenter.

The explosion tore through the ground, focused on one target. Asher. He didn't stand a chance. Her magic obliterated him to ash in seconds.

Drained, she heaved a breath as the Empryen tumbled to the ground where nothing more than a pile of ash remained of Asher.

She rose on unsteady feet. Her throat burned. The teal lenses receded as her vision cleared, revealing the devastation in her wake. All around her lay piles of ash where Fallen hadn't misted in time before struck by her wave of Raziel magic.

Fueled by heavenly light, her blast had ended the battle in one fell swoop.

They'd won.

Raven approached with slow, tentative steps, his swords hung by his side, a look of awe on his face. Slater materialized where Asher once stood and scooped the Empryen off the ground. The other Guardians moved in, surrounding her.

She held out her hand to Slater.

His expression tightened as though conflicted by her simple request. Her earlier thought returned.

Slater wants the Empryen.

Blaine materialized beside Slater, his face splatted with black blood. "That was quite the show."

She ignored him. "Give the Empryen to me, Slater."

Blaine smirked, glancing at Slater. "How sweet. She thinks you got the sword for her." He turned to Raine. "Sorry, love. Fate intended that sword for me. You just need to activate it and I'll be on my way."

Her gaze darted between Blaine and Slater. No, Blaine lied. The Empryen wasn't for him. Her destiny was to deliver the sword, not to Blaine, but to its final location.

Dread sank low in her belly. Heaviness streamed through the connection she shared with Slater. She crept closer, hardening her voice. "Slater, give it to me."

His lips pressed together as he tightened his hold on the sword.

Without warning, Blaine reached for the Empryen. Slater misted. She gasped as he reappeared beside her and grabbed her hand. The world spun. A second later, they materialized outside the bunker. Clutching her arm, he all but dragged her down the stairs, shoving them through the door.

Her heart raced, but underneath the adrenaline was the sour taste of betrayal.

Betrayal.

Slater had betrayed her.

The second they stepped inside the bunker, she flipped the dagger in her hand and held it at his throat, shoving him against the closed door.

River's words returned to her. *He's a Fallen…He'll betray you…You're fooling yourself.*

Her pulse swished in her ears.

"This entire time. You've lied to me," she said through clenched teeth, seething at him, unable to control the pain slicing through her chest.

He remained silent. He didn't defend his actions but didn't deny them either.

She pushed the blade harder against his throat. Blood welled from the cut, dripping onto the Purah, tarnishing the silvery surface. For the first time since she'd met him, she considered ending him, sending his soul back to Hell.

After she cut off his balls and shoved them down his throat.

"How could you?" Her voice shook. Tears burned in her eyes, but she refused to let them fall.

Not for him. Not for anyone.

River warned her. Aric warned her. Her magic warned her. Everyone in this fucked up realm warned her.

Why in the Fate didn't she listen?

With her free hand, she snatched the Empryen from Slater. Inside her hand, the Purah tingled, shimmering with a mixture of her own power and Fate's.

Fate.

Why did Blaine think Fate intended the sword for him? The Empryen was hers, not Blaine's. Fate paved this destiny for her.

Her breaths punched fast and heavy, as she glared at Slater. "You used me."

A shadow flashed across his face.

Did he regret his actions or only the fact she'd caught him?

When his hand slowly inched to the one that held the dagger at his neck, she pushed harder. Now, blood didn't just trickle, it oozed from the slice in his flesh.

She gasped. *What the...*

His blood wasn't black. It was...different.

"Raine," he whispered.

"Don't..." She composed herself, shaking off the weird sensations swirling through their connection.

Curling his fingers around her wrist, he eased the

dagger from his neck. Too shocked, she released it and it clanged to the floor beside their feet.

She retreated a step. How was any of this possible? She'd sensed something was different with him, that something had changed, but never expected...this.

Slater's blood wasn't black like a Fallen's. It didn't resemble the same color as the last time she'd made him bleed. Now, his blood was lighter, brighter, more burgundy.

What in the actual Fate?

Slater inched closer. "Let me explain."

His words snapped her to attention. She should kill him, not chat. He betrayed her.

"You lie to me. I should gut you."

He held back a grin. "And yet, you still haven't."

That almost made her punch him in the face.

Using the neck of his shirt, he wiped the blood trailing down his chest, and moved past her, farther into the bunker. She swiveled, tracking his movement. Why was she waiting? Why did she give him an opportunity to explain?

She knew why. That stupid connection firing between them had annihilated her common sense.

Slater paused with his back to her. His head lowered. "Before I Fell, Fate came to me with a deal."

She peered at the sword in her hand while every fiber in her body screamed at her to leave. She never should've trusted him.

He turned to face her. "Fate gave me the Empryen."

"Bullshit."

He held up his hand. "Let me finish. Fate agreed to give me the freedom I yearned for if I hid the sword in

Hell. Then, when the time was right, deliver it to a Raziel." His expression softened, but that didn't stop her from wanting to stab him in the eye. "You, Raine. I had to deliver the sword to you."

"That is utter—"

"Still not finished, princess."

She scowled at him, imagining a dagger slicing straight through his neck and slamming into the wall behind him. "My patience is wearing thin. Get to the point."

He dragged a hand over his smooth head. "When I arrived in Hell, I hid the sword where Fate told me to, but Zath found out I had it. I refused to bend to his will, so he banished me to the Pits."

A metallic taste filled her mouth as she bit her tongue to stop interrupting.

"In my darkest hours, Fate sent me visions of you. You kept me alive, Raine."

She rolled her eyes, so over his bullshit. "So, what? Skip ahead a few centuries, and Blaine freed you from the Pits so you could steal the Empryen for him?"

His chest rose and fell with a deep inhale. Black Fallen blood still dotted his face and arms, reminding her of the battle they'd just fought. Which now felt like a lifetime ago.

"Blaine freed me to locate the Dumahel twins when they were born. I didn't think he knew about the sword until recently."

"I'm so sick of hearing your lies. The entire time you've been with me has been one giant charade."

"You're wrong."

She scoffed. "And how the Fate did Asher end up with it if you hid it so well? Your story has so many holes it's about to flood the bunker."

He leaned over and splayed his hands on the desk, a weathered expression aging his face. "I don't know how Asher found the sword."

"Stop lying to me," she shouted.

The tight expression on his face nearly undid her. If she wasn't considering beheading him, she might have felt sorry for the Fallen.

"You want the truth? Fine. Here it is. I wanted the sword, yes and I knew you'd help me find it, but not so I could give it to Blaine. I wanted it so you could activate it, so I could fulfill my bargain with Fate and gain my freedom."

" 'Cause that's so much better than betraying me to Blaine. You still had a hidden agenda. You still lied to me and made me believe you wanted to find Asher, not the sword. Everyone warned me, but I thought..." The last words choked in her throat.

His gaze dragged to hers causing that fracture inside her chest to expand, sucking in all surrounding life like a giant black hole. She should stop speaking. This conversation was pointless. The only thing that mattered was the sword. But her feet wouldn't move, they refused to turn and walk out that door.

"What now? You want me to activate the Empryen so you can run off into the sunset a free immortal? Why did Fate want you to deliver it to me when I had it in the first place?"

He frowned. "I...don't know. I can't help feeling this was her plan. She wanted us to...connect. Maybe Fate needed you to activate the sword in the mortal realm before you took it back. She told me I had to protect you so you could fulfill your destiny."

She scoffed. Slater was delusional if he thought she needed protection.

She pushed off the wall, the Empryen still tingling in her palm as though it begged for her to activate it. "Why does Blaine want it?"

"He doesn't just want the sword. He wants you with it." Slater straightened. "And I'm not handing you over like some prized bounty. To anyone."

Bile rose in her throat. Was that what Fate planned? Was that what Blaine meant when he said Fate intended the sword for him? Had Fate weaved Raine's destiny with Blaine's?

Slater stood in front of her in an instant, invading her space as he had so many times over the past few weeks. His scent consumed her, stirring in her belly, but she wouldn't let him fool her again.

Her eyes were wide open now.

"Why the fuck do you think I misted us here? I don't know when it happened, or how, but at some point, everything shifted. Everything changed." He paused, searching her face. "Actually, I do know. When I called you princess in the forest at the Guardian mansion a few months ago and you swore to gut me if I ever called you that again. Right then, I knew you were mine. I knew Fate destined us to be together. I won't hand you over to Blaine."

Her heart thudded as the urge to punch him faded away.

She let his statement hang between them while heaviness sank low in her chest. He thought by misting her here, he could change her destiny.

If only.

He cupped the side of her face and her body

betrayed her, sinking into his embrace. "I'll protect you, Raine. Now and every moment for the rest of my existence."

Light exploded from the black hole in her chest, blasting heat through her blood. She'd felt the connection to him from the beginning but refused to acknowledge it. Sure, he'd had an ulterior motive, they both did, but she couldn't deny that while they'd been together, he'd always chosen her. He'd put her first. He'd protected her, fought with her, and saved her soul more than once.

Him betraying her was so much easier to swallow.

"Take the Empryen." He dipped his head, his warm breath whispered over her lips. "We'll figure this out. Once you return the sword, you can come back here. We'll both be free."

No, they wouldn't. Once she delivered the sword, her destiny ended.

He curled a finger around the band in her hair, slipping it free. Loose strands tumbled down her shoulders and back. "Will you deliver the sword tonight?"

For the love of Fate. Why did he keep asking questions she didn't want to answer? "I have to. I've lost enough time already."

"Stay here with me for a little longer. Please." He threaded his fingers through her hair. "I don't want you to go."

She held his gaze, and for a moment, she lost herself in his dark brown eyes, recognizing his soul as hers. To her, he wasn't just another Fallen, or whatever the change in his blood meant. He was her soulmate.

And for once in her existence, she wanted to choose a path for herself, if only for a night.

In this moment, she chose him.

Chapter THIRTY-EIGHT

A burning pull deep within his soul drew his lips to Raine's. A desire not to have her just in this moment but to reinforce the bond between them.

Somehow, and for some unknown reason, Fate had created a soulmate for him. He felt the connection the second he'd first seen her in the forest, and every moment since, it strengthened, securing its claws inside not only his soul but his heart.

She was what he'd fought for all along, not his freedom, but her. He just hadn't realized it until now.

Gliding his tongue along her bottom lip, she opened for him, and he let go. Through their bond, he poured all his emotions, his love for her, his hope for their future.

Ever since she'd healed him, those damn gray feathers had become as determined as her. Slowly at first, they regrew, until they now outnumbered the crimson on one wing. He'd felt the shift in his soul as well. At first, he'd thought maybe Raine's magic was still in his system, and that the changes would revert as her magic faded, but it didn't. And now, what remained wasn't only residual heavenly magic, but an unbreakable soulmate bond.

Raine moaned, scraping her nails at the base of his skull. He needed her now, more than ever. He needed to show her how much she meant to him.

Gripping the back of her thighs, he hoisted her legs around him, carried her to the bedroom, and sat her gently on the edge of the bed. When she peered up at him, he tuncd into their bond, and how her heart beat in time with his. A strong, constant thump, behind his ribs, as though they were one.

Raine reached to one side and leaned the Empryen against the wall, before scooting backward up the bed. He couldn't blame her for not letting the sword out of her sight, but she was safe with him. Sure, he hadn't figured out all the answers yet, but he wouldn't give the sword to Blaine. Once she activated it, he'd fulfilled his bargain with Fate, and Raine could return it.

He prowled between her legs, unable to stop the animalistic growl rumbling deep inside him. Things felt rushed the last time they were together. Adrenaline-fueled sex in the armory where anyone could've walked in on them. He never got the opportunity to worship her the way she deserved. No one knew of his hideout, not even Blaine. So now, their last time together until Raine returned to him, he'd take it slow and seal their bond how he should've the first time.

A whisper in their connection told him they'd end up together again in the same realm. That everything would work out. He just needed to be patient. He'd been patient for centuries, a little while longer wouldn't kill him.

Blaine was smart to want Raine on his side. However, the Fallen failed to anticipate what Slater would do to keep her safe.

One by one, he popped the buttons on her pants and slid them down her thighs. On the way back up, he trailed light kisses along the inside of her leg until he reached her apex. Starting gently, he nuzzled and kissed the center of her panties until she writhed with need beneath him. He hooked his fingers around the hem and slipped them off before returning between her legs to continue his exploration without the cotton barrier.

Raine moaned, clutching the sheets by her side, spurring him on. Using his hands on her thighs, he anchored her to the bed and devoured her. Tasting, kissing, entering. She tasted sweet and delicate on his tongue, like stolen, midnight kisses amongst the blooming jasmine. He couldn't get enough. He lapped and teased until her back arched off the bed and she shuddered beneath him, gasping for breath.

He'd never felt so much power, so much need. So much…love.

What had begun as a game for him, tormenting his fiery princess, had ended with her victorious. She'd captured his heart and soul, and he never wanted them back.

Crawling off the bed, he stripped off his clothes before returning between her legs. Sitting on his haunches, he coaxed Raine onto his lap and slipped off her shirt and bra to roll his thumbs over the hard peaks of her breasts.

She trailed her finger along his bottom lip. "Your tongue is as wicked as your shadows."

He held back the smirk. "A compliment? From you?"

She smacked him upside the head making him chuckle.

"Take it and shut the hell up."

Instead of replying, he crushed his mouth to hers, drowning in her taste. The feeling of her naked in his arms. He caught every one of her moans and stored it away in his heart for their time apart.

Lifting her hips, he slid inside her, joining their bodies as one, along with their hearts. Light exploded in his soul. The same light he originally mistook for her magic. It connected the two of them, fused their soulmate bond together, and swelled in his chest.

Tremors shook his body, zinging through his blood, building a tight coil of tension in his gut. A light sheen of sweat coated their skin as he rocked inside Raine. Still kissing him, she clutched his shoulders, digging his nails into the flesh.

He wanted this to last forever. Not just the here and now, but the feelings, the sensations of their bodies together as one, the way she gave herself to him. How he offered her everything—his body, his heart, his soul.

They'd find their way back together. Now wasn't their time.

Raine had to return the sword and finish her mission. He wouldn't deny her that. He had to face Fate before Blaine found him. Then, they'd be free together.

At some point, they lost control and kissing became too much.

He gripped her hips, driving into her. Raine tilted her head to the side and his mouth trailed down her neck. Heat consumed his blood, firing through his veins, overtaking all his senses until he only thought of Raine. Her stormy scent, her soft skin beneath his rough grasp, her platinum blonde hair tickling his face.

When she threw her head back and cried his name, clenching him from every angle, the need to ensure she never forgot him drove him into a frenzy. He rocked harder, faster, until the heady smell of sex and their combined scents filled the room. The tightly wound coil released, exploded with light, flashing one word in his mind.

Mine.

As tiny aftershocks quaked their bodies, he lowered Raine's back onto the mattress and lay beside her in a tangled heap of arms and legs, while their breathing steadied.

"That was…good."

He snorted. "Two compliments in one day. Are you feeling all right, princess?" Propping himself up on his forearm, he caught her faint smile. "You're beautiful. But when you smile, the secret ones when you think no one is watching, you're…breathtaking."

The smile faded and she turned her head away. "Don't say things like that. It'll make this harder than it already is."

He pinched her chin, coaxing her head back to face him. "This was always going to be hard. Our destinies lead us in opposite directions."

"What will you do about Blaine and Fate?"

He shrugged one shoulder. "I'll figure something out."

"I wish…"

She didn't need to finish the sentence. "Me too, Raine." He leaned down to kiss her forehead. "But we'll eventually land in the same place. I feel it. Soulmates always find a way."

He thought of Aric and Willow. Despite all that Fate put them through, Aric never gave up hope, fighting for his soulmate until they found their way back together. He'd never craved a soulmate, but that was before he knew Raine. Now, he'd fight to never let her go.

For the first time since he Fell from the Heavens, he had faith. Hope.

Wrapping her hand around his neck, she drew him down to her and kissed him, a gentle touch of her lips, lingering for a moment that broke his damn heart.

"One day," she murmured.

Instead of a vow, it felt like a damn goodbye.

****

They spent the next hour joined together, exploring their connection and their bodies, finding comfort tangled in each other's arms. He didn't bother speaking. Nothing he said would change their circumstances. He'd never ask her to defy her destiny for him, just as he knew without a doubt, she'd never ask him to forgo his freedom for her.

Separation, for a little while, was a small price to pay.

Eventually, Raine detangled herself to slip off the bed and dress. He followed, a sinking feeling weighing down his limbs, constricting his chest. Once dressed, he sank onto the edge of the bed and watched Raine pick up the Empryen.

She snagged his gaze, before clasping the hilt with both hands and balancing the tip on the floor. Lowering her head, her chest rose with a deep inhale. Power sparked, brilliant teal swirls shot from her hands, twisting and weaving around the blade. The sword glowed, humming with power.

Besides Raine, he'd never seen anything so spectacular. "I'm so in awe of you right now and, to be honest, feeling a little inadequate."

Raine lifted her head. "Because I activated the

Empryen?"

"Because you made a weapon capable of destroying realms. Because the magic from your hands is as beautiful as you. Because you're…mine."

Her lips rolled inward to a hard line.

Clearly, he missed his cue for compliments. "How do you get back given you can't mist?"

"The sword will mist me."

A weird sensation trickled through their bond, and he couldn't quite put his finger on it. He hated this. Why did it hurt so much? He'd take a Purah dagger over having to say goodbye to Raine.

He stood before her, the pulsing sword between them. "You're the strongest angel I've ever known. We'll get through this. I…love you."

Her gaze dipped to the sword as though she tackled some inner turmoil, fighting between leaving and staying. He fought the same battle only one part of him wanted to fall to his knees and beg her to stay. The logical part of him knew she couldn't.

"It's time," she whispered.

He nodded. "Before you go, tell me which realm in the Heavens. In case you don't make it back."

If his deal with Fate went pear-shaped, and he ended up back under her control, at least he could mist to the Heavens and find Raine. If Blaine didn't kill him first.

Raine slowly shook her head. "I'm not taking the sword to the Heavens." Again, her gaze danced between him and the glowing sword.

"I don't understand. If you're not taking the sword to the Heavens, where are you taking it?"

Violet eyes full of determination, fire, and strength

that hadn't been there a moment ago, locked with his. "To Hell."

His brain malfunctioned.

Did she just say Hell? Did he hear correctly? Had he imagined it?

"What the actual fuck?"

Raine lifted her chin. "I'm taking the Empryen to Pahadim to finish what I started."

Chills wracked his body. He'd hidden the sword in Pahadim when he'd first arrived in Hell. The exact realm Fate told him about. Did Fate make him hide it there for Raine to find? Was that her destiny?

"Why?"

"I forged the Empryen to kill Zath. To end his reign once and for all."

He stared at her, waiting for the punchline. Surely, this was a fucking joke. But Raine just stood there with her brows furrowed, her gaze alert, and a perfectly crafted mask hiding her emotions.

"No," he murmured. "You'll Fall."

"Did you hit your head? Of course, I'll Fall, but this is my destiny. I've trained my entire existence for this."

Clarity hit him so hard and fast it sent a bolt of pain through his skull. "That's why you never let anyone in. Why you keep yourself so distant, making sure everyone around you stays at arm's length. In a twisted way, you think you're protecting them."

"Why bother forming attachments when I'm destined to Fall?"

He rubbed the back of his neck. "What the fuck, Raine? What about River? Does he know?"

"Leave him out of this," she snapped. "He knows I

need to return the Empryen. If I don't, Fate threatened to revoke his immortality."

He shook his head. Just when his soul started to heal, she'd destroy hers. "There has to be another way. I won't let you do this."

"It's not up to you," she snapped. "I'm the only immortal who can wield the sword. It's meant for me."

She spun to leave. Lightning fast, he summoned shadows and shot them at Raine. She struggled against his grip, but he continued building the shadows until they twisted around her entire body like unbreakable rope.

"I won't let you Fall, not when you saved me, and we have a chance to be together."

She seethed at him. "You bastard. Let me go."

"No can do, princess."

Fate destined Raine to forge the Empryen and use it to kill Zath. But in doing so, their destinies had collided in the mortal realm, neither the Heavens nor Hell. Neutral territory. He wouldn't let Raine, his soulmate, destroy her soul for a quest. She deserved freedom from darkness, from hatred, from the poisonous blood that had infected his soul since the day he agreed to that deal with Fate.

Fate had known all along, hadn't she?

He still wanted to usher in a new millennium, a wave of change, to be more than he was in the Heavens, and he could still achieve that. His path would just look different than he first anticipated.

Plans changed all the time, as one gathered more information and details about the situation. Now, was one of those moments.

He had to save Raine. His fiery princess, the angel

who kick-started his heart and made it beat again. The Raziel who weaved her magic inside his soul.

For her, his freedom would be worth the price.

Moving closer, he raised a shadow to her head. Muscles tightened in her jaw as she fought against him, thrashing her head, but he held tighter.

"When you remember this, and I know you'll figure out a way to, I want you to remember this moment. The moment I chose you." He brushed his thumb along her chin. "Remember what we had was real."

She struggled against the bindings. He'd expect nothing less, but he'd make this sacrifice for her.

Raine's eyes widened as he pushed a shadow into her mind. He'd vowed never to enter her mind again against her will but doing this was the only way he knew how to save her.

"Let me in, Raine. It won't be permanent. I just need a head start. Remember what I told you about the Ariel."

When she remembered, she'd hunt him down, but by then, this would all be over.

"Don't do this." Tears welled in her eyes as she fought harder.

His chest squeezed so tight he struggled to maintain focus, but he just needed a few more seconds.

He forced the shadow deeper into her mind, rolling over the crumbled walls she'd once erected to keep him out. Inside, he searched for the memories. The ones of him. The memories of their time together. The reason she arrived in the mortal realm.

He cloaked every memory but kept those surrounding it. She'd remember her time in this realm, her brother, and the Guardians. Just not him or the Empryen.

When he cloaked the last memory, he planted one final thought in her mind.

Find Willow.

Recalling the shadows, he caught Raine before she collapsed to the floor, unconscious. He lifted her into his arms for one final moment, before misting her to a location he knew she'd be safe.

With a heavy, crumbled heart, he pried the Empryen from her hands and left.

Chapter THIRTY-NINE

Find Willow. Raine peeled open her eyes to dull light. Foreign scents of pine and...dirt drifted through her nose. She pushed herself up to sit, glancing around the...forest.

What the Fate?

The last thing she remembered was...Everything was fuzzy. Cloudy. As though she'd had too many of EJ's cocktails and couldn't remember what made her lay in the dirt like an animal.

She stood and brushed off the leaves from her pants. Luckily, they were leather. After, she wiped the tops of her heels on the back of her thighs until they were glossy again. The first beginnings of dawn filtered between the tree trunks. Had she fallen asleep out here?

Sunlight caught on a weapon by her feet. She picked up the dagger, turning it this way and that, inspecting the blade. A memory sparked in her mind but before she captured it, the memory retreated. She'd made the dagger for someone...but who?

She flipped the blade in her hand before tucking it in her belt. Why couldn't she remember?

Stumbling through the forest, she made her way across the lawn to the Guardian mansion. Dark patches of grass drew her attention. Had she fought a Fallen? Had she hit her head?

As she stepped up to the porch, Raven threw open

the door. A semi-healed cut ran down his cheek, the skin pink and angry.

Had she fought Raven?

"Where have you been?"

She screwed up her face. "Lying in the dirt apparently."

Raven's brows drew tight together. "After you obliterated Asher, Slater misted away with you. Where did he take you?"

She drew back. Now, her turn to frown. "Who's Slater?"

Raven tilted his head, studying her. "Slater. The Fallen you worked with to recover the Empryen."

Find Willow.

A sharp pain stabbed her temple. "I don't know what you're talking about. I went outside and…"

Everything after that was foggy. She couldn't remember how she made it outside or why. Given the tight expression on Raven's face, something had happened, but she had no idea what.

"Raine," his voice lowered, edged with concern. "Where's the Empryen?"

She peered at her open palms, expecting to find…something, but they were empty. River burst out the front door, skidding to a halt right before he barreled into Raven.

Her brother's frantic emerald-green gaze locked with hers. "Where's the Empryen, sis?"

"For the love of Fate, why does everyone keep asking me that?" She slipped the dagger free from her belt. "Do you mean this? I found it in the dirt."

River inched closer, acting strange. Concern didn't suit him. "Do you know what the Empryen is?"

"Clearly, not. I would've thought that part was obvious."

River narrowed his eyes. "Tell me why we're here in the mortal realm. The real reason."

She opened her mouth to respond but nothing came out. Why were they in the mortal realm? They'd been here for a couple of years now, staying with the Guardians while she searched for…what? She pushed harder, trying to remember. The sharp pain returned at her temples.

She squeezed her forehead. "I…don't know. I can't remember."

Raven swore. "Fucking Slater."

"The douche-canoe must've taken the sword," River said to Raven.

Raven's jaw tightened. "And wiped her memory."

They engaged in a conversation as though she weren't standing with them. She'd listen, but the swooshing in her head tuned out the world around her until all she focused on were…shadows.

She sensed them. Faint whispers of darkness swirling in the deepest corner of her mind. Weaved between them were two clear words.

Find Willow.

"What did you say?" Raven turned to her.

Had she said that aloud? "Find Willow?" She squeezed her forehead again. "It's all I can think about. Why does it feel like I'm drowning in shadows?"

Raven's eyes darkened as he addressed River. "Take her upstairs. I'll get Willow and summon Cole. We're gonna need all the help we can get. That bastard will pay for this."

Her brother reached for her, but she retreated out of

his grasp. "Tell me what's going on."

His shoulders sagged. "Slater wiped your memories before he took the Empryen."

Slater? Why was that name familiar? "Who the Fate is Slater?"

River's eyes widened for the briefest moment before his expression turned somber. "Sis, he's your soulmate."

Chapter FORTY

Slater knelt on one knee in the scorching, rough dirt of Pahadim, with the Empryen grasped between his palms, tip in the earth. He bowed his head, remembering everything that had happened until this moment. His longing for a more fulfilling existence, his deal with Fate, his torture in the Pits, and how Blaine had freed him. But most of all, he thought of the moments preceding his return to Hell.

In his existence, he never imagined meeting someone like Raine. A courageous angel who set not just his body on fire but his entire soul. Over the past few weeks, she'd slipped beneath his skin and filled his heart, until he couldn't imagine being without her.

Until that was his only option.

Better to have loved and lost her, than for her to destroy her soul.

Now, he was back where it all started.

After his Fall from the Heavens, he'd entered the gates and used his remaining power to mist to this spot at Fate's direction. He'd hidden the Empryen in the cavern now in front of him. Still healing and transitioning, he lacked the strength to leave, and instead spent countless days, weeks under the blazing desert sun, waiting for a sign that never came.

How naïve to think Fate would look out for him. She had no control over this realm.

He was in Hell.

Once fully transitioned into a Fallen, he'd misted back to the entrance of Hell where Zath awaited him. Despite Fate having removed Zath's powers before she banished him, Zath had still overpowered him. At the time, he hadn't known the Infernal Pits existed. Fate neglected to inform him. If he'd known, would he have still taken the deal with Fate? Probably. He'd always believed he was meant for something greater.

But in the end, he'd failed. Not just himself, but at keeping the Empryen safe as well. A sick chuckle quaked in his chest. He'd failed so badly he'd condemned himself to the Pits. Centuries that changed him. Visions of Raine came when he'd needed them most, but even they hadn't prevented his resentment.

Until Blaine freed him.

The Empryen pulsed in his hands, sparks of power tingled his skin, zapping his heart, connecting with Raine's magic. Raine had said she was the only immortal who could wield the sword. But what if that wasn't true? What if she only needed to activate it?

What if Fate set this whole thing up like a sick fucking joke?

He unfurled his wings, scanning the inside feathers. His transition, the healing gray feathers, had stalled. Just like when he Fell, he felt neither Fallen nor angel. The longer he stayed in Hell, the more Raine's magic would fade, the quicker their soulmate bond deteriorated. His wings would return to crimson.

Without access to the Heavens, he wouldn't fully change back.

And he owed it to Raine not to return to the mortal realm until he completed her destiny. Until he ended

Zath.

For Raine, he'd Fall over and over again. He'd choose saving her soul over his freedom every second of every day.

Beside him, the air rippled a moment before Blaine materialized. He didn't bother worrying about the Fallen finding him, or what he'd done at the Guardian mansion after the battle. If Blaine wanted him dead, the Fallen would've done it by now. Slater had given him enough opportunities.

Empryen still clasped in his hands, he rose from the dirt and turned to face Blaine.

"It's not often someone surprises me," Blaine said, adjusting the collar of his leather jacket.

He had no words. Only one explanation accounted for his actions, and he doubted Blaine would understand.

The Fallen wasn't meant to be at the mansion. Blaine wasn't meant to fight Asher. Slater had planned to retrieve the sword so Raine could return it to the Heavens.

He scoffed to himself, but the Empryen was never destined for the Heavens.

He lifted the sword, twisting it so the sun's rays reflected teal sparkles of Raine's magic. "I didn't plan it to happen this way."

Blaine peered at the sword for a long moment, before lifting his gaze to Slater.

"Destinies rarely change, my friend. Choices are disguised as alternate paths. In the end, we arrive at the same destination."

He thought that over. Alternate paths. Originally, he'd planned to use Raine to activate the sword, so he fulfilled his bargain with Fate. Then, for a split second, he considered giving the sword *and* Raine to Blaine. But at some point, his soulmate bond with Raine outweighed his loyalty to Blaine and his desire for freedom. As it turned out, to save Raine's soul, he'd given up everything.

Alternative paths? Or perhaps he accepted the path he hadn't known he wanted?

"What changed?" Blaine asked.

He motioned to a volcanic boulder for Blaine to sit. "Let me tell you a story."

Blaine threw his head back and laughed. "Oh, how I wish I had a comfy chair and smooth bourbon."

He cocked his eyebrow.

Blaine's lip hitched at the corner. "Very well, I'll make do without." Blaine perched on the boulder and gestured for Slater to continue. "Tell your story."

Absently, he dragged the tip of the sword through the dirt, creating a series of random squiggles. The sandy ground shimmered outward as though repelled by the blade. Raziel magic here in Hell. And he thought fighting Fallen was the strangest thing he'd experienced.

He inhaled a deep breath and began his story. "Once upon a time, there was an angel in the Heavens who believed in bigger things. That Fate destined him for more. An angel who believed he could change the mortal realm, change the universe. But one day, another angel preyed on that hope, the desire to better himself, and offered him a deal too good to resist."

Blaine tapped his chin. "I believe I've already heard this story."

He paused his doodling. "Let me finish."

Blaine waved his hand for him to continue.

"But before that angel sacrificed his soul to Hell, his queen appeared to him and offered a counter deal. One that would demonstrate his honor and loyalty and reward him with freedom. That angel became a Fallen, going through Hell to keep his word. Literally." He peered at the oversized sun, seemingly so low in the sky he could lift the sword and scrape the surface. "But everything changed the day that Fallen fell in love with an angel."

"Sounds familiar." Blaine scoffed. "Tell me, my friend, how does this story end?"

"I'm not sure yet. But during his journey, the Fallen finally figured out his destiny. His true purpose. The path Fate paved for him." He paused. "If something is worth giving up, then it wasn't important in the first place. And he'd give his soul, his bargain for freedom, his thirst for a greater existence, if it meant saving his soulmate."

By the hilt, he offered the sword to Blaine but held it just out of reach. "I know you wanted Raine and the sword, but I won't let her Fall. She's not some pawn in your twisted battle with Fate. She's my soulmate. I will defend and protect her until my last breath."

"And what do you suppose I do with this sword?

"I suspect you already know that answer."

Blaine smirked. "Perhaps I do."

Blaine reached for the sword, but Slater held it back. "I want to help finish this. Complete the mission Raine intended."

"As absurd as it sounds, I presumed the Fallen and the angel would want to run off into the fiery sunset together."

He lowered his head. "She'll never forgive me for betraying her." A heavy weight pressed on his chest, but he pushed through it to lift his chin. Before he left Raine, he'd vowed to complete her mission. He owed her that. "I'll finish this with you."

"The soulmate bond is a fickle thing." Blaine circled his finger in the air around Slater. "The guilt you feel is an irrelevant reaction spurred on by the heart. It'll pass."

He wasn't so sure.

Blaine pushed off the boulder and held out his palm for the Empryen. "Trust me, it'll fade until you forget what faith ever felt like."

Faith. He'd never thought he'd feel that again for one single purpose. "Why would Fate create a soulmate bond destined for different realms?"

"Stranger things have happened."

Blaine moved his hand to the sword and this time Slater let him take it.

The moment Blaine curled his fingers around the hilt, a burst of power exploded from the blade, the force so great, Slater staggered backward. As Blaine raised the Empryen in the air, an inscription in black lettering burned along the flat surface of the blade as though activated by his touch.

Slater gaped, reading the ancient letters as they appeared one by one. "Sarael."

Chapter FORTY-ONE

Raine stared at the angel before her, the one that resembled her brother, yet he said words that would never come out of her brother's mouth.

Ever.

"Soulmate?" She scoffed. "Don't you think if I had a soulmate, he'd be here? That I'd remember him?" She cocked her brow. "That I'd at least *know* who he was?"

River's lips formed a thin line. Fixing his gaze on her, he leaned in. "Where is the Empryen?"

She glared at him, seconds away from punching him in the face, brother or not. "What in the Fate are you talking about?"

River squeezed her shoulder. "Raine, listen to me carefully." He lowered his voice as though revealing a secret. "Fate sent you here to find the Empryen. A sword *you* created."

Something sparked in her mind, right at the back, locked behind that damn shadow barrier. A memory? She concentrated harder, trying to grasp it, but it slipped away every time.

She peered down the hall, scanning the living room. It all looked familiar. She knew where she was and who lived here. How did she remember some things and not others?

Had everyone gone delusional while she had a slumber party for one in the forest?

"How can I remember some things and not others? If this asshat Slater wiped my memories, why did he leave some? I know who you are, I know Raven, I know this house, I know I'm in the mortal realm." She paused. "I know I'm a fucking Raziel. Why didn't he wipe all that?"

River inhaled a deep breath, his shoulders dropping on the exhale. "He must've left those for a reason. Did you…" River grimaced. "Do something to hurt him? Make him retaliate?"

Her eyes narrowed. "As in slice him into pieces?" A memory sparked again, just out of reach. "He sounds like a shit soulmate. I bet Hailee would disapprove of him as a hero." She threw her hands in the air. "See? I even remember all those painful, nauseating romantic comedies."

River gave her a weak smile. Again, so unlike him.

"I'm the first to admit that finding out he's your soulmate threw me, and I have no issue telling you I fell asleep many nights wishing Aric would beat the bejesus out of him. But…"

"But what?"

"After the battle with the Fallen, once you defeated Asher with that awesome power blast, Slater misted you somewhere with the sword. Then a few hours later, you turn up here with no memory of anything relating to the Empryen." River paused. "Did he know something I didn't? Was he trying to stop you from taking the Empryen back? Or did he betray you and steal it?"

Don't do this…

She clenched her fist around the dagger in her palm. "Why would Fate bother creating a soulmate for me when I'm destined to…"

Her mind blanked.

"Destined to what?" River pressed.

I won't let you Fall…

She pinched her forehead. "I don't have a fucking clue."

With a heavy sigh, River ushered her upstairs. "Let's see if Willow can help."

She let River guide her to the entertainment room where the others waited. Cole had yet to arrive.

Fantastic. An audience for her amnesia episode. Just what she needed.

Willow rushed to her, taking her hand. "Raine, tell me how to help."

She stared at the Ariel. Vibrant red hair, a cascade of curls down her shoulders, bright hazel eyes. She sensed the regeneration powers streaming through Willow's blood.

Find Willow. The words tumbled around her mind.

She tightened her grip on the blade, wanting so badly to throw it at the furniture.

"Unless you know why I need to find you? That's the only thing I can think of."

Willow shook her head.

She snatched her hand free from Willow's to pace the room. Everyone stared at her as though she'd lost her mind. Maybe she had? Adjusting her grip on the dagger, she inspected the craftsmanship. She was sure she'd made it for someone. Did she make it for Slater? If so, why?

If he tried to remove her memories, why didn't she stab him with it? Unless she couldn't? Unless he'd captured her or made her…vulnerable. She grimaced at the idea. Her vulnerable? No way.

"Argh." She grunted, as she stabbed the dagger into the backrest of the couch. "My mind is full of shadows."

"What if Willow's magic can heal it?" Aric asked, moving closer to his soulmate.

She spun to face them.

Willow frowned. "My magic regenerates fauna, not memories."

Aric entwined his hand with Willow's. The leather band he wore on his wrist lit brilliant orange, the color of Ariel magic. "But what if together you can do more?"

Willow drew back. "That's ridiculous. I'm not powerful enough to regenerate memories. I don't even know how."

Another memory, beyond the shadows, sparked in Raine's mind. A time when Fate approached her about…something important. Fate had told her about unique angels who were more powerful than others. Angels who harnessed and drew on their connections to the Heavens to amplify their magic. A pair of these angels were stronger together as one.

Back then, she assumed Fate spoke of her and River. How her and her brother had the power to create and end life. She'd used that power to forge…something.

Was Willow like her?

Aric lifted Willow's hand to place it on his chest over his heart. "Draw on our connection, use it to strengthen your magic."

The air around the entrance to the entertainment room rippled a second before Cole materialized. His steel-gray eyes swung her way, pinning her with a deadly stare. "You didn't."

"Didn't what?"

The situation was so nuts EJ hadn't even made it behind the bar.

Cole marched straight to her without acknowledging the others. "Last week, you asked me if I could wipe memories. Certain ones, not all of them." His eyes narrowed into thin slits. "Which Azrael did you threaten? Because I sure as hell didn't do it for you."

"Hang on a minute, dicknose. I didn't threaten any Azrael. Why would I want to remove memories?"

Cole cocked a brow. "Because you felt things you didn't want to for a certain Fallen?"

That memory in the back of her mind reared its ugly head again.

An argument. A kiss.

A...Fallen.

She snagged the Azrael by the neck of his shirt and twisted. "Give them back."

He blanched for the briefest second before his brows furrowed. "I can't undo another Azrael's shadows. You should've thought of that beforehand."

Raven curled his fingers around her wrist and eased her away from Cole. "We'll figure this out, Raine."

She clawed at her temples with both hands. "It's there, I can feel it. It's right there, but I can't see it. Not knowing is killing me."

I need a head start...

"He's stopping me from doing something."

Willow touched her arm. Sparks of Ariel magic

danced at her fingertips. "Let me try."

Strange urgency screamed in her blood. They were running out of time, but she didn't know why. What was about to happen? She needed to stop…something.

Or someone.

The Ariel was her only option.

When she nodded, Willow led her to the couch and sank down beside her, placing one hand in Raine's and the other in Aric's. Raine closed her eyes, unsure why, instinct maybe? Brilliant warmth flooded her veins, like a stream bursting through a dam wall and gushing down the river, consuming everything in its path. She surrendered to the feeling, let the magic rush through her.

Ariel magic invaded her senses. Pine, wildflowers, stormy rain, cool spring mornings. It washed over her skin, seeped into her veins, and glided through her blood with one destination.

Her mind.

The second Willow's magic broke the shadows in her mind, crippling pain stabbed her temples. She gritted her teeth. If she made a sound, Willow would stop.

She had to push through it.

The warm magic swirled around the shadows, searching for a way through. Something lit up in the center. Her memories. But as soon as she noticed them, the shadows thickened, grew angrier and concealed them.

Imaginary needles jabbed into her head. The muscles in her jaw tightened as she clenched her teeth harder. With her free hand, she gripped the armrest, digging her nails into the leather.

Willow's magic intensified, battling the shadows. Her breaths came short and sharp. Aric grunted. Still, Raine kept her eyes closed, searching for the memories.

Willow tightened her grip on Raine's hand, both their palms sweaty and hot like the magic filling her blood.

A little further...

A crack appeared in the shadows, a weak spot, and the Ariel magic slipped in before the shadows retreated. Something shattered in her mind. She screamed, clawing her skull as the memories burst open.

Fate materialized inside the expansive tower, her floral summer dress fanning out on the marble floor behind her. She hadn't had a visitor in...forever. Locked away, protecting the Empryen, she'd lived an existence of solitude until the time came for Fate to release her. For her to fulfil her destiny.

Fate lifted her chin, her eyes illuminated with silvery specs. "The time has come, my Raziel."

Raine straightened, her muscles tightened, readying for battle even though her belly fluttered with what Fate expected of her. "I'm ready."

She knew this day would come, had trained her entire existence for it.

Beside her, on a raised dais, the Empryen hovered in midair in a cocoon of her teal magic, concealed to everyone but her and Fate. Not that any angels ever came here.

Fate glided to the dais. Reaching through the ripples, Fate curled her delicate fingers around the hilt, removing the sword for the first time since Raine had forged it.

Holding it in her hand, Fate turned to her. "When

315

you wake, arrive at my sanctuary with your brother."

"Brother?"

Fate had never mentioned she had a brother. Why hadn't she known? Why hadn't she met him? He hadn't trained for this, not like her. He would slow her down.

Fate inclined her head. "Yes. He'll be your reason."

Reason? For what?

Before she asked, Fate waved her hand in front of Raine's face. Misty, silvery clouds swirled around her head.

"Sleep now."

Raine cried out. Squeezing her temples as another memory exploded, this one more recent.

Slater...her activating the sword...the look in his eyes when his shadows entered her mind.

She bent forward, dry heaving as nausea churned her stomach.

"Are you okay?" someone asked.

She couldn't focus. She gasped for air, the pain in her head slowly receded.

Fate had planned this. No one stole the Empryen. Fate took it and gave it to Slater. That betrayal she could stomach, but...Slater's? All along, he planned to double-cross her. She was just a pawn in his quest to steal the Empryen back.

Killing Zath was her destiny, not Slater's.

He wasn't her soulmate. Nothing they had was real. He was a Fallen.

Her enemy.

Bracing on the armrest, she pushed herself off the couch to stand. Her legs unsteady but more determined than the day Fate removed the Empryen.

Reaching behind Willow, she ripped the dagger free from the leather and scanned the room until she found Cole.

She aimed the tip of the dagger at the Azrael. "Mist me to Hell. Now."

Chapter FORTY-TWO

When Slater first arrived in Hell, many centuries ago, he'd never expected to make that choice again, let alone attempt to use the Empryen Fate had given him.

He and Blaine stood together on the roof of a partly demolished church on Main Street. Well, no one had officially named the street. Streets in Hell didn't have names. He'd just dubbed it Main Street and it stuck.

All the action happened on this street. Fallen came and went, Devoid wandered aimlessly; he'd even established a training center off this street. At the far end, Azrael delivered souls destined for Hell.

Sulfur tingled his nostrils with every inhale. Hot wind blew along the ground below, and to pass the time, he imagined tumbleweeds bouncing down the street like in those mortal cowboy movies.

His fingers twitched to release shadows. Restlessness prickled beneath his skin, not from his impending battle with Zath but from something else.

Was Raine all right? Had Willow figured out how to unveil the memories?

Would his fiery princess ever forgive him?

No. He exhaled a ragged breath. Raine wasn't his princess any longer. But the desire to return to her tore through his middle as though any minute his body would rip in half.

Now, he understood why EJ stormed the gates of

Hell to rescue his soulmate.

That pull was like nothing he'd ever felt.

Provided Raine stayed in the mortal realm, she was safe.

Blaine clasped the Empryen in his hand, tip down on the roof. The inscription still visible along the smooth surface. All that time, Raine and he had wondered how the word Sarael linked to the sword. Now, they knew.

Blaine was the Protector of the Heavens.

Fate intended for Blaine to have the sword all along.

Impatient, he shot Blaine a look. "Why are we waiting?"

They'd sat on this rooftop for what felt like an eternity and in that time, Blaine had barely spoken. So unlike him. Blaine also hadn't summoned his Fallen army or shared his plan. How would they get close to Zath without his knowledge?

"The Dumahel."

He screwed up his face. "I presume you mean Ebony and not her twin. 'Cause you remember what happened the last time we took the sister, don't you? And why in the blazing Hell are we waiting for Ebony? She sided with Asher. Did she even survive Raine's explosion of power?"

Blaine's gaze roamed the street below. "She did."

That Fallen was more cryptic than fucking Fate. "How do you know she'll come?"

"She's a Fallen. She can't go to her sister. Her father is in the Pits, thanks to the Raziel. Ebony will realize the error of her ways and return here."

Fire billowed from a nearby building, spraying

glass onto the street below. Heat singed his cheek. Why did the heat only now bother him?

He wiped sweat from his brow before glancing at Blaine. "Tell me how you'll end Zath."

Blaine curled his finger around the hilt of the Empryen. "Over my centuries here, Zath has played right into my hands. I have him exactly where I need him. He may think that each soul I bring him rejuvenates his powers, but it also builds trust." His gaze swung to Slater. "Which we know is deadly."

Trust. Trust was deadly and dangerous, especially given freely. Raine had given him her trust and he'd destroyed her, tore her trust into pieces and fed it to the hellhounds.

An invisible fist constricted his chest.

At the far end of Main Street, the entrance to Hell materialized in the center of the road. Monstrous wrought iron gates licked with flames reached high into the sunburned sky. They only appeared when a soul entered Hell.

A moment later, the gates swung inward, and Ebony stumbled through, looking as though she hadn't slept in decades. She paused just inside as her gaze lifted to him and Blaine on the rooftop.

Blaine bumped his shoulder. "Told you."

A chill skated over his flesh, sprouting goosebumps on his arms, even though Hell was a thousand degrees. "Did you feel that?"

Blaine frowned. "Feel what?"

Before he answered, Ebony misted, appearing beside Blaine.

"Hello, love."

She threw mental daggers at Slater. "Your

Guardian sent my father's soul to the Pits."

He almost told her how many fucks he didn't give, but Blaine cut in.

"And you conspired with said father to kill me, using this very sword."

Take that, bitch.

"I think that trumps sending your father on a little tropical vacation, don't you?" Blaine said.

Ebony paled, but she held her ground. He recognized the same determination and fire in her twin.

"My father hated you. He said you'd eventually send us all to the Pits."

Blaine gave a dramatic gasp. "And yet, here you are. Not there." He switched the Empryen into his other hand, closest to Slater. "I have a final proposition for you."

"What could you possibly offer me?" She sneered.

"In exchange for dreamwalking me one final time, I'll free all the souls in the Pits. In fact, I'll end that entire realm."

Slater drew back. His heart thudded. "Say what? It's a one-use-only sword. You can't use it to kill Zath *and* destroy the Pits. I vowed to Raine—"

"Zath created the Infernal Pits. End Zath, end the Pits."

The niggling sensation inside his gut intensified until he could no longer ignore it. Tiny prickles scratched beneath his skin. Blaine remained unfazed. Was Slater the only one feeling it?

Something was wrong.

With Raine?

"How does this benefit me?" Ebony asked, with more snark than she should use in Blaine's presence.

She was lucky Blaine didn't end her just for her tone. He'd sent Fallen to the Pits for less.

"You're not exactly in a position to negotiate, love, but I'll humor you anyway. How about a promotion to knight?" He paused, finger tapping his lips. "What's the mortal term for a female knight?"

Slater gaped as though Blaine had sprouted wings from his ears. "A knight? What the fuck?"

Some foreign creature invaded his body, tearing at his chest cavity from the inside, desperate to flee. Warm pulsing light snapped his gaze to the gates. He scanned the street, failing to find the source.

His pulse hammered in his ears. What was happening?

"You're promoting her to a fucking knight when she conspired to end you? I gave you years of loyalty and even the Empryen, yet you never referred to me as a knight."

Slater turned away. He'd made a mistake. He shouldn't have given Blaine the sword.

He slammed the heel of his palm against his chest as wicked sharp pain spread through his limbs, igniting fire in his blood.

"Oh, Slater. Don't worry yourself over measly titles. You're about to depart this realm. Which, at first, I'll admit I was a tad disappointed about, but it seems your destiny doesn't end here. For that reason, I'm in need of a new second...knight...whatever you want to call it. Name it what you like, love."

Slater peered at the empty space where the gates had appeared earlier. What in the fiery Hell was wrong with him?

Blaine's strong hand clutched his shoulder,

drawing his attention once more. "It's been my honor, my friend."

"What?"

Blaine held his gaze for a moment before giving him a curt nod. He turned to Ebony. "Assemble the army, love. We have a king to overthrow."

"I told you I'd help finish this." He snagged Blaine's jacket. "I have to do this for Raine."

Crippling pain cut through his middle. He wrapped an arm around his stomach, grunting from the invisible force.

"I'll honor your request."

It all happened at once. Blaine misted away with the sword and Ebony. The gates of Hell materialized in the street. A brilliant teal light erupted from his chest, shooting to the gates.

He straightened, holding his breath as they swung inward.

Chapter FORTY-THREE

Raine stood before the gates of Hell as they materialized. They didn't scare her, but for the first time in her existence, something made her…reconsider a handful of choices that led her here. Did she regret them? No. *Reconsidered.* One in particular. If she hadn't trusted Slater, she wouldn't be here…swordless.

Back to square one.

Find the fucking Empryen.

Slater vowed to complete her mission, but once again, he underestimated her determination, her strength, her thirst to fulfill her destiny. To prove to Fate that she was more than a Raziel who possessed wicked skill with sharp objects. To prove to the Guardians that she was more than a pawn in Fate's plans.

To prove to her brother that dragging him to the mortal realm was worth it.

To redeem herself.

She wasn't a princess. She was a warrior, who had trained her entire existence to bring peace to the mortal realm.

Her. And only her.

The Empryen disappeared under her watch, but now she knew how. She would find it. And after she shoved it into Zath's chest and ended his reign, she'd use one of the daggers in her hand to end that traitorous so-called soulmate.

Chin held high, she advanced to the gates, but Cole snagged her shoulder. She glared at the Azrael. "Get your hand off me before I slice it off."

Cole grimaced and recoiled. "Are you sure this is your path, Raine?"

What a dumbass question. "This is the destiny Fate paved for me. I won't fail."

Cole inhaled a deep breath, looking as though he wanted to say something but held back.

"Spit it out, Cole."

He shoved his hands in his pockets. "I find it hard to believe that Fate would destine an angel like you to Fall."

Before she wasted a dagger on him, she turned away, facing the gates once more. During those long and lonely days spent locked in her tower, she'd thought the same. Why would Fate create a powerful angel and then send her soul to Hell? But she was the only angel trained to use the Empryen. No other angel could.

Fate intended this destiny for her.

She straightened, tightening her grip on the two daggers. "This is the only way to end Zath."

She took another step forward. Now wasn't the time to lose her confidence.

Fire erupted along the top of the gates as they swung open.

Slater appeared at the entrance.

Without a thought, she hurled a dagger at the Fallen, for once aiming straight for his heart. He deserved it.

The dagger flew true, slamming into his chest, all

the way to the hilt. Slater grunted, stumbling backward. She ignored the pang inside her own chest.

His wide-eyed gaze found hers. "Princess…"

She ignored him. Any second now, his body would explode into mist, sending his soul back to the Pits where he belonged.

Three…two…one…

Slater curled his fingers around the hilt and eased the dagger out of his flesh. "You stabbed me in the heart."

Clearly, she missed. First time for everything.

She flipped her second dagger to hold the tip. In one swift motion, she threw it at Slater, but he anticipated her move. Stepping to the side, he plucked it from the air as though it were a feather.

"Stop it, Raine."

Bastard. Traitor. Failed soulmate.

Something snapped inside her heart.

"Die already," she screamed, unsheathing two Kiel and throwing them at him simultaneously.

Slater misted, reappearing in front of her, so close they breathed the same hot, stale air. She swung at him, but he blocked her, gripping her wrist.

"Stop."

Her breath punched in and out. How dare he intercept her path. Again. "Where's the Empryen?"

"Let me explain."

She shoved out of his grasp. "Explain what? How you betrayed me? How you tricked me into working with you just so you could steal the sword back?" She clenched and unclenched her fists, wishing for more weapons to hurl at his black, evil heart. "How you made me feel…"

She retreated a step.

He matched her steps, closing in, not letting her out of his reach. "Made you feel what?"

She glared at him, refusing to answer. "Where's the sword?"

"Made you feel what, Raine? Tell me."

She couldn't breathe. The heavy air suffocated her.

Cole cleared his throat. "Ah, Raine, this is getting awkward. I'm not sure whether to step in and defend you or let you stab this loser in the heart."

She was done talking. She was done with Slater, and she was over the way he made her feel. How in a few short weeks, he made her yearn for a different destiny. One that didn't involve a suicide mission to Hell.

The sooner she ended this, the better. She sidestepped Slater, heading to the gates.

Slater swore, blocking her path. His almost black eyes narrowed at her. "In case you've forgotten, princess, I told you I won't let you Fall."

She shoved his chest. "Don't tell me what I can and can't do."

Slater grabbed her arm. Her stomach flipped. They materialized on the lawn outside the Guardian mansion.

"You asshole," she screamed.

She swung and punched him in the jaw, snapping his head to the side. The sickening crunch gave her more satisfaction than any orgasm.

"Fuck." Slater groaned, cradling his swelling jaw. "Stop it."

She didn't. He deserved all her frustration and anger. She'd never allowed herself to fall for anyone. Never opened herself up to anyone, even her brother.

He deserved this.

She battered her fist against his chest, unleashing her fury. The stupid Fallen didn't fight back and didn't even stumble. He took everything she threw at him.

If only she had more knives.

"Where's the Empryen?" she shouted over and over until her voice was raw and raspy. Tears streamed down her cheeks.

She'd failed herself and the entire universe. Every mortal in this realm would perish because she let Slater get too close.

She slipped up.

He weakened her.

She let him in.

When her shoulders sagged and her will to fight drained into the earth below her feet, Slater took her hands in his. By now, they'd attracted an audience. From the corner of her eye, she saw Raven storming across the lawn, a murderous snarl growing louder with each step.

The others stood at the edge of the lawn, no doubt waiting for the signal to kick Slater's ass. Though, inspecting the blood pooled on his shirt, she'd done a good job of it on her own.

"Raine?" Raven called, but it sounded foggy and distant, even though he now stood beside her. "What the hell's going on?"

She couldn't answer. Instead, her gaze drifted to her brother standing beside Aric. She'd failed River. Fate would revoke his immortality. Eventually, he'd age and die like an ordinary mortal.

And when Zath invaded, bringing Hell on Earth, they were all as good as dead.

Her pulse slammed inside her head, about to explode. She reached for a Kiel, but her fingers came up empty. Darkness flashed before her eyes. Her breath quickened, short sucks of air, never enough to satisfy her hungry lungs. Her chest constricted, pressing harder around her ribs, suffocating her second by second.

Someone touched her shoulder, light at first, then fingers curled around her arm, drawing her forward. She stumbled into the embrace, sucking in gulps of air. A hand guided her head to rest onto a firm chest as strong arms wrapped around her back, cocooning her in smells of rich leather, brimstone, and ash. A strong, steady heartbeat thumped in her ear. She sagged into the warmth, clutching the fabric of the shirt in both hands, never wanting to let go.

Soft, warm lips pressed a gentle kiss on the top of her head. "I've got you."

She couldn't pull away, didn't want to.

Why did Slater have to ruin this? Why couldn't he let her complete her destiny?

Why did he make her…care for him?

Gradually, air found its way into her lungs. Her breathing slowed and her heart rate steadied. When she was sure she wouldn't pass out, she lifted her head.

Slater loosened his grip but kept her within his arms.

He'd never looked so…broken. Hard lines creased his brow, his lips set firm, dark gray circles beneath his equally dark eyes. He looked as broken as she felt.

Why? Why did he do this?

Slater slid his arms from around her to cup her face. "I'm so sorry, Raine."

She couldn't speak. Her heart wanted to forgive

him, thanks to their soulmate bond it would always, but her head couldn't. No matter his intentions, he'd betrayed her in the worst possible way.

He'd told her to remember what they had was real, but she didn't know what to trust anymore.

How did she distinguish between the lies?

"Raine, what happened?" Raven asked.

Her gaze fell with her shoulders.

Slater stepped back, lowering his hands from her face creating an ache inside her heart. "I took the Empryen to Hell."

"We figured that. What I wanna know is why?" Raven snapped.

Slater lifted his chin, all defiant. They were so similar. Two immortals doing what they thought was best, at any cost. Did that make it right?

She retreated a step to stop mourning the loss of his warmth.

Slater held her gaze for a long moment before looking at Raven. "I gave the sword to Blaine."

She gasped. "No."

Slater continued as though she hadn't spoken. "Before I Fell, Fate gave me the sword and told me that when the time came, I needed to get Raine to activate it."

A lump thickened in her throat. That sword was hers.

"I kept it hidden, but Asher fucking found it. I came to the Guardians for help because I knew Raine was here looking for it." His gaze shifted to her. "When it came to choosing between betraying you and saving your soul, the choice was the easiest one I've ever made." He paused. "I'm sorry for how it happened, but

I won't apologize for saving your soul, Raine. Ever."

She shook her head as tears burned her eyes. "The Empryen was my destiny."

Slater's voice softened, while the creases in his brows deepened. "Princess, Fate intended for Blaine to have the sword. When he held it, black letters burned along the blade. He's the Sarael."

"No," she whispered.

Fate had used her to deliver the sword to Blaine. Blaine would kill Zath.

She staggered back. "He can't be."

A million unanswered questions raced through her mind.

How could Fate trick me?
Did Slater know all along?

She didn't know the exact time, but Slater Fell long before Blaine. Long before Fate exiled Raven and the others.

Fate gave him the sword before Blaine even Fell.

She'd lived nothing but lies. Her entire destiny unraveled before her.

Fate created her to activate a powerful weapon for someone else. She'd never felt more worthless.

Again, her fingers inched toward a Kiel that wasn't there.

"Raine." Slater reached for her hand, but she snatched it out of his reach.

"No. I created the Empryen. The sword is *mine*." She pointed her finger at him. "Again…you didn't give me a choice. You didn't even ask."

Without waiting for his reply, she stormed back into the mansion. Her feet didn't even falter when Slater roared her name.

Chapter FORTY-FOUR

Raven fired questions that Slater had no desire to answer. His ability to talk, to breathe, to fucking exist vanished the moment Raine turned her back on him. She flattened her palm against the outer wall before she entered the mansion, no doubt locking him the hell out.

He knew she'd hate him once she retrieved her memories, but he'd take the same risk again and again. Hating him was better than her Falling.

River followed his sister inside the mansion. No surprise there. Also, no surprise that Aric approached him, ready to launch with his fists. He recognized the glare from their many run-ins over the years. What did surprise him though, was Willow by Aric's side, looking just as deadly. He had a strange moment where his chest swelled, knowing the Ariel could kick some serious ass with a set of daggers. All thanks to him.

At least one good thing came out of this disaster.

"Slater," Raven snapped.

He swung his gaze to the head Guardian. "What?"

"Does Blaine intend to use the Empryen to kill Zath?"

He nodded.

"Surely he's not that stupid." Raven massaged the back of his neck. "You have to stop him."

Once maybe, but now, he didn't belong in Hell. Something had changed, no, shifted, in his soul when he misted Raine from Hell. As an Azrael, he could drop in and visit Hell, but he sensed he'd now given up permanent residency.

He was back in limbo. Nowhere was home, not without Raine.

What was freedom without her?

Even if it took centuries to earn back her trust, he'd do it. After all, he had all the time in the universe.

He glanced back at the mansion. "Blaine's got it handled."

"Fuck." Raven turned to Aric. "We have to stop him."

"I don't know if that's possible, man. It wouldn't surprise me if Fate planned it. If Blaine overthrows Zath, he'll be the new king of Hell." Aric paused. "I'm more concerned about what he'll do after."

Raven peered at the Heavens as though that would help. Yeah, right. Nothing could stop the inevitable.

Raven ran his fingers through his hair. "He has to plan it. He can't just grab the Empryen and charge into battle. We still have time to stop him."

Slater chuckled to himself when all the final pieces fell into place.

Blaine had steadily built an army of Fallen since the minute he'd arrived in Hell. He'd recruited angels over the centuries, syphoning Azrael and Raziel magic to enhance his Guardian powers. He'd freed him from the Pits to recruit Dumahel twins and used them to dreamwalk to Fate.

None of those acts were random.

Blaine had planned this moment for centuries. Somehow, he knew the Empryen would arrive in his hands.

Slater turned to the Guardians. "Blaine's been planning this for centuries. Nothing you do will stop him."

The air shifted beside Raven a second before Cole materialized on the lawn. Done with the Guardians, he had another matter to deal with.

He didn't waste a moment. He misted and reappeared in front of the Azrael, gripped his shirt, and smashed his back against a nearby tree.

Cole grunted.

Slater was three seconds from punching the Azrael's pretty face. "Don't you dare mist her to Hell again. She doesn't belong there."

Cole shoved back at Slater's chest, forcing him to let go. "In that, we both agree. But, as I'm sure you already know, she's quite persuasive when holding a dagger."

A chuckle quaked in his chest. That sounded like his fiery princess.

"True. But if you mist her there again, you'll have me to deal with." His nostrils flared. "And I'll make Raine look like a bag of pretty sunshine. Feel me?"

"Loud and clear." Cole straightened his shirt. "What's your plan now, lover boy?"

First, he needed to track down all Azrael and deliver the same threat, so Raine had no method of travel back to Hell. After that...

"I have no fucking clue."

****

For four days he'd parked his ass on the Guardian property waiting for Raine to come out. She'd hidden herself inside like a true princess. Only, her modified Raziel spell prohibited him from busting down the door to rescue her. It also prohibited him within fifty yards of the mansion.

He'd organized deliveries of flowers, expensive liquor, and even a shiny pair of heels from that designer she loved, misting all over this forsaken world in search of tokens to give her. Anything to coax her to see him, to hear him out.

She never did.

He leaned against his now favorite pine tree, the rough trunk scratching through his shirt. What would it take to get through to her?

All he wanted was to explain. Tell his side of the story.

Waiting became his obsession. *Again*. A challenge of sorts to see who broke first. His fiery princess had inner strength beyond any immortal he'd ever encountered. Beating her at this game would take everything he had.

So, he prepared himself for exactly that.

Letting his eyes drift shut, he angled his face to catch sunlight filtering through the tree canopy. The long-forgotten warmth tingled on his cheeks, trickling healing light through his blood.

Denying the changes in his wings, in his soul, was no longer an option. Each day his wings healed a little more. Silvery-gray feathers now outnumbered the crimson ones, and given the progress to date, he had a few more days until his soul completely aligned with the Heavens. With Fate.

Thinking back, his soul had switched sides the moment it connected with Raine. Even if she hadn't healed him, he guessed he would've still found himself in this same position.

So many times, he considered shouting to her, standing on the lawn with his wings outstretched, hoping that convinced her to at least listen to him. He'd hurt her, he knew that, but he meant what he said. To save her soul, he'd choose the same path again and again. But he held on to his secret. What if she didn't want the Guardians to know she healed him? What if it made her resent him even more? Did the Guardians know she could heal a Fallen's soul? Did Raine know?

And would Fate retaliate or was this her almighty plan all along?

Not only was his soul in limbo, so was his relationship with Raine and he'd do whatever it took to win her back. Including waiting out here until she was ready to face him. Given Fate still hadn't appeared to discuss their deal, he had all the time in the universe. Sooner or later, he'd wear down his stormy princess's resistance, and when he did, he'd pour out his heart and soul to her and hope it was enough.

Fucking Fate and her twisted plans.

Awareness buzzed along his nape, and he lifted his lids a fraction to find Aric striding across the lawn.

Just great.

Aric stopped a few feet away, arms crossed over his chest. "You're a determined fucker, I'll give you that."

He shrugged one shoulder, closing his eyes again. "I've got all the time in this world."

Aric huffed a breath. "Want some advice?"

"I feel like you'll give it anyway."

When Aric didn't continue, Slater opened his eyes. The Guardian raked his fingers through his hair, scanning the grounds. He'd never seen the guy so…concerned?

Finally, Aric pinned Slater with a hard stare. "Raine isn't a girly-girl if you haven't noticed. Flowers and shit won't work."

He knew that, obviously, but assumed every female appreciated gifts of flowers and chocolates, pretty things wrapped in glossy ribbon. "What are you saying?"

Aric's eyes closed briefly while he shook his head. "I can't believe I'm telling you this." He paused as though battling with the decision. "If you wanna get through to her, you need something bigger. Grander. Something she'll take notice of. Something to make you worthy of her attention. Fate did a real number on her, and you pulled a similar fucking stunt. But as much as I hate to say it, you need to fix this."

He thought for a moment.

Something grander…something to make him worthy of her attention…

"Think about Raine, what's important to her, why you…love her."

He scoffed to cover the thumping in his chest. Though, he did a shit job of masking it.

Aric rolled his eyes. "I don't know what the hell the deal is with you two, but there's no point denying it. The soulmate connection is as clear as the Heavens. Your battle is getting Raine to acknowledge it. She's more stubborn than Raven." Aric's gaze darted to the Heavens then back to Slater. "I also sense your change. She needs to know."

Slater remained silent. He'd been a Fallen for so long, he couldn't remember what it felt like for an angel to be in the presence of another. But the Guardians would sense the lack of darkness in his soul. They were Fate's warriors. They'd always been more powerful than other factions, until Fate stripped their power.

Aric continued, "That's the only reason I'm standing here now and not kicking your ass into the next realm. This changes everything. Not just for Raine but for Raven. He needs to know it's possible."

"I'm not sure she'll ever venture out from her tower."

Aric hardened his stare, his voice deepened. "Make it happen. Try harder. Fate banished us here centuries ago to save Blaine. A mission, up until this point, we all assumed was impossible." He pointed a finger at Slater. "You prove it's not."

An invisible fist squeezed his chest. "Do the others know?"

"Not yet, but it won't take long for them to sense it."

He couldn't deny that Raine and him were in uncharted territory. A Fallen had never returned to the Heavens.

Ever.

He'd be the first.

Aric crossed his arms again. "Just hurry the fuck up. Raine's a whole other world of stabby without you around and it'd be nice to live in the house without her throwing shit every time someone looks at her."

Slater chuckled.

Without another word, Aric strode back to the Guardian mansion.

Slater stood there for a bit longer, thinking of the Guardian's words.

Think about why you love her…

Aric was right. Raine didn't want pretty gifts. He'd gone about this the wrong way. He wasn't trying to court an ordinary angel. He wanted to win back his fucking soulmate. An angel he'd proudly follow into battle. One who he considered not just a fierce warrior, but an equal.

Raine didn't want tokens to make her feel special. She deserved something that made her feel powerful, fierce, and lethal.

Not a gift for a princess, but one fit for a queen.

Chapter FORTY-FIVE

Her heart bounced around behind her ribs like that psycho kitten. She peered out the second-story glass sliding door and found Slater once again standing at the edge of the Guardian property where her Raziel barrier started. This time, he was shirtless, wearing only black leather pants and boots which didn't help her stupid heart. He had twin dagger sheaths crisscrossed over his broad chest, looking like a deadly ancient warrior sent from another time.

Partly true.

The black scars marring his thick arms reminded her of the hell he experienced when he Fell. A path paved for him by Fate. He'd gone through that to protect the sword, to deliver it to her, and ultimately hand it to Blaine. The true protector of the Heavens.

So many questions remained unanswered.

But one kept repeating in her head. If Fate had given her the same task as she paved for Slater, would Raine have made the same decision? Would she have put her destiny above everything else? And everyone?

Yes.

Since he'd misted her from Hell, he'd stood by that same tree for six days, misting away for only short periods. Deliveries of gifts followed each day, but she made River return them. Slater couldn't buy her forgiveness. Aric had spoken with him yesterday and when she sensed him mist away, she thought he'd finally gotten the hint to leave her alone. But the persistent dumbass returned.

Enough was enough.

She couldn't keep staring out a window hoping to catch him glancing back at her. Once, she thought romantic comedies ruined her badass reputation. They had nothing on what Slater had done to her.

He'd turned her into a pining, raging, hollow shell.

She felt...empty.

With a huff, she threw open the sliding door and stepped out onto the balcony. Unfurling her wings, she coasted down onto the lawn and marched right up to him, halting a few steps away, out of his reach. Slater lifted his chin, locking his deep brown eyes on her.

She peered at the twin black Karambit knives held in his hands. Why the Fate did he have those? Fighting her wouldn't help his cause.

A ripple along her neck told her the other Guardians had filed onto the lawn but kept their distance.

Inhaling, she filled her lungs with his intoxicating fire and brimstone scent. It felt so good, as though her lungs filled for the first time in almost a week. Despite her anger that he'd stopped her from fulfilling her purpose, she couldn't deny that she'd...missed him. No matter how much training she did, how many insignificant objects she stabbed, it never eased the pain behind her ribs.

She ached for him. For his strong arms wrapped around her, murmuring secret words meant only for her. He calmed her more than any Kiel.

The furniture in the Guardian mansion would

agree.

When the silence became too much, she opened her mouth to say...something. But before she did, Slater lowered to one knee, laying the knives crisscrossed on the lawn between them.

He bowed his head. "They're not made from Purah, nor are they forged by the most powerful Raziel in the universe. They were made by an Azrael, filled with regret and remorse for the hurt he caused, his hope for a better future and his love...for his queen."

Her heart stilled.

Slater peered up at her. "I was wrong to call you a princess. You deserve for me to treat you as a queen. You're strong, powerful, and fierce. And right now, I bow before you, pledging my honor, my loyalty, and my soul to you for the rest of eternity."

Her heart cracked open, flooding her chest with brilliant white light. She'd hated him for stealing the Empryen, but she hated herself more because she understood why he'd done it.

He betrayed her to save her soul.

She would've done the same.

She peered at the knives presented to her by her...soulmate. She couldn't stay angry at him any longer. Not for the choices he made, not for his actions in this clusterfuck of a destiny, not for him putting her soul first.

That ache behind her ribs would only heal if she forgave him. A strange thrill zipped through her soul at the thought.

As a Fallen and an angel, their path would be difficult. But together, she sensed they'd make it. Their souls were destined.

As she bent to pick up the knives, Slater rose to his feet and offered them to her.

She inspected the curved blades, the smooth surface, sharp point, symmetrical circular finger loop. They weren't entirely bad. In her hand, the weight and balance needed improvements, but she could fix that with a touch of Raziel magic. "Why would you offer me something sharp that I could use to stab you? Are you that dumb?"

He chuckled, stepping into her space. "I want you to stab me. I want you to challenge me." He curled a finger beneath her chin, lifting her gaze to his. "I want you to fight me every step of the way, because I never want to become complacent again. I want you to push me to fight harder for you. I want to earn your heart, to be worthy of your love. I want to be the someone you need."

He cupped her face in his hands, dipping his head so they were eye level. Wild thrills sparked through her blood, centering in her…heart. It swelled, strengthened, came back to life.

"Needing someone doesn't make us weak, it makes us stronger. You make me stronger. You make me feel alive. You make me a better immortal." He searched her eyes. "You make me a better angel."

She drew back. "What?"

A smirk curled at the corner of his mouth. Lowering his hands, he stepped back and unfurled his wings. A brilliant explosion of light burst over the lawn, with Slater at the epicenter. He stretched his wings in a wide arc.

Her breath caught. No crimson feathers lined his wings, not one. Each feather was silvery-gray…the

343

color of Azrael wings.

When she held out her hand, Slater curled his wings around her, cocooning them. She brushed her fingers along the soft gray feathers. "How?"

"You, my queen." He cradled her face. "You healed me."

She thought back to the moment in the bunker right after he'd misted her, when she'd cut him. His blood hadn't been black. She'd sensed something had changed, something was different with him.

He knew.

"I took the Empryen to Hell because I wouldn't let you sacrifice your soul, not when you gave me new life. I'm going to spend the rest of my existence proving to you how worthy I am. I love you, Raine."

His fierce, deep brown eyes darkened, and she braced herself for a flash of crimson that never came.

What he said made sense, but she couldn't understand how she'd healed more than his wound.

She healed his soul.

"I can't give life. I can only..."

Back in the cavern, when she'd used her magic to protect his heart from the Purah seeping into his blood, she'd unknowingly forged something far stronger than any weapon. Heavenly light had consumed her, blending with her...concern for him. The combination magnified her powers until the magic had exploded from her fingertips in a giant rush.

His eyes softened.

The Guardians spoke of their love for their soulmates. How nothing rivaled the connection. How they'd move the Heavens and Hell to save them.

It finally made sense.

She felt that for Slater. The way her blood heated at the thought of him. The way her heart skipped when she caught him watching her. The hollowness she experienced when he wasn't there.

How she'd healed him because she couldn't imagine a future without him in it.

Did that mean she…

He brushed his fingers along her cheek. "This was our destiny. You created a sword that will end Zath. I delivered that weapon to Blaine, the Sarael. We found each other. Together, we will help usher in a new reign; we will save this realm."

His head dipped closer to her lips. Her pulse whooshed in her ears.

For the first time in her existence, she chose an unknown path. One that didn't have a clear beginning, middle, and end. A path she chose for herself.

"I…" A light shudder rippled through her as though she gulped gin straight from the bottle. "I…feel…"

The words scratched in her throat.

His face lit with a cocky smile as his wings wrapped around her back, drawing her flush against him. "I love you too, my queen. Forever."

Chapter FORTY-SIX

Slater dipped his head, easing his mouth to Raine's. She didn't need to tell him in words, he sensed her love colliding with his through their soulmate connection. Never had he experienced something akin to the brilliant, heavenly light threading between their souls, securing its anchor deep inside him.

He never wanted it to end.

And if having his soul aligned again with the Heavens under Fate's control instead of the freedom he thought he craved, if it meant being with Raine, then he'd make that choice every day.

For the rest of his existence, he'd strive to be worthy of her love.

Strange power hummed behind his soul, different than Raine's, more…pure and heavenly. Gradually at first, the power intensified, expanding through his soul, weaving itself into every cell in his body until it exploded.

He broke the kiss with a gasp. "Did you feel that?"

Raine tensed in his arms, her nostrils flared before she narrowed her violet eyes. She shoved against his wings until he withdrew them, ending their private moment.

The new power bloomed, an invisible force pulsing inside him.

Raine spun the knives on her fingers, staring at a

spot on the lawn. The other Guardians gravitated to the—

The ornamental cherry tree in front of the mansion exploded with pink and white flowers, the blossoms tumbling along the grass, caught in a gust of wind.

His heart thudded. What in the fiery Hell?

Air rippled around the tree, shimmering with a kaleidoscope of colors and heavenly magic. The blossoms stilled midair.

His pulse hammered, but he couldn't inhale a breath, as though a hand had reached into his chest and squeezed his lungs. It couldn't be…

As the thought formed in his mind, an apparition of Fate appeared, hovering a few inches above the grass. There, but not there at the same time.

Fate.

She'd come to recall his soul.

He wasn't ready. Why couldn't he have longer in the mortal realm? Longer with Raine? Just when they'd slain all their obstacles, when Raine had forgiven him and acknowledged her feelings for him in her own way, when he'd finally embraced his true destiny, Fate fucking recalled his soul.

He slid his hand over Raine's shoulder, coaxing her to turn around. She didn't. She widened her stance, a deep rumble hummed from her as though she were seconds away from throwing those knives at Fate. He'd never felt so fucking proud.

Moving behind her, he snaked his arms around her middle, holding her tight for the last time. "Throwing those knives won't end how you want."

On the opposite side of the lawn, Raven stepped forward, separating himself from the other Guardians.

"Fate."

Fate returned his nod before scanning the Guardians one by one. When her gaze landed on him and Raine, a triumphant glint lit her silvery eyes.

Raine tensed in his arms. So did he. He couldn't help it. What he'd give to let Raine throw those knives for the shit Fate pulled.

Lowering his arms, he moved to stand beside Raine, holding his head high. It had all been worth it. He'd do it all again if it meant being with Raine for what now felt like a fleeting moment. He'd wait for her until she returned to the Heavens, and they could start their new beginning.

"I didn't…" Raine bowed her head. "I failed."

Fate gravitated closer, hovering above the lawn. "You fulfilled your destined path, my Raziel."

"What?" Raine's gaze zeroed in on Fate. "You told me I was to end Zath. I trained my entire existence for that mission. A mission I was…never intended for."

Her fist curled around the blade as she prowled forward, but he slipped his hand around hers, holding her back.

Relax, my queen, he whispered in her mind.

As much as he'd love for Raine to throw that knife, it wouldn't end well for either of them. Especially if he cheered her on.

"All is how it should be. Your actions will result in the end of Zath's reign." Fate's gaze slid to his before returning to Raine. "You will remain in this realm with your brother…in your true forms. The Guardians need your skills. The end is near."

Raine glared at Fate but held her tongue.

Since Falling, he'd focused on nothing but his

damn freedom, when he now knew that was never the end game. Fate had sent him to Raine. She'd intended for them to meet.

He stepped forward. "What about...me?"

Raine and her brother were free of their obligation to Fate. They no longer had a threat hanging over their heads. He wanted...

"Still seeking freedom, Azrael?"

"I..." He lifted his chin. "I wish to stay here with Raine."

Silver power illuminated Fate's eyes. "Very well. You will return when your soulmate does."

Had he...What the hell just happened? Did Fate permit him to stay in the mortal realm with Raine? She didn't recall his ass to the Heavens. He was...free. Kind of.

Fate glided to stand before Raven. "The time has come, Guardian."

He frowned. "For what?"

"To bring him home."

In the stunned silence that followed, Fate's form faded into the ether until she was no longer there. Cherry blossoms frozen in midair fluttered to the ground before they also vanished.

What the hell?

While the Guardians discussed Fate's cryptic message, he turned to Raine, taking her hands in his and dipping his head, searching her eyes. "You all right?"

"Fate never intended for me to go to Hell. She never intended for me to end Zath. She just made me think that was my path, that I'd use the weapon I forged to kill him. How screwed up is that?"

He slipped a hand free from hers to cup her jaw.

"Your soul is too pure for Hell. Fate would never destine that, and I'd never allow it."

She nodded, though he sensed it would take time before Raine accepted the diversion in her destiny. But now, they had all the time they needed.

"Do you want to…come inside?"

His blood heated at the thought of devouring Raine, especially knowing they were safe and no uncertainty hung over their heads.

Damn good idea.

But he peered at the other Guardians still lingering on the lawn. First, he needed to do something. Something he should've done a long time ago.

"Meet me in the armory," he whispered against her ear, before snagging the fleshy lobe between his teeth.

Heat flashed through their connection. Without another word, he released Raine and didn't bother hiding the fact he watched her ass stride all the way across the lawn, flipping the knives back and forth in her hands. At the entrance to the mansion, she placed her palm on the wall.

Everything fell into place. He and Raine were together in the mortal realm, the Empryen was with Blaine, and he had his freedom, albeit different from what he'd expected.

When Raine slipped through the front door, he looked back at the Guardians, at River.

Some part of him wanted to…he didn't know, seek River's approval? As stupid as that sounded. Would he give a shit if River didn't give it? Probably not.

But it felt important that he at least tried. For Raine's sake, more than his.

Conversations between the Guardians ceased as he

approached.

Raven stepped forward. "Something to say?"

He'd rather not have an audience but doubted that would happen. "I want to be with Raine. Now that I'm no longer a…Fallen, I'd appreciate no issues when I want to come here to see her."

Raven shoved his hands in his jean pockets. "Yeah, well, given the recent developments, I don't have an issue. If Raine wants you around, that's good enough for me."

His heart thudded, flipping around inside his chest. He glanced at Aric and EJ.

EJ shrugged. "I'm all for a less stabby version of Raine. My nerves are frickin' shot."

Aric took a moment to answer. "I think you've proven your worth, man. Don't screw it up."

Warmth swelled inside his chest. Finally, he turned to River. Although Raven was the leader of the Guardians, in this instance, River's opinion trumped all the others.

River's green eyes sparkled with excitement. "You make my sister happy."

Someone snorted.

"Happy in a Raine kind of way." River pulled a bag of candy from his pocket, offering it to him. "Plus, I could use an ally when these douchebags give me crap about my shirts."

Aric and EJ groaned in unison.

He'd thought when he requested to stay in the mortal realm with Raine that he'd condemned them to an eternity as outcasts. That they'd live on the fringes of the Guardians, in their own existence. He never expected acceptance.

Aric made him see sense, that he had to fight to deserve Raine, not just win her heart. Raven had invited him into their home. And the angel whose opinion mattered the most gave his approval.

Slater dug into the candy bag and threw one in his mouth. "Deal."

Brotherly backslaps ensued and talk of the future, but he kind of zoned out. This was what belonging felt like. Freedom. Finally, he was free to live the destiny he chose, with the one he loved.

EPILOGUE

One week later

In the early hours of the morning, Raine tiptoed down to the armory, gravitating to the Purah basin as though drawn to it by some magical force. At the rim, she glanced inside. Her breath stalled. Crystal clear heavenly water gradually rose until it reached the top of the basin.

How?

Fate had told her she needed to fulfil her destiny before the Purah ran out. That Fate had linked the Empryen's powers to this basin. When the Purah ran out, the Empryen was powerless, but she hadn't fulfilled her destiny. As far as she knew, Zath was still alive. Albeit still trapped in Hell. If her destiny was to activate the Empryen so Blaine, the Sarael, could wield its powers and kill Zath, then she'd...achieved that.

She and Slater had both achieved their destinies.

As a drop of Purah dripped over the side of the basin, heavenly light burst through her soul, seeping into her skin. Beneath the heavenly power, her own Raziel magic felt revitalized, stronger, like she was back in the Heavens.

Purah trickled down the sides of the basin, spilling onto the stone floor, as a crazed chuckle burst from her chest. For the past few years, she'd been so careful, never wasting a drop or using more than she needed to forge weapons in case her supply ran dry. Now, all that changed.

Dashing to the workbench, she grabbed a pail and filled it with overflowing heavenly water. Vibrant colors glittered over the armory walls as the shimmering Purah swished back and forth, steadily rising to refill the basin.

Swapping out the full pail for an empty one, she repeated the process.

The basin refilled again.

Standing there with another full pail dangling from her fingertips, she stared at the endless supply of Purah. *Endless.* Think of what she could create with so much. Just like the Purah in the basin, the possibilities were…endless.

She could train other Raziel to forge weapons, they could protect the mortals, the Guardians would have more allies across this realm. Together they could prepare the mortal realm for the coming battle.

For some reason beyond her understanding, Fate entrusted Blaine with the Empryen, but the battle with Hell wasn't over. Even if Blaine overthrew Zath, they still had a long road ahead before they restored peace.

Before the Guardians saved Blaine.

But with Willow's regeneration powers, an endless supply of Purah, and her healing powers, their future, for once, looked…bright.

Back at the workbench, she fired up the freezing chamber and summoned her Raziel magic, transforming pails of Purah into bricks. She wrapped each one in cloth with precise instructions on how to blend the Purah with a Raziel's individual magic to forge not only swords, but weapons of all kinds, including the pieces of jewelry she'd made Hailee. She'd ask Slater to mist her around this realm to deliver the bricks to other Raziel so they were never defenseless again.

Someone punched in the code to the armory before the door swung open. Slater strode in like he downright owned the place.

He dumped a duffle bag inside by the door.

She secured the tie on the final brick. "What's in the bag?"

In an instant, he stood in front of her and took her mouth in a searing kiss that left her breathless. "I'm moving in…permanently."

"I never said I wanted you to move in."

He chuckled, pinching her chin. "Oh, we both know you do."

She scoffed, doing a shit job of masking the ridiculous giddy sensation in her belly that never dissipated with Slater around. Or when she thought of him. Internally, she rolled her eyes at herself. If the other soulmates ever found out, they'd probably shoot confetti cannons from the roof.

Hard pass.

A bulge inside Slater's jacket squirmed.

"For the love of Fate. If you brought that creature with you—"

Slater gasped, unzipping his jacket to cradle the ginger furball in his hands. "Peaches needs a stable home environment, not one where her parents come and go at all hours. Co-parenting might be all the rage with mortals, but it's not my thing."

The kitten gave a well-timed meow.

She opened her mouth to throw back a snarky

comment, but he held up his finger. "Not finished, my queen."

She rolled her eyes. He smirked, knowing damn well it irritated her.

"I've spent centuries mostly alone, without letting anyone in, so focused on my freedom. When Blaine freed me from the Pits, sure, it was great to know someone had my back. But I've never experienced the bond you have with the Guardians. Even back in the Heavens, I always felt adrift, different from the other Azrael."

"That doesn't mean—"

"Still not finished."

She growled. His brown eyes darkened until they were almost black, no longer at risk of turning crimson.

"You're surrounded by immortals who care about you. Me included." He curled his finger under her chin, lifting her gaze. "You have no excuse now, Raine. You're not destined for Hell. You're not destined to leave them. Let them in. Let them see you."

After a long moment, she finally spoke. "You finished yet?"

He chuckled, motioning for her to speak.

Asshat.

"If you want that furball to stay here, fine. But it's not staying in my room. I don't even like…"

Her throat constricted at the almost lie. Damn cat.

His smirk made her want to punch him upside the head. "Nice try, my queen. But it's *our* room now, remember."

For the love of Fate.

A soulmate, a free destiny, parenting a damn cat— she didn't even recognize herself.

She playfully shoved him in the chest to move past him, but he caught her hand, spinning her to face him, taking her mouth in a hot, fierce kiss. He thrust his tongue against hers and didn't hold back. She dug her nails into the back of his neck, hoping the intensity between them never faded. She wanted this feeling, this fulfillment, for the rest of her existence. Even if she wouldn't admit it aloud.

He'd told her that she made him fight to be a better immortal, but in fact he did the same to her. He pushed so many of her buttons, at times she didn't know whether to stab him or scream his name in pleasure. Their connection made her stronger, more powerful. Her Raziel magic buzzed under the surface with everything she did, as though his presence fueled it.

She clawed at the buttons of his pants—

The fluffball meowed, protesting.

With a groan, Slater stepped back and lowered the cat to the floor. It scurried off to explore the armory.

"Welcome to parenting," she deadpanned. "Constant interruptions by annoying small creatures."

Slater smirked, gripping her hips to pull her flush against his hardness. Despite his soul now aligning with the Heavens, he still carried the fire and brimstone scent she loved about him. Hopefully, that never dulled either.

"The mansion is full of potential babysitters for when we need grown-up time."

He cupped her cheeks and dipped his head, smiling down at her. The look in his eyes reflected more than the happiness flowing through their connection. It conveyed unsaid words and an intensity that still unsettled her, but she wouldn't shy away from their bond any longer.

Fate had a shitty, convoluted way of bringing soulmates together.

She could've just asked.

He nipped at her bottom lip. "Tell me again how much you love me."

She peered up at the male who'd unraveled her entire existence and pieced it back together again, stronger, tighter, and with more life than she'd ever experienced.

The Azrael she'd walk through the gates of Hell for.

The angel who made altering her destiny worth it.

Her soulmate.

A grin warmed her cheeks. "I guess...you're all right."

His throaty laugh lit her insides on fire. In one swift movement, he swept her up, curling her legs around his waist as he carried her to the workbench.

Standing between her thighs, he grabbed a nearby dagger and flipped it in his hand. "How 'bout you show me how much you love me?"

She snatched the dagger out of the air and grazed the tip along his jaw. "I thought you'd never ask."

Thank you for purchasing
this publication of The Wild Rose Press, Inc.

For questions or more information
contact us at
info@thewildrosepress.com.

The Wild Rose Press, Inc.
www.thewildrosepress.com